NIGHT CREEPS

AN ADULT HORROR STORY

MICHAEL D'AMBROSIO

ISBN
978-1-958690-62-8 (Paperback)
978-1-958690-63-5 (eBook)
978-1-964982-23-6 (Hardcover)

TABLE OF CONTENTS

CHAPTER I

HUNTER, HUNTED

Bob Schultz crept through the trees with his Browning 30.06 semi-automatic rifle pointed ahead of him. He was an elderly man, dressed in camouflaged fatigues and a floppy camo hat with combat boots. A tree branch snapped loudly in the cool evening breeze, catching his attention. Schultz held his hand up for his partner, Bo Davis, to freeze.

Bo, a short, stocky man in his early thirties, wore a fluorescent vest with fatigues and a baseball cap. He carried a Remington Genesis rifle with a night scope. Davis whispered, "See anything?"

Schultz ordered him quietly, "Wait here. I'll see if I can flush it out in the open."

Davis complained softly, "We've been at it all day. We earned this one."

Schultz whispered determinedly, "We sure ain't goin' home empty-handed this time." He slipped into the trees in pursuit of the sound.

Davis leaned against a pine tree with his rifle pointed toward the clearing. As he waited anxiously for the deer to emerge, he whispered to himself, "This could be the big one. We'll show them boys at the lodge." Perspiration dripped from his forehead as he impatiently fingered the trigger. He murmured, "Come on, Bobby. Flush him out where I can paint his sorry ass."

Schultz stepped cautiously through the bushes and trees. He approached several boulders near the base of the rocky ridge and climbed atop one of them for a better view. Several rocks cascaded down from the top of the ridge, catching him off guard. He dodged the first few but one caught him square in the shoulder, knocking him backwards.

Schultz bellowed, "Damn you, you son-of-a-bitch!" He staggered to his feet and climbed the rocks to the top of the ridge. He searched angrily for the cause of the small rockslide in the fading twilight.

Beyond the ridge was a streamlined, box-shaped spacecraft. Its side hatch was open, projecting a ray of light off the nearby trees. Schultz saw the spaceship and uttered in amazement, "Well, I'll be!" His heart raced as he considered meeting the world's first alien visitor.

Another branch snapped nearby. Schultz mumbled sarcastically, "I ain't got time for you now. I got an alien to bag." He cautiously approached the ship with his rifle poised to fire.

The outline of a strange creature stood in the doorway of the hatch. Schultz strained to see what the creature was but the bright light inside the ship blurred its features. He inched closer and shouted, "Come on out, ET, with your hands up!" The creature hid from the doorway.

Schultz complained, "I guess we're gonna have to do this the hard way." Creeping towards the hatch, he searched for the creature.

Inside the spaceship, instrument panels blinked multicolored lights. A large glass tube with a metal base was positioned in the middle of the floor, filled with pink fluid. A living, sponge-like creature was suspended in the fluid. Several conduits ran from the base, up a steel column and over to each instrument panel.

Schultz warned, "Don't make me come in there, ET! I'm giving you three to come out."

Branches snapped in the trees to his right. Schultz backed away from the ship and nervously called out, "Is that you, Bo! Don't be screwing around or I'll whoop your ass. We got an alien encounter here."

Schultz heard more branches break in the trees on his left. His heart beat faster as he moved fearfully toward the ship. His breathing became irregular and he shuddered. "Sons-of-bitches ain't gonna get away with this."

Schultz pointed the rifle into the spaceship and warned, "If you don't come out, I'll fill this tin can with so many holes, it'll never fly again."

A branch snapped to Schultz's right and startled him. He shouted frantically, "Alright, you really pissed me off now!" He stomped toward the trees and aimed his rifle.

◆••••

An alien creature exited the ship and hunted Schultz from behind. It was similar to humans in some ways: a pair of arms and legs, a head with eyes and a mouth.

The mouth was full of sharp teeth and opened wide. Its outer skin resembled that of an alligator - rough and leathery. Sixteen small appendages protruded from its chest in two rows of eight and quivered with drops of clear alien hormone, dripping from each one. The creature wore a metal band around its head that covered its left ear with a small flap and attached to its throat with two electrodes.

Two of the creatures emerged from the forest and stalked Schultz. Schultz panicked and cried out, "Holy Mother of God! What the hell are you?"

The alien from the ship grabbed him from behind and pulled the rifle out of his hands. Schultz struggled to get free but a pink tongue shot from the alien's mouth and wrapped itself around his throat. Small bristles emerged from the creature's tongue and injected a paralyzing agent into his throat muscles and vocal cords.

The alien dropped the rifle on the ground and held Schultz firmly in its grip. The tiny appendages retracted until Schultz's back was pressed against its chest. The appendages darted out and penetrated both sides of Schultz's spine, injecting him with hormone. He shuddered and his eyes rolled back in his head. The other two aliens watched eagerly. Their grisly teeth shone eerily in the moonlight.

The tubular tongue slowly released from Schultz's neck and retracted into its host's mouth with a slithering sound. It released Schultz and let him fall to the ground unconscious. A low-pitched whirr emitted from one of the control panels inside the ship, interrupting the eerie silence.

One alien became annoyed and asked another, "What do we do about them, Shurek? They're going to keep hunting us until they find us." Shurek approached the alien named Kroll and grabbed at a flap on his chest.

Kroll pleaded, "Please don't do that. I only asked you a question."

Shurek warned, "You let me deal with them. You and Grimwold just stick to the plan. Understand?"

Kroll nodded and replied humbly, "I didn't mean any disrespect, Shurek. I just wondered."

"Well don't wonder. Just do your job." Shurek released his hold on Kroll's flap and hurried into the ship.

Grimwold laughed and taunted Kroll, "You weakling. You always were soft."

Kroll delicately lifted the flap and inspected a gray worm, which hung inside a small, fleshy chamber. He poked at the worm and it curled up. Kroll sighed with relief and delicately closed the flap over the chamber.

He warned Grimwold, "You keep it up and I'll rip out your whole worm sac."

Grimwold laughed harder and teased, "And do what Kroll, make love to it?" Kroll glared at Grimwold with a chilling glaze.

"Ooh, I'm scared," Grimwold mocked.

Shurek returned from inside the ship and slapped Kroll in the back of his head. The metal band fell off Kroll's head and landed in the grass. Shurek chided, "Stop causing trouble, Kroll." Without the interpreting device, Kroll could only respond in his alien dialect. He crawled on all fours in the grass and searched for his band.

Shurek informed them, "Jasper's ship is still far away. They don't have coordinates on us yet."

Grimwold responded, "That should leave us plenty of time to build an army."

"We're not taking any chances. Now let's get moving."

Kroll picked his metal band out of the grass and placed it on his head. He connected the probes to his throat and warned Shurek, "Don't do that again."

"Or what? What will you do to me, Kroll?"

Kroll glared at him and warned, "One day you might need me to watch your back and I just might forget."

Shurek mocked him, "I don't think I'll ever need you. You're a mess."

Schultz got to his feet a short distance away from the aliens. His face swelled and his jaw protruded with two upper fangs and irregular, pointed teeth. His limbs grew longer and he hunched over like an ape.

Shurek remarked confidently, "I think he'll do."

Grimwold inquired, "Can we trust him?"

Shurek approached Schultz and asked, "Is anyone else with you?"

Schultz nodded and answered in a course, raspy voice, "Only Bo."

Shurek ordered, "Don't come back until you've killed him."

Foamy saliva dribbled off Schultz's lip onto his boot. His clothes stretched tightly against his growing limbs until they tore. "I'll eat Bo. I'm hungry."

Shurek was amused and ordered, "Get out of here, now!"

Schultz grinned, baring his crooked, broken teeth, and then trudged into the trees.

Grimwold remarked, "These humans might transform into better soldiers than we thought."

Kroll replied uneasily, "We still don't know how they'll mutate with the DNA compound and with the worms inserted in them."

Shurek looked at Kroll with disgust and barked out, "Why don't you shut up? You're really starting to annoy me." Kroll walked away in frustration and entered the ship.

Shurek pointed toward three lights in the valley. "We'll start with those residences, Grimwold."

Grimwold remarked arrogantly, "This'll be easy." The two aliens disappeared into the trees.

Moonlight cast an eerie glow from just over the ridge across the grassy clearing. Broken cloud cover created lurking shadows across lumpy clods of grass. Bo fidgeted as he waited impatiently. "Where the hell are you, Bob?" Fear took control of him and he stood up, holding his rifle tightly in his hands. He crept along the perimeter of the clearing and searched for any sign of his hunting partner. There was no sign of Schultz.

Bo grumbled angrily to himself, "You and me are gonna have a long talk about this, buddy."

Schultz waited patiently in the trees nearby, watching Bo trudge away from him. Bo paused to take out his flashlight and shined it around the perimeter of the clearing. He flashed the light briefly in Schultz's eyes. Schultz became irritated and burst out of the trees. He rushed at Bo, snarling and growling.

Bo was horrified at what Schultz had become. He aimed his rifle while holding the flashlight and ordered, "Stop right there. Bob! If this is a joke, I'll kick your friggin' ass!" Bo now saw the horrible creature that Schultz had become. The fangs convinced him that this was no joke. He fired at Schultz from about ten feet. Schultz staggered and covered his chest with his left claw. He paused and snarled again at Bo. Bo aimed the rifle again but this time Schultz lunged at him. The two tumbled across the ground as Bo desperately tried to defend himself against the much stronger creature that Schultz had become. Bo's rifle and flashlight lay nearby in the grass out of his reach.

Schultz sat on Bo's chest and savagely tore into his right arm with his teeth. Bo gouged at Schultz's eye with his left hand but only angered the creature more. He ripped off Bo's right arm and beat him with it. He shoved his clawed hand through Bo's abdomen and ripped out his intestines. Bo's cries carried across the dark forest, unheard by anyone. Schultz held his entrails in the air like a prize and howled.

When Schultz finished devouring the flesh from Bo's body, he staggered through the trees to a trail. Schultz looked down at the bullet wound in his chest and grunted. After three more steps, he stumbled and fell to the ground dead.

Bo's body was a heap of broken bones and bloody pieces of flesh. His head lay sideways in the grass with his eyes frozen wide-open, displaying the fear he died with. A short length of spine extended from the severed neck and quivered briefly as his right eye twitched one final time.

————— ⁺⁺⧫⧫⁺⁺ —————

Two college students hiked along the trail up the side of Grahams' Mountain in the early morning hours. The woman wore a gray sweatshirt and pants with a red headband holding her long blond hair behind her. She walked ahead of her partner.

The young man wore sweat shorts and a tank top. A dark blue bandana was tied around his shaven head. He carried a black backpack over his shoulders and panted as he attempted to keep up.

The young woman teased, "Come on, Steve. I thought you were in shape."

Steve complained, "I am, Jill. Remember, I worked all night while you slept."

"Oh, stop whining." She saw someone lying motionless on the ground and paused.

Steve stopped next to her and asked, "What's wrong?"

Jill replied uneasily, "Look. There's a body on the ground."

Steve cautiously approached Schultz's body. Jill was frightened and stayed back. "Is he alive?" she asked.

Steve saw the gunshot wound in the chest and knew Schultz was dead. The deformed face and teeth of the corpse stunned him. "You'd better call the sheriff," he replied. "This isn't pretty." Jill opened a small pouch tied to her waist and took out her cell phone. She dialed the Sheriff's Office and waited patiently.

Steve saw pieces of stringy flesh caught between the dead man's teeth. The two fangs in the top of Schultz's mouth intrigued him. He muttered, "What in the hell happened to you?"

Sheriff Lamar Whittington sat at his desk flipping through photographs. He was a large African-American man in his early thirties, dressed in a blue uniform. He took the position of sheriff in Parmissing valley when he was blamed for his partner's death, but was given the option to leave town quietly. He figured, "How much could possibly happen in a hick town like this?"

Deputy Johnny Watkins entered through the front door and kidded, "Internet's faster if you're looking for a handsome young guy for tonight, Sheriff." Johnny wore the brown work uniform a little undersized for his physique. He worked out a lot and liked to show off to the ladies. He was in his middle twenties and easily the most sought-after bachelor in Parmissing Valley. He and Lamar became friends over the six months that Lamar served as sheriff.

Lamar put the photos down and replied sarcastically, "For your information, Deputy Know-it-all, we have four missing persons reported this morning. All unrelated but all from the vicinity of Graham's Mountain."

Johnny suggested, "Maybe they went for a hike or something."

"No, I don't think so. A mother doesn't leave three young children to go for a hike. Furthermore, her door was bashed in like maybe a bear came through."

"Did the kids hear anything?"

"They're a little young to tell. An infant, a two-year-old girl and a three-year-old boy."

"Where's the father?"

"Don't know. Hasn't been around in a few days. Neighbors say he was looking for work outside of town. I have a few of my men asking around for him. The kids need a parent."

"Who else disappeared?"

"A security guard from a gated community on the ridge; a sixty-year-old man without his wheel chair; and a pizza delivery boy."

"All last night?"

"Uh-huh."

The phone rang. Johnny quipped, "This could be your big break, Sheriff. Ed McMahon of Reader's Digest – Sheriff Whittington, you've just won …"

Lamar snapped, "Shut up, will you!"

Johnny chuckled and poured himself a cup of coffee from the urn on the counter.

Lamar answered the phone, "Parmissing Valley Police Department - Sheriff Whittington speaking." He sat up attentively and wrote on a piece of scratch paper. "Slow down, ma'am. Are you sure he's dead?"

Johnny's expression turned serious and he pulled up a chair next to the sheriff's desk.

Lamar instructed her calmly, "Just relax, ma'am. We'll be there in thirty minutes. Stay right there." He hung up the phone and sighed, "Seven thirty in the morning and it's already one of those days." He rubbed his temples with both hands and covered his face.

"Well, what happened?" asked Johnny.

Lamar leaned back in his chair and answered, "Two hikers on the Pomona Trail found a dead person, they think."

"You mean they can't tell if the guy's dead? What morons."

"No, he's dead alright. They just aren't sure if he's a 'he'."

Johnny remarked sarcastically, "That's pretty messed up if they can't tell if it's a male or female."

Lamar stood up and stated angrily, "The corpse doesn't look human, you friggin' retard!" He strapped on his gun belt and loaded his pistol.

"You're serious."

Lamar glared at him and ordered, "Get your shit and get in the truck. We're going up there to find out what the hell's going on. If this is a joke, I'm gonna bust some heads." He hurried out the door and climbed into the police SUV.

Johnny gulped down his coffee and tossed the Styrofoam cup in the trashcan. He grabbed a shotgun from the cabinet and a box of shells. Amused, he mumbled, "A HE or an IT. This ought to be interesting." He held the gun over his shoulder with one hand and walked out the door.

Lamar started the engine and put the truck in drive while keeping his foot on the brake. Johnny opened the passenger-side door and climbed in. He noticed the sheriff was unusually tense and commented, "You're not playing around today, are you?"

"Missing people and unanswered questions don't make for good job security even in a small town like Parmissing Valley."

Johnny suggested, "I'll call Kaz and tell him to stand by."

"No, tell him to head up there. The hiker is convinced the body is deceased, no matter what it is." Johnny took out his cell phone and dialed.

Lamar stared ahead glumly and drove toward Graham's Mountain.

⸻ ✦ ⸻

George Kazmerski was the Parmissing Valley coroner. He lived in a small home on the outskirts of town. He was short, fifty-two years old and Asian. He took the job of coroner ten years ago to get out of the big city rat race and to enjoy country living in his senior years. He sat at a table on his back porch and sipped coffee while reading the PV Daily Press. His telephone rang, ruining the peaceful atmosphere. George grumbled, "So much for hot coffee."

He reached inside the back door and answered the phone on the wall, "Hello. Kaz speaking." He stepped inside the kitchen and sat down at the table.

Johnny replied in a professional tone, "Good morning, Mr. Kazmerski. This is Deputy Watkins of the Parmissing Valley Sheriff's Department."

Kaz chuckled and asked, "Okay, Magnum, what can I do for you?"

Johnny kidded, "Kaz, you're supposed to respect the law, not make fun of it."

Kaz replied, "Sir, yes sir."

"That's better. We have a cold one for you up on the Pomona trail on Graham's Mountain," Johnny informed him. "Can you meet us there?"

Kaz thought for a moment and then asked, "Do you have a name?"

"Not yet. A couple of hikers found the body. Why?"

"Two of my friends went hunting yesterday and didn't come back."

Johnny became concerned and inquired, "Who were they?"

"Bo Davis and Bob Schultz. Emily Schultz called me this morning and asked if I heard anything. Didn't she call you?"

"Maybe she left a message," Johnny replied, growing more concerned.

"I told her not to worry. Maybe the boys had a few drinks and were sleeping it off."

"I'll let the sheriff know. Thanks, Kaz."

"Anytime. See you soon." Kaz hung up the phone and closed the sliding glass door. He took his ring of keys from a hook on the wall and exited the front door.

✦

Johnny paused for a moment, arousing the sheriff's wrath.

Lamar inquired impatiently, "Well, is he coming?"

Johnny put the cell phone inside his jacket and replied, "Kaz says two of his friends went hunting yesterday and didn't come home. One's wife called him, asking if he knew anything."

"You got names?"

"Bo Davis and Bob Schultz."

Lamar's eyes widened and he remarked, "No shit. I've known Schultzy for years."

Johnny suggested, "Maybe they got drunk and slept it off somewhere."

"I hope so. Otherwise, our list of missing persons just grew to six."

"Why six? The kids' father is still missing. That could be seven."

"Johnny."

"Yes, Sheriff."

"Shut up."

Johnny stared ahead and said nothing the rest of the ride.

Grimwold hid in the trees and watched the two hikers. Shurek lurked in the trees near Schultz's body. Jill kept her distance from Schultz's corpse and complained to Steve, "Why can't we get out of here. This place gives me the creeps."

Steve knelt with his back to Jill. He pulled open Schultz's mouth and studied the fangs and teeth. He answered, "We might have found a missing link or something like it. This guy can't be human."

Grimwold crept toward Jill from behind. Jill complained, "We've been together over three years and you've become more insensitive to me instead of less." Steve ignored her and probed Schultz's temples and cheek for bone structure.

Grimwold's mouth opened wide and his tongue slithered toward Jill. She stared nervously at Schultz's body with her arms folded against her body.

Grimwold's tongue whipped around Jill's neck and tightened. Short needles ejected from the tongue and penetrated Jill's throat. She tried to scream but the chemical from Grimwold's tongue numbed her vocal cords. Grimwold pressed her against his chest and quivered as sixteen appendages injected themselves into either side of Jill's spine. Jill's eyes rolled back in her head and her body shook violently.

Steve quipped, "You know what you need, Jill?" He turned around and was horrified. "Oh, my God! Jill!" Jill's fingers extended toward Steve in desperation until she lost consciousness. Grimwold retracted his tongue and released his hold on Jill. She fell to the ground, unresponsive.

Shurek stepped out of the trees behind Steve. His tongue extended from his mouth and hovered behind Steve's head. Steve turned to run but Shurek grabbed him and wrapped his tongue around his neck. Steve grabbed the tongue and tried to pull it away but to no avail. He tried desperately to scream but no sounds came from his mouth.

Grimwold approached Steve from behind and pulled him against his chest. His appendages injected alien hormone into either side of his spine.

He emitted mock laughter as Shurek's tongue throbbed and pulsed on Steve's neck. Finally, Shurek retracted his tongue and backed away.

Grimwold threw Steve's unconscious body over his shoulder and remarked, "This is gonna be easier than we thought."

Shurek warned, "We still have a lot of work to do. Don't get cocky." He picked up Jill's limp body and placed her over his shoulder. Her cell phone fell from her hip pouch and landed in the grass.

The two carried their prey into the forest toward the spaceship. Grimwold commented arrogantly, "I'm gonna enjoy making slaves of these people. They're so damn fragile."

Shurek scowled and ignored him.

━━━━━━ ·◆◆◆◆◆· ━━━━━━

Lamar and Johnny arrived on the Pomona Trail and parked near Schultz's corpse. Lamar remarked dryly, "Funny that the hikers ain't around. I told them to wait here."

Johnny opened the door and stepped out of the vehicle. He scanned the area and pondered, "I wonder where they went."

Lamar replied sarcastically, "Maybe they went for coffee and doughnuts! I don't know."

"Come on, Sheriff. Lighten up."

Lamar stepped out of the SUV and loaded his shotgun. He shouted, "Anyone out here?"

Johnny reached into the back seat and took out a rifle. He loaded it and scanned the area again.

Lamar shouted again, "Hello! Anyone here?"

The two men surveyed the area with worried expressions. Johnny remarked, "Don't see nothin' peculiar, Sheriff."

Lamar approached Schultz's corpse and warned, "Keep your eyes open and your mouth shut until we figure out what's going on here."

"Yes, sir."

Lamar knelt over the corpse and uttered, "It's Schultz alright or at least it used to be."

Johnny paced around the perimeter, searching for clues. He glanced back and inquired curiously, "What killed him?"

Lamar examined the bullet wound and replied, "Ordinarily, I'd say a bullet to the chest. In this case, I have no friggin' idea what happened to him."

Johnny found Jill's cell phone and picked it up. "Hey, Sheriff, looks like someone lost their cell phone."

Lamar took a handkerchief from his pocket and handed it to his deputy. He chastised him, "That's right, screw up the evidence, you muttonhead. This is a crime scene, you know."

Johnny took the handkerchief and wrapped it around the cell phone. He replied apologetically, "Sorry, Sheriff. I wasn't thinking."

Lamar returned to Schultz's corpse and examined it. He uttered nervously, "If I didn't know better, I'd swear he was poisoned and shot, but this would certainly be the worst damn case of rigor mortis I've ever seen, though."

Johnny saw a small pool of glistening substance on the dirt and grass. He knelt down and studied it. "Hey, Sheriff, there's something on the ground here."

Lamar left the body and approached him. "What do you got?"

"Looks like clear syrup."

Lamar knelt down and stirred the substance with a stick. The substance was viscous and dripped slowly from the stick. He directed Johnny, "Get the sample kit out of the truck. Get as much of this stuff as you can without the dirt."

"Right away, Sheriff." Johnny went to the truck and opened the rear hatch.

Lamar eyed a rough trail through the grass and trees. He considered following it but thought better of it.

A man's voice came over the radio in the police SUV, "Sheriff, it's Flores. Come in, please."

Lamar plodded to the vehicle and reached inside for the mike. "Go ahead, Flores."

"We found traces of a strange substance on Noel Kemmerman's wheelchair."

Lamar quipped cynically, "Let me guess; it's thick and clear and syrupy."

"Sure is."

"Finish up there and report to Pomona Trail on Graham's Mountain ASAP. Bring Nickerson with you."

"Will do, Sheriff."

Lamar tossed the radio mike on the seat. Johnny brought a small plastic container to him. "Here it is, Sheriff."

Lamar growled, "Well put it in the truck already! What do you want me to do with it?"

Johnny knew that the sheriff only acted like this when he was worried. He understood and learned to tolerate the sheriff's lousy attitude when things got tough.

Kaz pulled up in his Suburban marked Parmissing Valley Coroner's Office. Lamar waved him over to the body.

Kaz got out of the Suburban, carrying a black bag with him. Lamar greeted him somberly, "Morning, Kaz."

"Hey, Sheriff, what do we have today?"

"Bullet hole in the chest but I'm not sure if that's what killed him."

Kaz glanced at the body and uttered in mild surprise, "Geez, Schultz was a friend of mine. Sure doesn't look like him, though." He put on a pair of latex gloves and checked for a pulse.

Lamar remarked, "I guess he's got rigor pretty bad."

Kaz examined the teeth and replied, "Shouldn't do this to him, though. I'll need to get an autopsy on him immediately. He looks pretty messed up for being dead less than twenty-four hours." Kaz laid out the body bag on the ground. He looked up at Lamar and remarked, "You know the drill."

Lamar ordered, "Johnny, get your ass over here and give us a hand."

The three of them maneuvered Schultz's corpse into the body bag and lifted it into the rear of the Suburban.

Johnny complained, "Chris' sakes, Mr. Schultz could've stood to lose a few pounds."

Lamar chastised him, "Watch your mouth, boy. Don't be usin' the Lord's name in vain."

Johnny was embarrassed. "Sorry, Sheriff. My bad."

Kaz took off the latex gloves and tossed them on the bag. "Well, Sheriff, I'll take our boy back and see what I can find out."

"Thanks, Kaz. I'll stop by later."

Kaz shook hands with the two men and kidded Johnny, "Keep the Sheriff out of trouble, will you?"

"Sheriff's a handful but I'll try."

Kaz climbed in the Suburban and drove off. Lamar ordered, "Let's take another look around. Keep your eyes open and your gun ready."

"I got you covered, Sheriff."

The two men searched the trees for an hour and found nothing. Lamar scanned the area once more while Johnny waited impatiently inside the truck. Once inside, the sheriff started the truck and muttered, "Flores and Nickerson should have been here by now."

Johnny picked up the radio mike and called, "Come in Flores. This is Deputy Watkins. Come in Flores."

"You got the right channel?" Lamar asked.

"Of course, I do, Sheriff."

Johnny again called, "Flores. Nickerson. Come in, will you?" There was no response. The two men glanced at each other nervously.

Lamar drove the vehicle down the mountain trail. He recalled that he came to Parmissing Valley just so he wouldn't have to deal with situations like this. He knew he was a coward after his experience with big city police politics but he learned to play a tough guy here in Parmissing Valley. Johnny suspected as much but valued his friendship with Lamar. He pandered to him in most situations.

Lamar took out his cell phone and called the local news station. He informed them of Schultz's death and his pending investigation. Johnny questioned him, "Do you think that was smart, Sheriff?"

"They'd find out anyway and then they'd be after my hide. Media's a dangerous animal, you know."

Grimwold and Shurek watched their latest victims mutate on the spaceship floor. Jill spasmed and quivered as her face throbbed. Her jaw extended and her teeth became disjointed. Two short fangs grew out of her upper jaw. Her back snapped as it hunched and her groans became snarls.

Steve moaned as he rolled across the spaceship floor. His cheeks enlarged and his eyes rolled back in his head momentarily. His limbs grew and his back hunched with a loud crack.

Shurek remarked, "Looks like they're reverting to a primitive stage of their evolution."

Grimwold suggested mockingly, "Maybe they were never that smart to begin with. How long will they mutate for?"

"Who knows?" replied Shurek cynically. "Maybe they'll never stop."

Kroll entered and announced, "I found a cave nearby for these things to stay until we need them. I turned two more humans from the cabins we struck last night."

Two disfigured humans entered the spaceship wearing tattered police uniforms. The nametags read 'Flores' and 'Nickerson'.

Shurek looked pleased with him and quipped, "Maybe you are worth keeping around, Kroll."

"Very funny, Shurek."

Shurek took Flores' pistol from his belt and examined it. His claws were too big to work the trigger. He complained, "We need to find someone to teach us about their weapons."

Grimwold suggested, "We could implant DNA compound inside them."

"No, not in the mutated humans. Their brains are already a mess."

Kroll advised, "I don't think we should mess with that. You don't know what will happen."

Shurek scoffed, "That's why we have these, you fool." He lifted the fleshy flap that covered a small cavity in the right side of his chest, revealing a gray worm about two inches long. It dangled from the roof of the cavity.

Grimwold remarked, "Clever idea, Shurek. We can control them after we give them the DNA."

Kroll shook his head in disbelief and warned, "You'd better be careful. You don't know what they'll become."

Shurek chided, "Don't you have something better to do, Kroll, than to irritate me to no end?"

Kroll glared at Shurek disgustedly and then ordered the mutants, "Follow me. I'll take you to your new home." The mutated humans obediently followed Kroll out of the ship.

Kaz pulled into the parking lot of the Parmissing Valley City Morgue and backed his vehicle toward the double-doored entrance on the side of the building.

The morgue resembled an old firehouse, made from red brick. It stood two stories high, square in shape and had few windows on either of the floors. The parking lot on the right side was just large enough to hold five vehicles. In a small city like Parmissing Valley, the morgue didn't get much action except for the elderly when they moved on to a higher plane of life. Crime was almost nonexistent.

Kaz got out of the Suburban and walked around to the rear. He looked sullen as he opened the rear door. A large woman dressed in an unsightly sundress, Greta, opened the double doors and propped them open with two wooden wedges. She remarked, "Looks like we're working a little overtime, huh, George?"

"Yeah. Unfortunately, it's a friend of mine."

"An old geezer?"

"No, a younger friend."

"What happened to him?"

"Gunshot wound and possible poisoning."

"Damn. We can't afford to lose healthy, young men around here, especially when there's good-hearted, single women like myself on the market."

Greta reached into the Suburban and unzipped the body bag enough to see the face of George Schultz. Horrified, she added, "Although, in his case, I would have thrown him back for the other women to fight over."

Kaz smiled at her remark. Greta always knew how to make him laugh. "Greta, you're a trip; you know that."

"Just making an honest assessment," she replied stoically.

"I'm sure you are."

Kaz slid the gurney halfway out of the vehicle and struggled to lower the wheels on it. He broke a sweat as he held the gurney tightly.

Greta offered, "Why don't you let me help you out with that?" She reached underneath the gurney and unlatched the wheels.

"Thanks, Greta," replied Kaz gratefully. "I don't know what I'd do without you." The wheels descended slowly and locked in.

"You're getting old, George? You never had trouble with the gurney before."

"I don't know what happened to Schultz but his body weighs a ton."

Greta patted him on the back and suggested, "That's what Viagra's for. It'll make you feel like a new man."

Kaz snapped, "I don't need Viagra, Greta! He's just really heavy." He strained as he pushed the gurney through the doors.

Greta kidded, "Nothing to be ashamed of, George. Young men are getting primed with that stuff, too. Women love it."

Kaz pushed the gurney past Greta's desk through another door and into a dim hallway. Greta closed the outside doors and followed him into the hall. "Why don't you replace some of these lights, George? Maybe you'll be able to see where you're going."

"Greta, don't you have work to do."

"I get the point, George. I'll leave you be."

"Thank you."

Kaz was relieved as he watched Greta disappear into the lobby. He pushed the gurney into room four and chocked it next to a steel table. He leaned against the wall and sighed.

Chapter II
Mutilations and Mutations

Dr. Joseph Beauchamp, the general practitioner for Parmissing Valley General Hospital took a rare vacation and planned on spending time with his wife, Suzie, and their two daughters. Joe was twenty-five and his good looks always drew stares from the women in the neighborhood.

Suzie was the same age and very attractive. She wore her long blond hair down over her shoulders and, even in a sweat suit, looked attractive. She enjoyed staying active, even while raising the two girls.

Suzie became pregnant and gave birth to the twin girls while Joe was in medical school. Times were tough then for the two of them until Joe graduated and took the job in Parmissing Valley. The rural atmosphere and small town was perfect for raising the girls.

Four SUVs parked in front of the Beauchamp residence. The mothers gathered and conversed on the sidewalk as their daughters, young Brownies, chatted excitedly about their camping trip.

Joe and Suzie sat in the living room on a love seat. Joe complained, "It's a shame the girl's camping trip is this weekend. I really looked forward to spending some time with you."

"It's only one weekend. They go back to school on Monday and we'll be alone."

"If you say so."

Suzie nestled against Joe and asked nervously, "Um, can I talk to you about something?"

"Sure. What's on your mind, Honey?"

"I know we decided not to have any more kids but, I was thinking, I'd really like to have one more. Do you think we could, Sweetie?"

Joe was surprised by Suzie's request and unprepared to answer. He replied hesitantly, "Let me think about it. I never expected that topic to come up again." Suzie's face saddened and she turned away.

Joe felt bad and pulled her back to him. He whispered into her ear, "Maybe we can make room for one more."

Suzie blurted excitedly, "Thank you, Joe! You've just made me the happiest woman in the world."

Joe teased, "You mean you weren't before this?"

"How can I not be? I have the best husband in the world."

Their two young daughters, DeeDee and Sarah, burst through the front door. They shouted excitedly, "They're here, mommy! They're here!"

Suzie reluctantly stood up and said, "I guess it's time to go." She picked up her sleeping bag and a backpack.

Joe offered, "Let me help you." He carried her sleeping bag in a roll for her under one arm and escorted her from the house. "Don't forget to call when you get there," he reminded her.

They kissed again by the SUV. Suzie promised, "I won't. Try to relax this weekend."

"We'll see. It seems something always comes up." They hugged again.

Two of the mothers, Jane and Pam noticed. Jane complained, "Once upon a time, my husband treated me like that."

Pam remarked, "You're not alone. Did he give you a reason for his change of heart?"

"No. It's just a matter of time before he asks for a divorce, though. It's obvious."

"I'm sorry, Jane."

"Don't be. I'll get over it."

Pam was a husky brunette, plain-faced with her hair in a bun. She had muscular arms and broad shoulders.

Jane, an attractive, young African-American mother who stood about five-feet tall, wore her hair in a ponytail that reached beyond her shoulders. She saw her daughter and niece step into the street and shouted, "Girls, come over here, right now."

Suzie noticed their anxiousness and relented, "Looks like I have to go. The girls are getting restless."

"Be careful of the animals," he cautioned her. "You never know what's roaming around in those woods at night."

Suzie kissed his cheek. She hurried to her SUV and ordered, "Let's go, everyone. Time to move out." The women and girls hurried into their vehicles.

Suzie suggested to Jane, "Why don't you and your girls come with us? We have room."

Jane replied cheerfully, "I'd love to. Thanks, Suzie."

Suzie asked, "Where's your stuff, Jane?"

"It's packed in Pam's truck."

"Then get your butt over here so we can hit the road."

Jane and her two girls climbed into Suzie's SUV and closed the doors. The vehicles drove away in a procession.

Joe stood on the doorstep with his hands in his pockets, looking somber. He exclaimed in a low voice, "Another kid! Is she crazy?" He went inside the house and sat down in the kitchen. After pouring a cup of coffee, he read the newspaper.

His German Shepard, Krauss, approached him and rested his head on Joe's lap. Joe reached down and patted him. "Well, Krauss, looks like it's you and me and a nice quiet weekend." The dog wagged his tail and lay on the floor nearby. Joe flipped through the paper on his way to the sports section until an article caught his eye - "Strange Lights on Graham's Mountain". He became annoyed and uttered, "Oh, please, not the UFO story again. These people belong in an asylum."

⁘⁘⬧⁘⁘

Kaz wrestled with Schultz's corpse and attempted to roll it onto the steel table but couldn't. He complained, "Damn, Bob! What the hell happened to you?"

Kaz peeled the body bag open and slid it down from underneath the corpse. He threw it disgustedly in the corner and muttered, "Viagra! The nerve of her." He rolled Schultz halfway over and noticed several holes along either side of his spinal column. "What do we have here?"

He leaned into the corpse with his shoulder and rolled it halfway over onto the steel table. After a deep breath, he exclaimed, "Whew! Now we're getting somewhere."

The corpse looked peculiar, lying on its side. The eyes were wide open and eerily blank. Kaz became irritated and uttered, "This isn't gonna work." He forcefully pressed both eyelids closed on the corpse until they remained closed. "Now, keep 'em closed! I don't need this right now."

Kaz slid a small tray with surgical tools and clamps on it next to Schultz's corpse. He took the scalpel and made a neat incision in the skin along the spine. Gently, he tugged the skin back with a forceps and pinned it open.

Greta burst through the door and asked, "Who are you shouting at, George?"

Kaz jumped back and covered his heart. He complained, "Geez, Greta! Can't you knock first? You scared the crap out of me."

Greta looked hurt and embarrassed. "Well, sorry for caring."

Kaz answered defensively, "I wasn't talking to anyone. I was thinking out loud."

Greta offered, "You sounded a little tense. Do you want me to start a report on Mr. Schultz?"

"Yeah, why not?"

"What do you think happened to him?"

Kaz became annoyed and shouted sarcastically, "I don't know yet, Greta!"

"I take it that's an 'I don't know'. Thank you, George." She left the room as quickly as she entered.

Kaz examined the flesh and bone around the spine. The discs were enlarged and flattened. He probed the flesh under the bone and found enlarged green tendrils. "What the hell are these?"

Kaz took a short steel bar and pried the discs apart. He located the spinal cord and pressed on it with a probe. It swelled with fluid. He cut through one of the holes in the flesh and discovered that whatever was injected into Bob Schultz directly affected the nervous system.

Kaz backed away from the table and wiped his brow. He never saw anything like this before and felt worse knowing that his friend suffered from this horrible, unknown affliction before his death. He wondered, *Was this caused by a person, a creature or a maybe even a machine?* Kaz removed his latex gloves and picked up the phone. He dialed Joe Beauchamp's number.

———— ·+·+♦+·+· ————

Joe sipped his coffee and read the sports page. The phone rang, breaking the silence. "I knew it was too good to last." He reluctantly got up from the table and answered the phone, "Dr. Beauchamp speaking."

The excitement in Kaz's voice immediately caught Joe's attention. He ranted, "Joe, I've got something here I think you need to see."

"I'm supposed to be on vacation, George," he complained. "What is it?"

"Well, a man appears to have been shot to death. Sheriff called me this morning to pick him up on the Pomona Trail."

"That's it – a man was shot to death?"

"There's more to it, Joe. His body is … Well, you'd better come down and see this for yourself. It ain't normal."

Joe rolled his eyes and took another sip of his coffee. He replied grudgingly, "Alright, George, I'll be down shortly."

"Thanks, Joe."

Joe hung up the phone and sighed. He muttered, "One week out of the year. That's all I ask."

Joe filled the dog's bowl with water and set it on the floor. He patted the dog on the head and said apologetically, "Sorry, boy. Gotta' go."

The dog wagged his tail as Joe picked up his keys from the counter. When he left the kitchen, the dog rested his head back on the tile floor and slept.

Joe locked the front door and walked toward his pickup truck. He pondered, *What could George possibly be so concerned about? What would he consider 'not normal'?*

Joe started the truck and backed out of the driveway. The morgue was four miles away and took only ten minutes by freeway. He turned on the radio and listened to the last few bars of a song before the local morning news came on.

The newswoman said somberly, "Highlighting today's news, Bob Schultz was found dead on the Pomona Trail early this morning. Bob's wife reported that he went hunting with a friend, Bo Davis, yesterday and never returned. There's been no sign of Davis as of yet. Sheriff Whittington expects to have more information later this afternoon."

Joe commented cynically to himself, "It sure didn't take long for that to make the news."

⋯⋯✦✦✦⋯⋯

Lamar and six of his men searched through the forest on the west side of the Pomona Trail. Johnny and another searched the east side. Shortly after, he found red splotches of blood on the grass at the edge of a clearing and shouted, "Hey, Sheriff, I found something!"

Lamar trudged through thick bushes toward him and complained, "This better be good, Watkins."

Johnny pointed to the stained grass. Lamar knelt down and examined the stains. He spotted small chunks of flesh in the grass as well. He looked further and saw a pool of blood.

Lamar wiped sweat from his brow and tried to hide his nervousness. He stammered, "Looks like somebody's been butchered pretty good."

Johnny inquired, "Where's the rest of the body? You'd think it'd be close by."

"If this is Davis' remains, he's no doubt dead. Take a sample of the blood and send it over to Milmont. They'll confirm the identity."

Johnny ordered, "Jones. Mayberry. Get a sample of this and get it over to Milmont."

Jones volunteered, "I'll get the kit." He went to his vehicle and opened the trunk.

Lamar instructed Johnny, "Let's head back to the morgue and see what Kaz found so far."

Johnny was surprised and asked, "Is that it for the investigation?"

"Unless the blood is someone else's, I don't see a need to waste manpower up here."

"But what about the killer, Sheriff?"

Lamar glared at Johnny and repeated sternly, "We'll see what Kaz has found so far. Besides, it was probably just a bear or something."

"Yes, sir." Johnny then directed the other officers, "Hang out until Jones gets his sample, then head back to town."

◆ ⋯

The policemen congregated and stared at the bloodstains in the grass. Officer Mayberry asked, "What if the murderer comes back?"

Johnny responded impatiently, "Apprehend him and call us."

"But what if it's an animal?"

Johnny became irritated and exclaimed, "Then shoot it! Do I have to think of everything?"

"Just wanted to be sure we're clear on our objectives."

Johnny groaned and followed Lamar to their police SUV.

Lamar chuckled and teased, "How does it feel to be bombarded with stupid questions when you're trying to think?"

Johnny asked humbly, "I'm not that bad, am I?"

As Lamar climbed into the truck, he responded playfully, "What do you think?"

<hr>

Joe's truck pulled into the morgue's parking lot and parked next to the entrance. "Well, let's get this over with," he mumbled to himself. "Maybe I'll get home in time for an afternoon nap."

Joe entered the morgue and saw Greta seated at the desk. *No friggin' way. Spare me,* he thought to himself.

Greta smiled at Joe with crooked teeth and thinning hair. She greeted him cheerfully, "Good morning, Dr. Beauchamp!"

Joe tried not to make eye contact with her as he replied, "Good morning, Greta."

"Are you still married to that stick of a woman?" she teased.

Joe became annoyed and replied tersely, "Yes, Greta and I always will."

"Ah, your one of those 'til death do us part' people. Nothing lasts forever, you know. If you ever change your mind …"

"No, Greta, I won't change my mind. Can you tell George that I'm here, please?"

"Sure, Honey. Anything for you." Joe rolled his eyes and paced the floor impatiently.

Greta pressed the button on the speakerphone. She smiled again at Joe and said coyly, "Hey, George, that handsome friend of yours is here - Dr. Beauchamp."

Kaz chuckled and replied over the intercom, "Send him back, Greta."

"You heard him, Sweetie. Want an escort?"

Joe pushed the door open and answered cynically, "No, I'm sure I can find him."

Greta leaned out of her chair and eyed Joe from behind as he left the lobby. When the door closed, she groaned, "What I would do for a piece of that man!"

Joe opened the door to the lab and peered in. Kaz wore a plastic apron and latex gloves. He cut into the nape of Schultz's neck with a scalpel when Joe commented, "I heard this is the hot party in town."

Kaz ceased cutting and greeted him, "Hello, Joe. Thanks so much for coming."

"Good to see you, Kaz." Joe approached him and eyed the corpse. He commented wryly, "You know, you're cutting into my vacation time."

Kaz pointed to an apron and gloves on the countertop. He instructed Joe, "Suit up. I think you'll find this is well worth some of your vacation time."

Joe put on the apron and inquired, "What's so special about your corpse or did Greta put you up to this?" He stretched on the latex gloves and approached the gurney.

Kaz ribbed him, "Come on, Joe. She's a lonely old woman and she likes you."

"Gee, I couldn't tell." He approached the corpse and browsed at the neck and spine areas.

Kaz noticed Joe's hesitancy. "Something wrong, Joe?"

"I, uh, prefer to work on the living. I've never had much luck with cadavers."

"They make you queasy?"

"Just a little," he replied, somewhat embarrassed.

Kaz peeled the skin back with the forceps and pointed to one of several holes along the spine. "See this? Something was injected into Bob's back. There's eight of these holes on either side of his spine."

Joe leaned closer and probed the hole with his gloved fingertip. He asked, "Any idea what from?"

"No. I discovered this and called you right away."

Joe studied the broadened disks and felt underneath them. He noticed the swollen tendrils and spinal cord between the separated disks. "Can you get a fluid sample from the spinal cord, Kaz? Judging by the color, I don't think this is an infection."

Kaz went to the counter and opened a drawer. He retrieved a syringe and uncapped the needle. "Any thoughts so far, Joe?"

Joe studied the spine and remarked, "The disks look disfigured."

Kaz quipped, "Or mutated." He inserted the needle into the spinal cord and removed a small amount of the fluid. Next, he dispensed the contents into a glass vial and set it on the table.

"Can you have Sam Berman come over and check this out?" requested Joe. "I'm sure he can explain some of this."

"Of course. I'll contact him when we're done."

"The disks are enlarged and flattened. The spine as a whole looks as though it degenerated into a row of bony plates."

"What could cause something like this?" asked Kaz, baffled.

"Beats me. I don't know of any diseases that can do this to an adult." Joe lifted the eyelids of the corpse and shined a small light at the eyes. The pupils were large and dark with very little white showing.

Kaz warned, "You make sure you close those eyes when you're finished. They give me the willies."

"Very interesting," Joe remarked.

"That's the damnedest thing I've ever seen," Kaz mentioned. He pressed the page button and requested, "Greta, see if you can get a hold of Sam Berman."

Greta answered coldly, "Say 'please'."

"Alright, Greta, I'm sorry. Please get Sam on the line for me."

"Oh, alright," she replied. Kaz released the page button and returned to the table.

Joe suggested, "How about we roll him over and take a look inside?"

"I hope you're up for this. He's a little on the heavy side."

Joe teased, "Come on, Kaz. You used to manhandle corpses all by yourself."

Kaz remarked cynically, "Yeah, we'll see how you do with this one." He reached over the table and grabbed the corpse's hips as Joe pulled on the left arm and shoulder. Together they rolled Schultz's body on its back.

Joe groaned, "His body is damn heavy."

Kaz suggested, "Rigor mortis?"

"No way. Something else is going on with Mr. Schultz."

"How'd you know his name?"

"Heard it on the radio on the way over."

Kaz pounded his fist on the steel table and complained, "Damn that Sheriff Whittington! He can't keep his yap shut."

Joe asked, "Is it that big a deal?"

"Well, I thought he'd have enough sense to realize we have to be careful with this. Suppose Schultz has some contagious disease?" Kaz explained, "Whittington never could resist being the center of attention. He's always trying to sell himself to the town. He doesn't realize that nobody cares."

"Well, it doesn't matter now," Joe remarked. "Let's cut him open."

The two men stared at each other for several seconds. Then Kaz realized that Joe waited for him to cut open the body.

Kaz said humbly, "I thought you wanted to do the honors, Joe."

"No, thanks," Joe responded. "I work with the living; you work with the dead."

"You make it sound so dead," joked Kaz as he took a small rotary saw off the tray and plugged it in. When he leaned over the corpse and attempted to cut through the sternum, the blade slit the skin, which was leathery and gray, but failed to cut through the bone. A small plume of smoke rose from the blade as Kaz leaned harder against the chest.

Surprised, Joe questioned him, "Is the blade supposed to do that?"

Kaz grew frustrated and replied, "Not really."

Joe took the saw from Kaz and tried to cut through the bone. Again, the blade emitted a plume of smoke. "That's the toughest damn bone I ever saw."

Kaz opened the door to one of the lower cabinets and retrieved a circular saw. He quipped, "Time to get serious." Joe looked surprised and stepped back.

Kaz plugged the saw in and leaned over the chest. "Meet my new friends, Black and Decker," he joked. It took the better part of an hour to cut through the ribs and sternum. When he finally cut through the last piece of bone, the ribcage sagged heavily into the body. Kaz unplugged the saw and set it on the counter.

Joe strained to lift the rib cage off of the body. "Shit! This thing weighs a ton."

Kaz returned to the table and remarked, "I told you so."

Together they lifted the ribcage and set it on the counter nearby. Joe wiped sweat from his forehead with his sleeve and sighed. Kaz felt redeemed and kidded, "Greta says that Viagra will fix this problem."

Joe tapped on the bone with a scalpel. It sounded like hollowed cement. He exclaimed, "Kaz, his bone structure resembles petrified wood!"

"That's one possibility."

Joe pointed to the corpse and said, "You're up."

"Thanks, buddy. I thought you were on a roll." Kaz picked up a scalpel and probe. He sliced open the abdomen of the corpse and folded back the skin. "The skin's pretty tough. It's like cutting through leather."

Joe felt the skin between his thumb and forefinger. Even with the latex glove on, he felt the odd dexterity of the skin. He examined the face more closely. The cheekbones were raised and the temple area enlarged. Joe pressed against them with his fingers. "You see this, Kaz?"

Kaz looked over at the face and asked, "What's that?"

"There's bone over the temple area and the cheekbones are enlarged."

"How did that happen so quickly? I just saw him two days ago and he didn't look like this."

Joe surmised, "Something strange is going on here. Schultz looks like he was mutating into something foreign."

"What do you mean foreign?"

Joe explained, "This might sound stupid but it's like an alien life form was changing his physical structure."

Kaz looked surprised and stepped back from the body. "How the hell does a human being suddenly mutate into an alien life form?"

"Believe me, Kaz, if I knew, I'd tell you. I'm only guessing for lack of a better reason." Joe looked at the open abdomen and remarked, "The intestines are discolored and enlarged. Take them out."

Kaz frowned as he removed four feet of intestines, hand over hand. He chided Joe, "Can you at least cut it off for me?"

Joe looked surprised and asked, "Is that it – only four feet?"

Kaz tugged on it and replied, "Sure looks that way."

Joe took a scalpel off the stainless-steel tray and sliced both ends of the large intestine. He held up one end and studied it. It was blue and smooth, like a snake. Attached to the inner wall were many small roots that dangled freely inside the intestine.

Kaz asked, "Well, are you going to say something?"

Joe looked shocked. "This definitely doesn't look human! I've never seen anything like this." He held the end of the intestine for Kaz to examine.

He inspected it and asked, "What are those tendrils?"

"I really don't know. Perhaps they pull the nourishment out of whatever passes through them."

Kaz suggested, "If he was alien, then maybe that's why his intestine grew so short."

"Imagine how fast he would be able to digest his food if that were the case," Joe pointed out.

"Maybe we should call the authorities in. This is getting weird."

"Not yet. Let's keep going."

"But your vacation?"

"Come on, Kaz. This is serious."

Kaz removed the organs one at a time and set them in a steel tub. Joe dissected each organ and carefully examined it.

Lamar steered the police SUV onto the main highway, staring ahead in silence.

Johnny asked, "Do you think we're dealing with a carnivorous creature?"

Lamar rubbed his chin and pondered for several seconds. "I really don't know what to think. See if you can get Flores and Nickerson on the radio, will you?"

"What do I tell them if they answer?"

"Send them up to Pomona Trail to search for Schultz and Davis' guns. Who else is available?"

"Borden and Reyes."

"Send them, too."

Johnny picked up the radio handset and called, "Flores. Nickerson. This is Deputy Watkins. Come in." He tried several times but there was no response.

Lamar became uneasy and complained, "Where the hell are they?"

Johnny called again on the radio, "Flores. Nickerson. Come in. This is Watkins." He waited a few minutes and then called, "Borden. Reyes. This is Watkins."

Reyes voice crackled from the radio, "This is Reyes. Go ahead, Johnny."

"You and Borden head up to the Pomona Trail. Look for Schultz and Davis' hunting rifles."

Reyes replied, "We're near Graham's Village about two miles away."

Lamar grabbed the mike from Johnny and instructed them, "While you're there, ask around if anyone's seen Flores or Nickerson lately. We can't raise them on the radio."

"Will do, Sheriff."

Lamar tossed the mike on the seat. Johnny placed it back on the radio and asked, "Do you think it's safe for the two of them to go up there?"

Lamar looked agitated and answered, "How the hell should I know?"

"Sorry, Sheriff."

Lamar parked the vehicle on the side of the road and put his head against the steering wheel. "I'm sorry," he said apologetically. "I don't know what to think right now."

"We'll get through this, Sheriff. I know we will."

"I'm glad you're so confident."

"I'm sure the killer isn't hanging around Parmissing Valley now that the news is out. Besides, there's got to be a clue or two that will explain what happened."

"You're right, Johnny. There's got to be a logical explanation for this mess. Maybe Kaz found something by now."

Lamar drove back onto the road and sped toward the next exit. His silence made Johnny nervous. Johnny noticed the sweat on Lamar's forehead and realized that the sheriff was really worried. He always suspected that Lamar took the sheriff's position in Parmissing Valley to be away from the tough city streets, but Lamar always looked after him and taught him a lot about finding clues at the scene of the crime. He wondered how he knew so much for having so little experience.

The SUV pulled into the parking lot beside the morgue. The two men got out and entered the morgue. Greta smiled at them and said, "Good afternoon, Sheriff Whittington. Hello, Johnny."

Lamar replied, "Hello, Greta. We're here to see Kaz."

"He's in room four with Doc Beauchamp." Greta smiled coyly at Johnny and waddled toward the door in an attempt to wiggle seductively.

Lamar looked at Johnny with empathy and asked, "You got a hot date or something, Greta?"

Greta paused by the door and replied, "I wish, Sheriff. Just going to check for the mail."

Lamar kidded, "I hope you're behaving yourself. I don't want no calls about you carrying on and chasing men all over town."

Greta beamed and suggested, "Maybe I ought to chase after you, Sheriff."

Now Johnny chuckled at him. Lamar replied stoically, "Good day, Greta."

Greta added, "You know how to get a hold of me. Don't you, Sheriff?"

Lamar shuddered at the thought and hurried through the door toward Kaz's lab.

Johnny responded, "Sheriff's having a bad day, Greta. Don't mind him."

"I understand. If you need anything …"

"No, I'm fine, Greta. Thanks." Johnny chuckled to himself as he walked out of the lobby and headed down the hall.

⋯⋯✦✦✦⋯⋯

Kaz lifted a large purple organ from the corpse's chest and held it up. Joe examined it and concluded, "I believe this was his heart, although it hardly looks like one." He snipped the arteries and veins that connected to it.

Kaz set the organ in the tray and rolled it over. The two men noticed a small hole in it. Kaz uttered, "What do we have here?"

"Let's find out." Joe took a forceps and pressed it into the hole.

Lamar and Johnny entered the room and casually approached the table. Lamar inquired, "So, do we have a cause of death, Kaz?"

Joe pulled a bullet from the hole in the heart and held it up for the men to see.

Kaz examined it and announced, "Looks like a single shot into the heart, Sheriff."

Lamar picked up a plastic bag from the counter and instructed Joe, "Drop that bad boy in here and I'll get it over to forensics."

Joe placed the bullet inside the bag and Lamar sealed it. "You know, Sheriff, something happened to our boy Schultz that caused him to transform into something unhuman."

Lamar kidded, "What was your first clue?"

Kaz reminded him, "Whatever did this to Schultz is still out there."

Lamar grumbled, "Don't you think I know that?"

"I'm just making an observation, Sheriff. Maybe we should contact the authorities."

"I am the authority around here. I'll handle it."

Johnny approached the body and studied it. Lamar taunted, "See something you like, Johnny?"

"I was just thinking about how things might have played out for Mr. Schultz."

"And that is, Einstein?"

"Schultz became something unhuman and attacked Davis. Davis shot him in self-defense but Schultz killed him anyway."

"So what happened to Davis' body?"

"Maybe animals got him or even Schultz himself."

Kaz added, "That could be. Schultz developed some strange teeth formations like those of a carnivore."

Lamar stared at the bullet and replied, "Well, I'm going to get this over to forensics. Call me if you figure this thing out." He hurried out the door. Joe, Kaz and Johnny glanced at each other, unsure of the sheriff's new focus of attention.

Johnny said meekly, "We'll be in touch. Thanks, guys." He hurried after the sheriff.

Joe remarked, "What changed his attitude? He looks anxious to close this case."

Kaz shrugged his shoulders and countered, "Why's he worried about that bullet? That should be the least of his concerns."

"I don't think it's the bullet. That's just a cover for what's going on up there on that mountain."

Kaz suggested, "Let's keep going. We still have a lot to do and I'm tired of this mess already."

Joe prodded him, "No word from Sam, yet? We're going to need his expertise on this one."

"I'll check with Greta." Kaz took off his gloves and pressed the page on the wall. "Greta, did you reach Sam yet?"

Greta's voice blared from the speaker, "It's ringing now. Why don't you talk to him?"

Kaz picked up the phone on the table and pressed 'line 1'.

<hr>

Sam Berman was a handsome, dark-skinned forensics expert. He shaved his head to keep his youthful appearance and drove a red 1964 Corvette. He left a restaurant on the outskirts of town after a dinner date and was escorted by a young female. She wore a slinky, red dress and red heels.

Sam placed his arm around the young woman's waist and kidded with her until his cell phone rang and interrupted the moment. Sam excused himself when he recognized Kaz's number on the display. "Hello, Kaz. What can I do for you?"

Kaz replied, "Hi, Sam. Are you busy?"

"Yes, I am, at the moment."

"I have something I need you to take a look at."

Sam asked curiously, "Is this related to a murder?"

"I guess you could say that. I also have a sample of fluid I'd like you to analyze."

"I'll come by in the morning and see you. I'm tied up tonight."

"Thanks, Sam."

Sam put away his phone and complained, "That's the problem with being important. Everyone calls when they need an expert."

The young woman giggled and nestled against Sam's side as they walked. Sam asked, "Am I important to you?"

The young woman, named Alicia, answered, "I called you, didn't I?"

"Yes, you did." Sam smiled proudly and kissed her on the forehead.

<hr>

Officers Reyes and Borden talked with an elderly couple outside a log cabin. They stared at another police cruiser at the edge of the woods. Reyes asked, "When did you last see the two policemen."

The woman replied, "They went into the woods early this morning and never came out."

Reyes remarked, "That's strange. I wonder if they got lost."

Borden suggested, "Why don't we head over to the Pomona Trail. It's a few miles from here. They might have heard something over there and went on foot."

"Alright, but we're driving. I'm not hiking through no woods when people are disappearing all over the place."

Borden chided, "Stop it already, Reyes! You're spooking me."

"Well how else do you explain what's happening around here?" The elderly couple heard him. They anxiously went inside the cabin and locked their door.

"Nice work, Reyes. You scared those people out of their wits."

"Oh, shut up." The two policemen walked back to their vehicle.

••••••

Lamar pondered inside the truck over the gravity of the situation. He considered, *Maybe it's a good time to change careers.*

Johnny got in and stared patiently at him. "Alright, Sheriff, what's eating you?"

Lamar explained somberly, "Me and the Lord have had our differences over the years. We don't talk much lately."

"We all have our moments, Sheriff."

"Well, I think I'm going to resolve some of those differences and speak to the Man."

Johnny felt uncomfortable seeing him rattled like this. He wondered if the sheriff would stand up and face whoever or whatever murdered Schultz or would he bail on his men?

Reyes voice startled them from the radio. "Sheriff, are you there? It's Reyes."

Lamar anxiously picked up the radio handset and answered, "Go ahead, Reyes."

"We found Flores' vehicle. An old couple says he and Nickerson went into the woods this morning and never came out."

Lamar whispered, "Shit. Now I'm really worried."

Reyes continued, "We're going over to the Pomona Trail. Maybe they heard something and went to check it out."

"I want you guys out of there before dark. Understand?"

"Yes, sir."

Lamar handed the mike to Johnny and informed him, "Tomorrow morning, we're all going up there. Whatever's doing this is going to pay."

"What are we going to do when we get up there?"

"What do you think, jug head? We're taking every gun and round of ammunition with us. We're going to track this thing down and kill it."

"Now you're talking, Sheriff!"

· · + + + · ·

Suzie and five other mothers pitched tents at a campsite three miles west of the Pomona Trail. The young girls watched excitedly as their mothers set up the last tent. Suzie stepped away from the group and took her cell phone from her sweatpants' pocket.

Pam inquired, curious, "What are you up to, Suzie?"

"Just calling Joe to let him know I'm okay. I'll be right over."

Suzie dialed the phone and waited as it rang four times. The message mode turned on: "Dr. Beauchamp is not available to take your call at this time. Please leave a message and he'll respond promptly."

Suzie replied after the beep, "Hi, Honey. We're here at the campsite. Just checking in. I'll talk to you later. Love ya'." She turned the cell phone off and tucked it back in her sweat pants.

Pam kidded, "That was quick."

"He didn't pick up. I guess he's in the middle of something important."

"Men are always in the middle of something important. Maybe one day, we'll meet that criteria."

"Yeah, it seems there's always some emergency or crisis in their lives."

Suzie's girls, Sarah and Dee Dee, rushed to her and hugged her. They raved excitedly, "We love you, mommy."

Suzie knelt down and hugged them back. She said, "I love you, too, girls. Now go find the marshmallows. We're making a fire and we'll have a lot of fun." The girls raced to the truck and pulled out two bags of groceries.

Pam watched admiringly and commented, "You are so patient with your girls."

"Not always. There were a lot of times, though, that I felt like they were all I had. When Joe was in medical school, I had no one else."

"I wish I could be like you."

"Oh, stop it, Pam. You're every bit as good with the kids as I am."

"But you seem satisfied with life. I'm not. My life is missing something and it's depressing."

Suzie asked seriously, "What do you think you're missing, Pam?"

"A sense of purpose. I guess I don't feel appreciated by my husband or my daughter. Jenny gets so excited when she sees her daddy but couldn't care less about me."

"Be patient with them. I'm sure they care."

"Thanks, Suzie. I really wish that were the case."

⋅⋅⋅◆◆◆⋅⋅⋅

Borden and Reyes drove up the Pomona Trail until they reached the site where Schultz' body was found. Reyes parked the police cruiser and got out. Borden checked his .50 caliber Desert Eagle semi-automatic handgun and made sure it was loaded.

Reyes shouted, "You gonna get out and do something today or what?"

Borden reluctantly climbed out of the cruiser. He was a stocky, middle-aged man with balding hair. "I'm coming. Hold your horses," he muttered.

Reyes was a small, Hispanic man with a goatee. He complained, "It's getting late. Let's finish and get out of here."

"What are you afraid of, Reyes?"

"I got a bad feeling about Flores and Nickerson."

"Me, too. That's why I brought this baby." Borden holds out the Desert Eagle for Reyes to see.

Reyes laughed at him and teased, "What are you aiming to shoot with that cannon - a friggin' dinosaur?"

Borden replied coolly, "Just want to be prepared."

Reyes pulled out a switchblade and declared, "See this. If I find a killer, human or otherwise, I'll dice and slice that bitch into a flesh salad."

Borden was amused and chided, "That I'd like to see." Reyes spun the switchblade skillfully and deposited it in his vest pocket.

The two men followed a rough trail through the bushes to the clearing where Davis' blood was found on the grass. Reyes pointed to the markers and commented, "If those boys were really attacked by some animal and had weapons, then I'm sure their guns are around here somewhere. No animal I know of belongs to the NRA."

"You think that's going to shed any light on what happened to those other people?"

Reyes suggested, "Maybe. Let's spread out and do a quick search."

"You sure you want to do that?"

"Yeah, but don't go far."

"It's getting dark. Believe me, I'm not going far."

The two men split up about thirty feet apart and headed northwest toward higher ground. A quarter mile from the vehicle, Reyes discovered a cave in the side of the mountain. He crept closer to it and found a femur lying at the entrance. He shouted, "Borden, I found something!" Reyes aimed his flashlight inside the cave. He heard something move in the darkness.

Borden emerged from the woods and quietly approached Reyes. He tapped Reyes on the shoulder. Reyes was startled and spun around frantically. He held his pistol up to Borden's forehead and yelled, "What the hell is wrong with you?"

Borden nonchalantly pushed the barrel away from his head and requested calmly, "Please don't ever point your gun at me again."

Reyes trembled and replied defensively, "You scared the shit out of me!"

Borden noticed the femur on the ground and remarked, "Looks like an adult male's leg." He took his flashlight off his belt and aimed it inside the cave. He focused his eyes inside the cave but couldn't see anything. "Looks like we're going inside, Reyes, unless you're afraid of the dark."

"Kiss my ass, Borden." Reyes picked up a stone and threw it inside the cave. They heard the stone skip for a distance. He suggested, "Maybe we should call the sheriff first."

"Not yet." Borden held the flashlight in one hand and the Desert Eagle in the other. He cautiously entered the cave.

Reyes followed and taunted him, "Are you sure you can handle that thing?"

"Reyes, shut up!"

"I'm serious. That's a big ass gun to use in a cave."

Borden ignored him and proceeded further. He noticed a trail of various broken human bones leading deeper into the cave. He covered his mouth briefly with his hand and pistol.

Reyes complained, "It stinks in here."

Borden grumbled, "Bat piss. Get used to it."

Reyes whispered, "I know I heard something move in here and it wasn't bats."

"You really think so?" Borden stooped down and picked up a stone. He threw it at the ceiling about twenty feet up. Bats squealed and swarmed around them before disappearing deeper inside the cave. He chastised him, "That's what you heard, Amigo – bats."

"You'd better hope it was only the bats."

Borden stumbled and fell forward. He yelled angrily, "What the hell…?"

Reyes aimed his light on the ground and saw a Browning 30.06 rifle. He exclaimed, "Look, Borden, a rifle!"

Borden got up and dusted himself off. "Now it's time to call the sheriff."

The two policemen exited the cave and stood outside. Reyes took out his phone and dialed.

••◆••

Two men in suits sat next to Lamar's desk waiting patiently. Each was in his late forties and clean cut. Lamar and Johnny entered the station just as the phone rang.

Lamar kidded, "Well, looks like we got a visit from the Feds. Hold on while I take this call." He answered the phone, "This is Sheriff Whittington."

Reyes spoke excitedly, "Sheriff, we found one of the rifles in a cave! The place is littered with bones."

Lamar glanced at the two men in suits and replied, "Good work, Reyes. Come on back and we'll discuss our next course of action."

"We're leaving now, sir."

"Roger. Thanks, Reyes." Lamar hung up the phone.

The two men stood up and extended a hand to the sheriff. The taller of the two announced, "I'm Agent Melendez and this is Agent Cox. We'd like a little information on your missing persons."

Lamar chuckled and replied, "We're not exactly sure they're missing yet." Johnny looked confused by the sheriff's response.

Lamar suggested, "Hey, Johnny, why don't you take a walk down to the bakery and pick up some doughnuts?"

"Uh, sure, Sheriff." Johnny left the office, wondering what was going on.

Agent Cox inquired, "You do have reports on several missing persons today, don't you?"

"There were some parties up on the mountain last night. A few people haven't been heard from."

"So, what are you doing about it?"

"We did a preliminary search of the area and we're planning to go back tomorrow with a full search party."

Agent Melendez responded, "So you haven't found anything unusual with these disappearances, I assume."

"No, sir. One thing you learn in this business is never jump to conclusions."

"You know you're obligated to share information with us."

Lamar's heart raced as he chose his words carefully. "Missing persons and murders don't happen much in these parts. We want to be sure what we have before word gets out to the locals. I don't need a panic on my hands."

Agent Melendez handed him a business card and said, "Call me tomorrow and let me know how your search goes."

"Sure thing. Why the interest?"

"Just making sure it isn't something bigger than a few disappearances. We're ready to take the appropriate actions if necessary." The two agents stood up and walked toward the door.

Lamar kidded, "You boys are welcome to stay for doughnuts and coffee."

The two agents looked back at him unemotionally. Agent Cox answered sarcastically, "We don't eat doughnuts." They left the office and closed the door behind them.

◆••••

Lamar chuckled and quipped, "Too bad. Maybe you guys need a little sugar in your diet."

⚬⚬⚬

Kroll stared at the wall of the ship and read the thoughts of one of the mutated humans in the cave. Grimwold noticed his glazed look and inquired, "What are you doing now, you idiot?"

Kroll turned and glared at him. "Two humans have discovered the cave where our mutants are."

"Can you see who they are?"

"They wear uniforms like the other two." In his mind he saw the mutants huddled in the rear of the cave. He scanned the cave and saw the two men standing outside the cave. "There are two humans at the cave," he revealed. "We should take care of this now."

Grimwold threatened, "If you're wrong, I'll rip your tongue out and beat you with it."

"Can't you shut your mouth for just once?" shouted Kroll. "Useless babble. That's all you do."

Grimwold laughed sarcastically. He rushed out of the spaceship and into the woods. Kroll followed but from a distance. *Perhaps, Grimwold will walk into a trap. One can only hope.*

⚬⚬⚬

Reyes urged his partner, "Let's get out of here. We found one weapon."

Borden replied, "Not yet." He went further into the cave with his flashlight and Desert Eagle aimed ahead of him.

"What the hell's wrong with you, Borden? Let's go!" Reyes shouted angrily.

Borden saw more bones and cringed as he thought about what might have happened there.

Jill and Steve's mutated bodies slithered along the rocks to Borden's left. Flores and Nickerson's mutated bodies crept to Borden's right. Their arms were longer than before and their legs shortened. They moved like primates with their knuckles nearly dragging along the ground. None of their faces were recognizable any more. They had leathery, ogre-like appearances. Foamy saliva drooled from their mouths and pooled at their feet.

Outside the cave, Reyes paced back and forth nervously. He muttered, "Son of a bitch! This is messed up." He reluctantly entered the cave with his pistol and his flashlight aimed ahead of him. Borden was well ahead of him and out of sight. Reyes crept cautiously through the darkness and stepped on a bone. It snapped loudly under his boot.

Reyes shuddered and leaned against the cave wall for support. He mumbled quietly, "Mother of God! Get me out of here in one piece and I'll never swear again."

Borden sensed that he wasn't alone. He turned to his left as Jill lunged toward him. He quickly aimed his Desert Eagle at her face and fired.

The blast from the powerful handgun took half of her face and skull off. She shrieked and fell backwards several steps from the point of impact before landing on her back.

Reyes froze in fear for several seconds. Finally, he shouted, "Borden! Are you alright?"

Borden replied shakily, "Yeah. I got the son-of-a-bitch." As he turned, Steve knocked him to the ground. His flashlight bounced off the rocky floor and extinguished. Borden threw Steve off and got to his knees. He called out, "Reyes, I can't see! Get in here fast!"

Flores and Nickerson lunged on Borden and knocked him backwards. Steve crawled rabidly across the floor on all fours and bit into Borden's shoulder. He let out a horrific scream.

Reyes hurried through the cave, trembling in fear. "Borden! Where are you?"

Nickerson and Flores, tore into Borden's stomach and thigh with their sharp fangs.

Borden screamed and blindly fired the gun at the creatures. His first shot put a large hole in Steve's shoulder and knocked him away. The second shot ricocheted and nearly struck Reyes in the head.

Reyes crouched down and shouted, "Borden!" He crept closer and shined his light on Borden. He was horrified when he saw Flores gnawing on Borden's leg. Nickerson greedily shoved his claw into Borden's abdomen and pulled his intestines out. Borden looked at Reyes with a glazed stare. He put the gun to his head and shot himself.

His brains splattered across the cave wall. The gun flew from his hand from the force and bounced off the wall. The round ricocheted and struck Reyes in the arm. Reyes cried out and fell to the ground. He clutched at his arm and sobbed.

The mutants stopped feeding and looked at Reyes hungrily. Reyes cried out, "You bastards!" He fired several shots at the creatures, then scrambled to his feet and raced out of the cave.

Steve staggered and fell to the ground dead. Flores eyed the bullet wound in his chest and grinned sadistically. He howled and pursued Reyes. Nickerson chased after him as well.

Reyes sobbed hysterically as he raced through the darkening woods. Grimwold and Kroll waited for him as he unknowingly approached them. When Reyes saw them in his path, he froze in his tracks. He shook nervously and urinated in his pants.

The two mutants, Nickerson and Flores, waited behind him as Grimwold and Kroll approached him with sinister grins on their faces. Reyes pointed his pistol and pulled the trigger but the gun was empty. He took out his switchblade and pointed it at the aliens but it did nothing to deter Grimwold or Kroll.

Reyes muttered, "Oh, please help me, God!" He tried desperately to run past Flores and Nickerson but they grabbed him and shoved him backwards into Grimwold's clutches.

Grimwold's tongue wrapped around Reyes neck and cut off his screams. Grimwold's appendages penetrated Reyes back and secreted alien hormone into him.

Reyes shoved his switchblade into Grimwold's thick skin but inflicted little damage. He then stabbed his own abdomen and savagely cut into his organs in a desperate suicide attempt. He shuddered until his last breath left him. Grimwold released him and watched disappointedly as Reyes fell to the ground dead.

CHAPTER III
THE CAMPSITE

Nightfall set in and the girls sat around their campfire singing songs. The mothers wore sweat suits and the young girls wore their Brownie uniforms. The girls toasted marshmallows on sticks while their mothers supervised them.

Jane, Pam and Suzie sat on a log, watching the group. Jane commented, "I think you girls missed your calling. This looks like a real camp. Look how neat the tents are lined up."

"Dinner wasn't half bad either," Pam added.

Suzie confessed, "It's kind of hard to mess up burgers and hotdogs."

Jane admitted sadly, "I'm not used to having a meal in a cheerful environment. Usually it's so quiet in my house, you'd swear someone died."

Suzie stood up and announced loudly, "Alright girls, its bedtime. We have a busy schedule for tomorrow."

The girls moaned in disappointment. They joined their mothers and moved into their tents a short distance away.

Suzie suggested to her friends, "Let's tuck the girls in and we'll talk."

"I'd really appreciate that," Jane replied gratefully.

Suzie escorted her twins, Dee Dee and Sarah to their tent and tucked them in. Dee Dee asked, "Why do we have to go to bed, mommy?"

"Because we have a lot of things planned for tomorrow. All this fresh air will tire you out fast."

Sarah asked, "Are there boogie men out here, mommy?"

Suzie laughed. "If there's a boogie man out here, mommy will kick his butt. Now get some sleep."

Suzie kissed each of the girls and left the tent. She returned to the campfire and sat down on the log. She pondered about having another child and whether or not Joe would really go for it. She recalled their early years together. Sometimes, it seemed that Joe stayed away from home on purpose just to avoid the girls. There were many nights she cried herself to sleep, thinking how her unplanned pregnancy changed their lives. She loved her daughters but she also loved Joe. It seemed like he moved on with his life and left her behind.

Shurek, Grimwold, and Kroll hid in the trees with four mutants. Grimwold boasted, "This should be easy pickings."

Shurek warned, "I don't want to hear a sound. We'll each take a tent and finish them off quickly."

Kroll asked, "What about captives? We can use them."

"Only if you subdue them quietly."

Grimwold warned the mutants, "I don't want to hear a sound out of any of you. We'll leave you the spoils when we're done." The mutants grunted in satisfaction and quietly dispersed.

Jane returned to the campfire and sat down next to Suzie. Suzie sensed that something was wrong and asked, "Are you okay?"

Jane fought back tears and replied shakily, "Are you kidding? That bastard Sam has me so depressed."

"Are you sure there isn't something else on his mind. Maybe it's not you."

"No, I'm sure it's me. I'm surprised he hasn't asked for the divorce already."

"I'm sorry to hear that."

Pam returned with a small backpack and set it on the ground. She caught part of the conversation and asked, "Why is he acting like a schmuck to you, Jane?"

Jane replied somberly, "Since I'm not the skinny-mini I used to be before Jenny, he thinks I'm a slob. I'd like to see him give birth and keep his shape."

Pam remarked angrily, "You look fine. What do you mean you're not a skinny-mini?"

"Sam likes a skinny woman. I guess I don't fit that category anymore."

"I think men get spoiled sometimes," complained Suzie.

Jane continued, "I think he's got someone else on the side. Men can't go long periods without getting even a quickie. It's been over a year since we've been near each other so I know he's getting it somewhere."

Pam blurted, "What a jerk!"

Suzie suggested, "Maybe you need to turn the tables on him. Stop cooking for him and cleaning his things for a week. That'll teach him."

"I don't know what to do anymore. It's like a slow death."

Suzie suggested, "Then maybe it's time to move on."

Jane asked, "What about you, Pam? You never mention your husband."

"That's because there is none. Well, once upon a time there was. He disappeared one day and I never heard from him again. For all I know he's dead."

Suzie and Jane were wide-eyed with surprise. Jane felt embarrassed and said humbly, "I'm so sorry, Pam. I didn't know."

"No sweat. It's like he never existed, both figuratively and literally."

Jane grumbled, "I wish we had a chance to teach them a lesson, once and for all."

Suzie chuckled and responded, "I'd love to make Joe appreciate what I really do for him. I love him but I do feel very under-appreciated."

Pam looked uncomfortable and said, "I'll be right back. I think I have to relieve myself and I'd better do it quickly."

Suzie warned, "Don't go far. You'll get lost and then we'll have to look for you."

"Don't worry about me. I'm right at home out here." Pam took a roll of toilet paper from the backpack and held it up. She quipped, "You'll have to be patient. This might take a while, if you know what I mean." She hurried into the trees.

Suzie and Jane chuckled over her theatrics.

Grimwold watched anxiously and whispered to Shurek, "I'll take care of this one. I'll be back shortly." He anxiously pursued Pam.

Shurek suggested to Kroll, "Why don't you follow him and make sure she doesn't get away. I don't want to take any chances."

"I understand." Kroll disappeared into the trees after Grimwold.

Suzie blurted giddily, "She's insane! I don't know how she manages."

"She probably keeps it inside," suggested Jane. "One day she'll lose her cool and tear some poor guy apart. We'll hear about her on the news and be surprised."

"I sometimes wonder what I'd do without Joe if something happened to him."

"You know, Suzie, you just don't realize how much you depend on someone until they're gone."

"I guess that's why I care about the big jerk so much. I depend on him to keep me happy."

Jane uttered bitterly, "Well, it sucks depending on men."

"It's not all of them, Jane. There's a good one out there for you. You'll see."

"No there isn't. I'm just a useless piece of flesh. I couldn't get laid if I tried."

The two women stood up and hugged as the fire faded to glowing embers. Suzie promised her, "I'm here for you, Jane, whenever you need someone to talk to. That's what friends are for."

Tears rolled down Jane's cheeks. She placed her hand on Suzie's cheek in affectionate appreciation. She suddenly felt an attraction toward Suzie that she never felt before. When she kissed her, Suzie became breathless and looked wide-eyed at Jane.

Jane suddenly felt foolish and turned away. "I'm so sorry. I lost control of myself."

Suzie took a moment to absorb what just happened but felt sympathy for her friend. "Jane, it's alright."

Jane turned back and faced her. "I haven't felt the warmth of a friend or husband in so long. I didn't mean it."

Suzie felt her heart break for Jane and placed her hands on Jane's cheeks. "You're a beautiful person, Jane." She kissed Jane softly. Jane looked so relieved and peaceful for a brief second. Suzie kissed her again with a passion she hadn't felt in a while. She gently maneuvered Jane to the ground and positioned herself on top of her.

After a moment, Jane pushed her away and looked up at the sky. "Suzie, you don't want me. You have a husband and two beautiful daughters."

Suzie rolled on her back and gazed at the stars. "I know but Joe's not all he's cracked up to be. Maybe he's been a disappointment for me as well."

"Really?" replied Jane, surprised by Suzie's revelation.

"Yeah, I'm not living in a perfect world either."

Jane leaned forward and kissed her again.

⋅⋅⋅◆◆◆⋅⋅⋅

Pam pulled her sweat pants up and bent down for her roll of toilet paper. She noticed a faint glow through the trees and her curiosity got the better of her. Pam crept toward the source for a closer look. The light emanated from the open hatch of the spaceship. The ship itself was shaped like a bullet, about the size of a tractor-trailer.

Pam became frightened and turned to run but Grimwold stood before her with his fiendish smile and bared his sharp teeth. His tongue wiggled in and out of his mouth several times.

Kroll appeared behind her and wrapped his tongue around her neck. Small needles emerged from the tongue and injected a powerful numbing agent into her throat muscles. Pam struggled to get free and tried to scream but could only gasp for air. Her eyes were wide with fear.

Kroll released his tongue and shoved her into Grimwold's clutches. Grimwold glared at Kroll and chastised him, "How dare you interfere with my prey!"

Kroll replied smugly, "Shurek sent me to make sure you don't screw it up."

Grimwold hissed at him and pulled Pam against his chest. His appendages grappled into Pam's back and penetrated her. Clear drops of hormone dribbled from the puncture wounds. Grimwold's eyes bulged with perverse glee.

Pam hyperventilated and shivered until the appendages retracted. She slid limply from Grimwold's grip to the ground. Her eyes were half open but she wasn't conscious. Grimwold took a deep breath and exhaled. He taunted Kroll, "Did you enjoy watching?"

Kroll rebuked him, "If I didn't interfere, her scream would have awakened the others. You're reckless, Grimwold."

"And you're a disgrace! Stay out of my business if you know what's good for you."

◆⋅⋅⋅

Kroll shook his head in disgust at Grimwold and walked away. Grimwold glared as Kroll disappeared into the trees. He picked Pam up and carried her over his shoulder to the spaceship. Since Grimwold escaped from his world with Shurek and Kroll, he never quite trusted them. He often considered creating his own army of mutants and disposing of the two.

Grimwold entered the ship and laid Pam down on one of three steel tables. He retrieved a star shaped device from a nearby cabinet and placed it on Pam's head. When he pressed the hub on top of the device, probes emerged from each arm of the device and burned through Pam's skull into her brain. Tiny nanochips were inserted into her brain and immediately transmitted the aliens' history, behavioral patterns, habits and expectations into human form and programmed her to behave as a subservient mutant.

The hormone injected earlier initiated the mutation of Pam's body, nervous system and brain to assimilate certain alien traits into her physiology. Unfortunately, it was a degenerative process that made her become a lower-level creature.

Grimwold's tongue emerged and slid into Pam's mouth. Slimy mucus covered Pam's lips as the tongue penetrated past her tonsils and down her throat. He strained until a lump of DNA compound formed and passed through his tongue into Pam's throat.

Pam gagged unconsciously and her eyes rolled back in her head as she heaved. The compound was quickly absorbed into her body and stalled the degenerative process of the hormone. Her cheeks were already enlarged and her skin texture turned leathery brown. Her arms and legs became muscular and strained the sweat suit until it tore in several areas. Flattened bony plates grew out of her discs and protruded from her back, raising her slightly off the table.

Grimwold retracted his long, tubular tongue from her throat. He lifted a flap on his chest and retrieved a small gray worm from his cavity. The worm quivered back and forth between Grimwold's claws. He snickered as he laid the worm across Pam's upper lip. The worm slithered into her nose and penetrated her nasal passage until it ate its way into the frontal lobe of her brain. Blood mixed with pink fluid trickled from Pam's nose and streamed down the side of her face, staining the table. Inside her skull, tiny tendrils emerged from the worm and attached themselves to Pam's frontal lobe and monitored her thoughts. Grimwold was satisfied when he could read her thoughts. He saw her struggle to retain thoughts of her human life.

Pam was confused as she sorted out the alien world from her own. The change took a few hours before she fully made the transformation into Grimwold's pseudo-species. The one benefit was that he could control her thoughts and sensations through the worm. He felt confident that she was progressing satisfactorily so he left the ship and hurried back to the camp.

Pam retrieved her phone from her pocket and attempted to type a message. After struggling to make it legible, she sent the text. Pain shot through her brain and she smashed the phone against the wall. Her memories faded and she was helpless to do anything about it.

Shurek watched as Suzie and Jane embraced. "Interesting the way humans behave. Better for me, though. I doubt they'll be interrupted." He crept up to one of the tents and crawled inside. His vision allowed him to see the shapes of one mother and three girls in their sleeping bags, fast asleep. He studied them briefly and made his move. His tongue lashed out and coiled around the mother's neck. It tightened and crushed her throat. He grabbed two of the girls' throats with his claws and ripped them apart.

Meanwhile, Shurek motioned Kroll toward the third tent while he crept into the second tent where Suzie's daughters slept alone. He shoved a claw into each girl's throat to prevent them from screaming. Then, he raised their chins, thus exposing their necks, and tore into their throats with swift bites. Blood spattered across the tent walls and the quilts. Shurek thought sadistically, *Ah, fresh, young meat.*

Kroll slithered into the third tent and found three sleeping girls. He thrashed their throats and plunged his teeth into their tender abdomens. The taste of blood made him drunk with lust and hunger.

Jane glanced at the shaking tent and remarked, "Looks like the girls are restless. I'd better check on them."

"I'll wait for Pam. I certainly hope she doesn't make this a career move," Suzie commented impatiently.

Jane chuckled and kidded, "Pray that she's down wind. She tends to make a big issue of going to the bathroom, if you know what I mean."

"Thanks, Jane. I really needed to know that."

"I'd better turn in for the night. If not, we'll both have pneumonia."

Suzie hugged Jane again. "We have a bond that will never be broken."

"You're a good friend, Suzie," Jane complimented her and retired to her tent.

Kroll waited against the tent wall and debated whether to slide out or attack Jane. Jane entered and knelt down over the dead girls, unaware of their fate. She whispered, "Good night, girls. Momma' loves you." She stooped over to kiss each of them but Kroll made his move and leaped on her back. His tongue coiled around her neck and numbed her throat and vocal cords. His weight pressed Jane face first into the entrails of her daughter. She was mortified but helpless to move. Kroll pressed his chest evenly against Jane's back. His appendages darted cleanly into Jane's back on either side of her spine and hooked into her spinal cord. His head bobbed drunkenly until he retracted his tongue from Jane's neck.

Jane's eyes stared coldly at her dead daughter. Tears rolled down her cheek and she slid into unconsciousness.

The embers were barely noticeable as darkness swallowed the camp. Suzie paced uneasily and whimpered, "Come on, Pam. Where the hell are you?" She fixed her clothes and saw her breath in the chilly night air. Shivering, she complained aloud, "Oh, you pain in the ass, Pam." The moonlight broke through the clouds and cast an eerie glow through the haze on the camp.

Suzie mumbled to herself, "Shit! Something's wrong." She reluctantly stormed into the forest in search of Pam.

Shurek and Kroll watched Suzie disappear into the trees. They gutted the corpses in the last two tents and then emerged into the night air, covered in blood and entrails.

Kroll informed Shurek, "I've taken one for transformation."

"Take her to the ship. I'll wait here while the mutants feed."

Kroll returned to Jane's tent. He lifted her limp body over his shoulder and carried her back to the ship. Shurek called the mutant humans from the trees, "Come, my pets, and feed."

Four of them rushed past him and greedily tore the tents apart. They lunged onto the dead carcasses and gorged on the warm flesh in an orgy of blood.

Suzie stepped through the trees and called out, "Pam, where are you?" She listened but there was no reply. As she pushed through several branches, she saw the roll of toilet paper partially unraveled on the ground and became concerned. Again, Suzie shouted, "Pam, answer me!"

Suzie noticed the glow from the spaceship's open hatch and peered through the trees. She grew terrified and thought, *What the hell is going on here?*

Kroll appeared out of the trees carrying Jane over his shoulder. He crossed the clearing and approached the ship. Suzie wasn't sure who or what Kroll carried until he walked up the ramp and entered the ship. Then she recognized Jane by her hair and clothes. Several branches broke behind her and she screamed. Shurek reached through the trees and grabbed her arm. He threw her to the ground and perched over her, baring a sinister sneer with sharp, jagged teeth. Drool streamed from his jaws and pooled next to her.

The sight of Shurek appalled Suzie. She desperately crawled away and tried to get up but Grimwold stood behind her waiting. His appendages emerged, quivering excitedly. Clear hormone dripped from each of his appendages as they reached hungrily for Suzie like tiny fingers. Shurek warned Grimwold in their language, "Don't touch her. She's mine."

Grimwold taunted him, "Can you handle her?"

"I think you should watch yourself. You're testing my patience."

Suzie sensed they were at a discord and tried to run. Grimwold grabbed her by the back of the neck and shoved her into Shurek's waiting arms. Suzie struggled to get free as Shurek's tongue wrapped around her neck. She felt the needles penetrate her throat and paralyze her vocal cords.

Her breathing became restricted and she lost her ability to inhale. Shurek pressed her against his chest as she squirmed.

Suzie battled and turned partially sideways as the appendages penetrated her back, missing her spine. Only one row of the appendages came close to her spinal cord. The other row struck the fleshy part of her back and inflamed her skin like an infection.

Shurek relished the feeling of subduing a human female with as much fight as Suzie had. He felt an orgasmic, satisfying feeling as he pumped his hormone into her body. His eyes turned opaque as he breathed heavily, overcome with elation. Grimwold realized that Suzie would die if Shurek continued to inject her with hormone. He grabbed Shurek's shoulder tightly.

Shurek dropped Suzie to the ground and took a fighting stance toward Grimwold. He challenged, "How dare you?"

Grimwold warned sarcastically, "You were killing her. Humans can't take that much hormone."

Shurek bellowed, "Says who?"

Grimwold reminded him, "Remember the female in the cabin? She exploded all over the place."

Shurek glared at him and lowered his claws. He conceded, "Maybe you're right. I'd hate to waste this one. She's awful feisty for a human." He carried Suzie's limp body into the ship.

CHAPTER IV

THE TURNING

Kaz jotted notes in a copybook as he probed one of Schultz's lungs on a stainless-steel tray. Joe dissected sections of the spine and brain on another tray. He slit open the spinal cord at the base of the neck and noticed smaller cords had formed inside. "Son of a bitch!" he exclaimed. "Will you look at this?"

Kaz glanced over and asked, "What did you find?"

Joe revealed that the interior of the spine and brain were being destroyed by the formation of a new nervous system and brain. "Something's using Schultz for a host," he concluded.

Kaz grew somber as he slid his chair near Joe's. Joe pointed with a ceramic probe to the tiny cords inside the spinal cord. "Well, I'll be," uttered Kaz.

"I don't understand what's happening to him," Joe confessed, baffled by his discovery. "If he was transforming into something else, why would these new tendrils form inside him."

Kaz suggested, "Maybe it's modifying his body to accommodate its essence."

"What the hell are you talking about?" blurted Joe, growing more concerned about their findings.

"Essence. It's like a soul or a conscience."

"I couldn't even begin to guess," Joe grumbled. "This defies all logic that I know of." He then peeled apart the lobes of Schultz's brain. A much smaller, darkened piece of matter formed between the lobes and sprouted tendrils into the different lobes. Each area of contact on Schultz's lobes was deteriorated and showed swelling from infection. "Then something was taking over Schultz's body," he reiterated.

Kaz slid his chair back to the other tray and slit the heart open. He found a strange new organ growing inside Schultz's heart. This organ had only two chambers and was much simpler in relation to the human heart. He announced in amazement, "His heart was being replaced as well. The old one would deteriorate and be absorbed into his body."

Joe declared uneasily, "We do have an alien life form on our hands."

Kaz backed away from the table and asked apprehensively, "What do we do now?"

"Seal everything up. We need to notify the authorities. That's it for tonight."

"What about tomorrow?" asked Kaz.

"I'll have to make a call and see what the protocol is for this. We may need to quarantine the place." Joe looked up at the clock and muttered, "Damn. Nine-thirty already."

Kaz complained, "What a day?"

"Yeah, but at least we know that our buddy here did do a Jekyll and Hyde act."

"You know, Joe, that's exactly what he reminds me of - Jekyll and Hyde."

"Maybe the sheriff will have more info for us in the morning," suggested Joe.

"I certainly hope so." Kaz bagged the organs one at a time and marked the plastic bags.

Joe left the lab and entered the locker room. He stared in the mirror while washing his hands. *Aliens. Is it possible?*

As he left the building, he searched for his phone. "Damn it! Suzie's probably ticked off at me now." Inside the truck, he found the phone on the console where he left it. "Ah, there you are." He picked it up and checked for messages.

Suzie's message played back to him, "Hi, Honey. We're here at the campsite. Just checking in. I'll talk to you later. Love ya'."

Joe was disappointed but figured, "At least she's not mad at me." He stowed the phone in his shirt pocket.

Three tables were arranged in a row in the middle of the cargo bay at the rear of the spaceship. Each table had a base made from hardened, ceramic-like material. The top was stiff, spongy fiber made to contour to its user's body.

Pam lay on the first table, still unconscious, but mutating into a humanoid. Grimwold snickered despicably as he studied her. He forced Pam's mouth open and admired her new traits. Her cheeks grew and her jaw protruded as two longer, sharper teeth formed like fangs. Also, her tongue retracted into her throat until it couldn't be seen and her limbs were bigger and muscular.

Grimwold pressed the center of the programming device and it slowly retracted its probes from Pam's skull. He tossed it on the counter and glared at Kroll. Kroll inquired sarcastically, "Now what?"

Grimwold pointed to Jane and replied, "Your turn, great warrior."

Kroll leaned against the table with both claws and stared at Jane with a sick and evil gaze. He opened his mouth wide and heaved as if something were stuck in his throat. His tubular tongue slithered out toward her with a lump of DNA compound about a foot from the end. His tongue probed her lips before entering her mouth. She coughed as it pushed down her throat and then the lump of DNA slid into her esophagus. She gagged and convulsed for almost a minute.

Kroll studied Jane's behavior during her transformation and worried. If she was to be loyal to him, he didn't want her to suffer. He needed her to watch his back as he and the others implemented their plans. He knew better than to trust Shurek and Grimwold.

When Jane became still, Kroll took the star-shaped programmer and placed it on her head. He pressed the central hub and the device launched its probes into her skull. A sickening smell of burning flesh forced Kroll to back away as the probes burned through Jane's skull into the various sections of her brain.

Grimwold kidded, "Not bad. It's a good thing you don't have to install those probes by hand. You'd never make it."

Kroll replied angrily, "Someday you'll get yours, Grimwold. I'll see to that." Grimwold shoved him against the wall and the two snarled at each other.

Shurek entered the cargo bay carrying Suzie. He saw Grimwold and Kroll clinging to each other and ordered, "Separate now! One more time and I'll kill you both." He laid Suzie onto the third table and commanded them to finish the conversion.

Kroll reached under the flap of his chest cavity and retrieved his worm. He held it over Jane's nose but hesitated. Grimwold taunted him, "What's the matter, Kroll. Never seen a human cross over before?"

Kroll warned, "Don't worry about me. You've got your own creation to deal with."

Grimwold laughed hysterically and remarked, "You are amusing if not pathetic, Kroll. That's the only reason I let you live." Kroll glared at him but said nothing more.

Shurek interceded and warned, "Grimwold, shut up before I rip your tongue out and strangle you with it."

Grimwold chuckled at him and replied cynically, "I'd like to see that."

Shurek approached him, "Don't push me. My patience is limited." Grimwold became silent and backed down. Shurek removed another programming device from the cabinet.

Kroll discretely stowed the worm back in his chest cavity without the others noticing. Shurek returned to the table and placed the programming device on Suzie's head. The probes burned through her blonde hair, leaving black, singed spots.

Grimwold shook Pam's chin and commanded her in his alien tongue, "Get up, slave! We have work to do."

Pam opened her eyes and smiled deviously. She slid off the table and stood on the floor, face to face with Grimwold. "I am not your slave."

Grimwold was embarrassed by her insubordinance in front of Shurek and Kroll. He shouted angrily, "You'll never defy me again, you wretch!" He excited the worm in Pam's head and stimulated intense pain in her.

Pam screamed with her hands against the sides of her head. She pleaded, "Stop! I will obey." Grimwold continued to inflict pain on Pam. She fell to the floor and cried. Blood streamed from her nose and her eyes bulged.

Kroll chided, "I hope you get pleasure out of this. I'd like to see how loyal she is to you when you treat her like this."

Grimwold stopped hurting her and snarled at Kroll. "If you don't shut up, her first task will be to eat you alive."

"Watch your back, Grimwold," warned Kroll. "Watch your back." Kroll then stood by Jane and shook her gently. Jane awakened and looked surprised. She sat up on the edge of the table and flexed her muscular arms. She was impressed with her new self. Kroll asked, "Are you ready to hunt with me?"

Jane placed one of her clawed hands affectionately on his arm. She replied eagerly, "I'd love to." Kroll grinned with his reptilian mouth at Grimwold and helped Jane to her feet. Together they exited the cargo bay.

Shurek chuckled and suggested, "Perhaps you could learn a thing or two from Kroll."

Grimwold became enraged and pushed Pam toward the hatch. He shouted, "We'll see who's in control around here."

Shurek responded cynically, "Certainly not you." Grimwold and Pam left the ship.

Shurek turned his attention to Suzie. He whispered, "And now it's your turn to make the crossing." He closed his eyes and, after a deep breath, he exhaled and his tongue emerged. His body was rigid as his tongue landed on Suzie's sweatshirt.

Suzie's arms and legs became muscular and her cheekbones enlarged. Her skin turned a lighter shade of brown than the other girls. Her fangs were shorter and her teeth sharp although they remained arranged in a neat, normal dental pattern.

Shurek's tongue felt its way up to her mouth and massaged her lips. It pried her mouth open and slithered down her throat. He gulped and a large lump of DNA compound traversed the tubular tongue and deposited itself inside Suzie. Shurek gulped again and another lump of DNA compound passed through the tongue into her throat. Suzie shuddered and convulsed but Shurek's tongue remained inside her mouth.

Shurek weakened and nearly fell when the second lump left him. His tongue retracted into his mouth and he backed away from Suzie. He leaned against the wall and breathed heavily. He declared weakly, "You'll be the consummate mutant. You'll exceed all my expectations."

Shurek gathered his strength and staggered across the control room toward several cabinets. He opened the first cabinet and retrieved a metal case from among the supplies. The case was no bigger than a shoebox and was sealed by an electronic lock with a glass pad. Shurek placed his claw on the glass pad and pressed the blinking electronic lock. The lock made a loud click and the case opened slightly, emitting cold vapors out into the warm air.

Shurek opened the case and gazed inside with an adoring look. Inside were three clear containers, each with an egg in a briny solution. He removed one of the containers and studied it. The egg was translucent pink with the outline of a small creature inside, curled up in a ball.

Shurek carefully removed the top of the container with his claws. His tongue emerged and slithered inside the container. He strained his entire body and watched as the egg was withdrawn into his tongue. His eyes bulged and disappeared in the back of his head for a brief instant. He fertilized the egg through sacs located at the base of the tongue. It was a mind-numbing experience, and quite pleasurable for Shurek. The egg pulsed and throbbed inside his tubular tongue until the process was completed.

Shurek looked around suspiciously to ensure the others wouldn't see what he was about to perform. He stood over Suzie and gently laid his tongue on her waist. It wiggled and slid underneath her sweatpants. His body became rigid once more and he gripped the end of the table tightly with his claws. Soon, he drifted into a euphoric comatose state while his tongue worked its way between Suzie's legs and pressed inside of her.

Suzie moaned softly and placed her hands on her head. She inadvertently pressed the top of the programming device and terminated the process. The probes retracted but the device was held in place by her hands. Shurek was unaware that the device was turned off because of his mental state and Suzie was still semi-cognizant of what he was doing to her. The tongue throbbed and worked itself inside of her. It massaged and moistened her until it could safely insert the egg inside her womb.

By not receiving the full dose of hormone from Shurek when she was first attacked, Suzie's mental capacity and nervous system didn't degenerate like the others, although it was altered somewhat. When she interrupted the programming process, she was able to retain her human consciousness by minimizing the probes' damage to her brain's lobes. The initial dose of DNA compound initiated a transmutation of her body giving her strange new characteristics and abilities. The second dose that Shurek inserted inside her allowed her to develop her alien characteristics into a more advanced form. She became a hybrid with the most desirable traits of both species instead of an obedient, higher-level mutant slave.

Shurek retracted his tongue and uttered arrogantly, "Now we'll see who rules this wretched planet. With you by my side, the others are expendable." Suzie lay motionless with a look of contentment on her face.

A monitor beeped on one of the control panels. Shurek groaned, "What the hell do they want?" He approached the panel and pressed one of the six buttons along the bottom of the monitor. The face of another alien appeared on the screen.

The alien, named Jasper, threatened Shurek, "We know you're on Earth and we're coming to get you."

Shurek laughed at him and replied, "I'd think twice if I were you. I'm assembling a welcoming party for you when you get here."

Jasper warned, "We have seven battle cruisers with us and we'll take that planet apart piece by piece if necessary until you, Kroll and Grimwold are dead."

Shurek countered, "If you don't leave us alone, I'm going to give you a surprise you'll regret the rest of your shortened life. Don't screw with me, Jasper." Shurek turned off the monitor. Suzie's eyes flinched as she overheard the conversation.

Shurek glared at the screen for a moment then turned his attention back to Suzie. He snorted and brushed his clawed hand across her forehead. He whispered in his language, "You will be my secret weapon."

Shurek shook Suzie but she pretended to be unconscious. He grew impatient and stormed away.

᛭᛭᛭᛭᛭᛭

Four of the mutants returned to the campsite. Their faces had grown more grotesque with elongated jaws and serrated teeth. Their black, bulbous eyes receded into deep sockets in their large skulls. Each one placed some of its weight on its hands when it moved. Their arms were becoming legs as they degenerated into a primitive alien species. They no longer resembled anything human. The creatures picked through the remains of the girls' carcasses around the tents, even lapping at the bones to savor the taste of human flesh.

Grimwold entered the clearing, accompanied by Pam. She walked beside him and said nothing. From time to time she'd glare at him, wondering if he could be overtaken at some time.

Grimwold complained to her, "We'll need many more than this for our army." Pam said nothing, fearing that Grimwold might lash out at her.

Kroll and Jane arrived and joined them. Kroll suggested to Jane, "If you're hungry, go feed on the remains."

Jane smiled and pushed two of the creatures out of her way. When she pulled a torn section of tent out of her way, she found one mother's half-eaten carcass. As she gorged on the remains, she noticed shreds of clothing from a young girl. She paused and looked closer, realizing that it meant something sad to her. Jane lost her appetite and returned to Kroll's side. The programming wiped out most of her human memory and replaced it with alien history and culture, but those bloody pieces of cloth rekindled a piece of memory still intact in her brain.

Kroll realized what happened and suggested, "Let's hunt for fresh prey." Jane forced a smile and nodded.

Shurek entered the campsite and shoved Grimwold out of his way. He snarled at the mutants and glared at Grimwold and Kroll. The mutants scrambled out of his way and huddled by the trees. Kroll asked, "What's wrong, Shurek?"

Shurek chastised him, "We came here to build an army and conquer this planet! You sit here dining on old meat."

Kroll replied obediently, "We agree completely. We should find more prisoners and fresh meat."

Grimwold chuckled at Kroll, angering Shurek all the more. Shurek shouted at Grimwold, "What's so funny?"

Grimwold replied, "You. Kroll. This whole situation." He grabbed Pam by the arm and the two walked away from Shurek.

Shurek warned, "You're pushing your luck, Grimwold." Grimwold chuckled and shoved Pam forward with enough force to knock her over. Jane recalled that her and Pam once had some connection and felt pity for her as she scrambled to her feet.

Suddenly, Pam lunged at Grimwold's leg and bit into it with her teeth. Grimwold screamed in pain and pulled her off. He slapped the side of her head and grabbed her by her throat. Jane leaped at Grimwold and pinned him against a tree with her claws against his throat.

Shurek and Kroll watched curiously. Grimwold warned Kroll, "Get her out of my face before I kill her."

Kroll suggested to Jane, "Perhaps you might want to leave Grimwold alone. He has issues." Jane sneered and retreated to Kroll's side.

Grimwold faked a low-pitched laugh and walked away. Pam looked back at them briefly with frightened eyes and followed him.

Jane muttered, "Someday, she's gonna kill him."

Shurek was amused and remarked, "I welcome that day."

Kroll informed Shurek, "We will hunt and take prisoners."

"Take two of the mutants with you. They will protect you while you work."

"We'll return with the beginning of our new army."

"I'm counting on you."

Kroll hurried into the woods, followed closely by Jane.

Moonlight shined eerily across the parking lot of a rural roadside bar as random clouds passed in front of it. A dozen cars and pickup trucks were parked randomly about the parking lot. Across the street from the bar was a seedy hotel, a truck stop and gas station. Eighteen-wheelers pulled in and out at varying intervals for fuel. Kroll and Jane peered out of the trees and scanned the area. Two mutants waited anxiously behind them.

A man and woman, both in their thirties, left the bar holding hands and walked toward a silver Lexus at the edge of the parking lot. Both were intoxicated and laughed giddily while conversing. The woman wore a light blue blouse with a short denim skirt, denim vest and loafers. The man wore slacks, shoes and a collared shirt. Both were overdressed for the area and looked to be tourists.

Kroll stepped out of the trees toward them but Jane grabbed his arm and restrained him. He stared at her with a surprised look on his face. Jane gestured with her claw for him to be patient. Kroll nodded and retreated into the shelter of the trees. He turned his attention back to the couple.

The man opened vehicle for the woman and attempted to kiss her. She pushed him away and smiled. He watched as she set her pocketbook on the seat and unbuttoned her vest. Jane pointed to the woman and then to Kroll. Kroll understood and waited.

The man grew impatient and walked around to the driver's-side. He opened the door and sat down sideways in the seat with his feet still on the ground. When he started the car, music blared from the stereo, creating quite a ruckus until he turned it down.

The mutants became anxious as they sensed live prey nearby. Jane motioned for the mutants to stay put and be quiet.

Two young females exited the bar. They chatted loudly as they walked toward another corner of the parking lot. Jane instructed the two mutants, "Bring them back alive." The mutants crept along the perimeter of the parking lot toward the girls. They hid behind vehicles and trees as they drew closer to their prey.

The woman tossed her vest in the back seat of the Lexus and unbuttoned the top three buttons on her blouse. Jane and Kroll stepped out of the trees and quietly approached the Lexus.

Kroll opened his mouth in grotesque fashion. His tongue shot out and wrapped around the woman's neck before she could scream. Small needles penetrated her throat. They numbed her vocal cords and inhibited her breathing. Kroll pulled her against his chest and held her tightly. His appendages penetrated either side of her spine and injected his hormone into her nervous system. His eyes looked passive as he savored the moment.

Jane stooped over the man and surprised him. She grabbed him by the neck and pulled him from the car. He struggled to scream but could only whimper as she nearly choked off his ability to breath with her claw. The man's eyes widened with fright as he stared in horror at Jane's alien form. He shuddered and urinated in his pants when she opened her mouth, baring her sharp teeth and fangs. Drool streamed from her stiff, leathery lip onto his dress shoes. She hissed at him and latched her teeth into his throat, tearing out the tender flesh.

Blood spattered across her face but she didn't care. Her tongue extended from her mouth and lapped at the warm fluid. It wasn't fully developed into the tubular tongue that the aliens had but it was long enough to enable her feed. Jane thrashed the man's abdomen open through his shirt and pants with her sharp claws. She tossed him on the hood of the car and ripped out his intestines. She held them up to the moonlight and devoured them.

Kroll turned his victim around to face him and laid her across the trunk. She wore a blank expression and looked up at the starry sky as if saying goodbye to her world forever. His tongue emerged from his mouth and slithered halfway down her throat before pausing. He gulped as if he would choke until a large lump of the DNA compound formed and traversed the tongue into the woman's throat. She gagged and coughed but Kroll held her firmly until he was satisfied that the lump was implanted. It would be a few minutes before the compound disseminated throughout her body and initiated the change. Slowly, he retracted his tongue from inside her. The woman's face turned ashen and she looked very ill. Kroll dismissed it as part of the transformation.

Jane paused to observe Kroll. She realized the woman was too drunk to be of any value and instructed Kroll in the alien tongue, "Leave her be. She's worthless." She then gnawed on the man's shoulder until only bone showed. Blood spilled from her lips onto his still corpse.

Kroll suspected that Jane was jealous of him and disregarded her advice. He reached inside his chest and removed his worm. Eagerly, he placed the worm on the woman's upper lip. The worm slithered inside her mouth and moved toward the back of her throat. It crept to her nasal passage and attempted to squeeze inside on a route to her brain. The woman gagged and vomited. She fell to the ground and convulsed. Kroll was startled and leaped away from her.

Jane stopped feeding and walked around the car to Kroll. She learned from her programming that the alien males only had one worm to control their selected mutants while the females always maintained eight or nine worms at a time and could control several mutants.

This was one fact that Shurek and Kroll overlooked, leaving Grimwold as the only one safe from this anomaly. He was the only one who successfully implanted his worm into his mutant.

If Pam developed her cache of worms and spread them among any mutants that she converted, Grimwold would have control of them and would always be superior to her and her tribe of mutants. Kroll chose not to implant his worm in Jane since he wanted an equal to share his reign with.

◆ • • •

Shurek figured he had time before he needed to implant his worm into Suzie. He was cautious and didn't want to risk losing it if she didn't survive the transformation.

The woman vomited again and, after a final gasp, stopped breathing. Jane saw the worm wiggle feebly in the vomit briefly before expiring. She hissed in a quiet rebuke of Kroll, then grabbed him by the shoulder and pulled his face close to hers. She chastised him, "You fool! You wasted your worm."

Kroll asked shamefully, "What happened?"

"She was too intoxicated to accept the worm. You should have left her or waited until later."

Kroll poked at the worm, hoping for some sign of life, but it was dead. He replied apologetically, "I should have trusted you."

Jane put her clawed hand on his shoulder and looked compassionately at him. She offered, "Whatever mutants I control will be at your service. We are one."

"Thank you. I hoped for a long time to find someone like you to be my partner."

"You have to choose a name for me, Kroll. What will it be?"

Kroll smiled at her and suggested, "How about Vega, after the Vega constellation?"

Jane asked, curious, "Why would you choose that name?"

"Because you are the bright spot in my life."

"Then Vega it is. Now let's feed."

Kroll joined Jane, now Vega, in devouring the body of the man on the hood.

━━━━━━ ✦✦✦✦✦ ━━━━━━

The two mutants stalked the two young women from behind. They crept quietly behind them and tackled them. One of the girls let out a moan and rolled over to face her assailant. The mutant scrambled to its feet and slapped the woman on the side of her head. She slumped over sideways and sobbed, while covering up. Not realizing what she was attacked by, she pleaded, "Please don't hurt me."

The other woman was stunned as her head banged against the asphalt when she fell. The mutants picked each of the girls up and slammed them face first into the side of their van. The two girls were semi-conscious and incoherent. The mutants dragged them by their arms and loped across the parking lot.

Vega and Kroll watched excitedly from behind the Lexus. Vega announced, "Looks like we have new play toys."

Kroll remarked anxiously, "I'm looking forward to this." The two snickered and waited.

The mutants appeared before them and dropped the women on the ground behind the Lexus. Vega chided them, "Easy. You'll damage them." The mutants waited eagerly for permission to eat them.

Kroll asked, "Should we turn them loose on the humans inside the building?"

Vega eyed the bar and then replied, "Of course."

Kroll pointed at the bar and the mutants raced toward it.

Vega grabbed each of the women by the back of the neck and hoisted them up in the air. She asked Kroll, "Which one would you like?" Kroll pointed to the brunette.

Vega tossed her in the air into Kroll's waiting arms. She enjoyed the strength that came with her new body. The woman grunted as Kroll caught her in his arms. He set her on her feet backwards and held her tightly against his chest. His appendages grappled into her spine and injected her with his hormone. The woman shuddered and hyperventilated. Her eyes bulged and rolled back in her head. Kroll's appendages quivered wildly as they pumped hormone into her body.

Vega noticed how excited Kroll became as his hormone was secreted into the woman. At first, she felt envious. Then she realized she had the same opportunity to self-gratify in whatever ways she deemed. She gently lifted the blonde woman to her feet and sat her on the edge of the passenger seat. Vega lapped playfully at the young woman's neck. Her gentleness briefly lulled the injured woman into a restful trance. Vega tilted her head upward and gagged as she strained to extend her newly developed tongue. At first, she had difficulty but, after coughing up a plug of mucous, the tongue emerged and hovered in front of her. She inserted the tongue into the woman's mouth, working it in and out slowly until it slid smoothly down her throat.

A small lump of DNA compound was all Vega could muster so far, but it traveled through her tongue and was deposited deep inside the woman's digestive tract. The woman trembled in horror as she briefly regained consciousness. She soon became lost again as her metabolism was altered and her consciousness was blurred. Her eyes glazed over and she no longer had the ability to sit up on her own.

Vega placed both of her clawed hands on the woman's shoulders and held her up. She retracted her tongue from the woman's mouth and caressed her lips with it. Subtly, she cast a glance over at Kroll as he clumsily shoved his tongue into the other woman's mouth. That woman unconsciously gagged and convulsed with each attempt.

Vega released the blonde and allowed her to fall across the seat. She was annoyed with Kroll's inexperience with humans so she stormed around the car and grabbed his tongue. She made a low humming sound to him. Kroll panicked and attempted to retract the tongue but Vega's soothing sounds relaxed him. Vega explained, "You have to be gentle with a female, Kroll." She moved Kroll's tongue slowly in and out of the woman's throat. Each time she inserted it a little further.

Kroll became very excited and produced a huge lump of DNA compound. The lump moved slowly and painfully through his tongue. Vega shook her head at him in disappointment. She massaged the lump through the outer layer of the tongue until it became longer and flatter. It moved much smoother as it continued through his tubular tongue and into the woman's mouth.

Vega stroked Kroll's tongue through the insertion of the lump, much to his delight. Her tongue slithered out of her mouth and gently wrapped around his. Each coil slid back and forth rhythmically across his exposed length of tongue. Kroll shuddered with excitement as Vega toyed with him. His appendages emerged and shot hormone at the woman's blouse and skirt.

When the lump was deposited, Kroll anxiously retracted his tongue and nearly swallowed Vega's. She quickly grabbed his tongue and unwrapped hers from it. She released her hold on his tongue and allowed him to finally retract it. Vega stroked his face and said soothingly in his alien dialect, "Easy, my special one. You must control yourself if you want to experience full pleasure."

Kroll leaned against the car for balance and inquired exhaustedly, "You mean there's more?"

"There could be if you stay loyal to me."

"This is why I chose not to control you. It wouldn't be the same."

Vega informed him, "Now I have my own business to take care of." She returned to the passenger-side of the car and knelt in front of the woman. Her tongue slithered under the woman's blouse and massaged her breasts.

Kroll laid his prey across the hood of the car and wandered over to watch Vega.

⸻ ·•◆•· ⸻

Three muscular bouncers conversed at the door as country music played in the background. Five couples line-danced to Billy Ray Cyrus' "Achey, Breakey Heart". Cigarette smoke filled the bar area as a dozen older patrons sat comfortably on stools, sipping beer from half empty mugs. Suddenly, the mutants burst through the front door.

The bouncers backed away in horror, stunned by the horrific creatures. The mutants leaped at them. With quick thrusts and swings from their sharp claws, they inflicted lethal wounds on the bouncers, leaving their stomachs slit wide open. The three men lay helplessly on the floor, desperately holding their organs inside their abdomens. Blood and bodily fluids littered the dirty wooden floor.

The mutants rushed at the dancing couples and lashed out at them before they realized what was happening. Each mutant struck at the throats of the couples until they lay helpless on the floor, clutching at their torn throats.

Two men at the bar threw their mugs at the mutants. One of the mugs struck a mutant and stunned it. The mutant fell to its knees with a dazed expression. The other mug sailed wide and struck the wall with a thud.

A trucker pulled a switchblade from his pants pocket and attacked the standing mutant. He stuck the knife into the mutant's side but the mutant grabbed him by the throat and threw him over the bar. Another man grabbed a mug and slammed the kneeling mutant in the side of the head. It staggered to its feet and swung aimlessly at him. He grabbed a stool and broke it over the mutant's head.

The second mutant lunged angrily at him and ripped his face off with one swipe of its clawed hand, leaving only the front of his skull intact. His eyes hung limply over the bony remains of his cheeks.

The bartender smashed the top off a bottle of 151 proof rum and tucked a strip of rag inside. He lit it with a cigarette lighter and fired the flaming bottle at the mutant. The bottle bounced off its head and burned slowly against the base of the wall.

The stunned mutant attacked the bartender. It grabbed him by the neck and tore into his throat with its teeth. The bartender's head hung awkwardly from his neck as the creature continued to feed off of him. The other patrons seated at the bar fled through the fire exit and raced to their vehicles.

The two mutants hurried after them, leaving a carnage of bodies lying across the bar floor. Some of the victims were barely alive and tried desperately to stop the bleeding from their lethal wounds.

A plume of smoke rose into the night sky from one of the bar's open windows. Across the street, a trucker filled his rig with fuel. He noticed the smoke rising from the bar and quickly called 911 on his cell phone.

••••••

Vega yanked the young woman's underpants off and tossed them inside the car. Her tongue massaged the woman's breasts as she unbuttoned her blouse. Vega felt a strange sense of pleasure that she hadn't known in some time. Was it part of her humanness or part of her new alien conscious? Maybe both. She didn't know and didn't care. It felt good. Vega became light-headed and leaned against the side of the car. She continued caressing the woman's breasts despite the spell.

Kroll noticed and became concerned. He inquired, "Are you okay, Vega?"

Vega retracted her tongue and answered, "Of course. I think I just finished another stage of my development." Kroll wondered what she meant.

Vega's tongue rolled out again and slithered under the woman's skirt along her inner thighs. Small bristles emerged from her tongue and injected a liquid opiate into her victim's upper thigh. The opiate acted quickly and kept the woman in a relaxed trance. Her tongue eased itself inside the woman and prepped her for the insertion of an egg. She leaned closer to the woman's hips and pushed her legs apart.

Kroll became aroused as he watched Vega perform in front of him. He looked back at his victim and grew more aroused. When he approached the brunette, his tongue emerged from his mouth like a snake and waved anxiously in the air. He used it to lap at his victim's neck. After a few moments of savoring the taste of her skin, he moved his tongue underneath the woman's clothing and massaged her breasts. He worked his tongue under her skirt and lace underwear. After several unsuccessful attempts to moisten her, he became frustrated and quit. Unfortunately for Kroll, she was injured from the jarring attack and couldn't respond to his attempts at foreplay. He watched Vega as she seductively maneuvered her tongue in and out of the blonde until the shape of the egg appeared.

Males of Kroll's species couldn't generate eggs, but could transport and insert them into a womb. Kroll considered that Vega could help him learn the technique of foreplay so he could insert an egg from the space ship inside Vega or another female mutant.

Kroll was more surprised that Vega could generate an egg so soon after transmutation. He wondered what other surprises she was capable of. Never had he adopted a cross-species that behaved like this before. He was pleased with Vega.

The insertion process took over an hour and Kroll became impatient. Vega glared at him and motioned for him to relax. He returned to his victim and attempted once again to stimulate her but his clumsy attempts didn't work well with a human woman. He lifted the woman's ankle high in the air and bit into the back of her thigh. He enjoyed the warm blood flowing from the severed artery as he sucked from it. Pieces of tendon and muscle dangled from his teeth but he didn't care. When the flow of blood slowed, he gnawed the leg until only bone was left.

The woman shuddered again before becoming motionless. She barely breathed and the loss of blood hastened her death.

••••••

Lamar drove down the highway, pondering the day's events. His deputy, Johnny Watkins, rode in the passenger seat, scanning the side of the road for stranded motorists. Concerned about what was to come, Johnny asked, "What about the spooks, Sheriff?"

Lamar countered angrily, "What the hell are you talking about?"

"You know – the feds."

Lamar was slightly embarrassed for not understanding Johnny's reference to the two agents that visited him earlier. He replied modestly, "What about them?"

"What are you gonna tell them?"

Lamar thought for a moment and then answered, "It's an ongoing investigation that could take several days."

"Think they'll buy it?"

"Of course, they'll buy it! They're feds."

Lamar's cell phone played "Ain't no mountain high enough" from Diana Ross and the Supremes."

Johnny chuckled and commented, "I never imagined you for a Supremes kind of guy, Sheriff."

Lamar glared at him and said, "Johnny, shut the hell up. Will you please?"

Lamar answered his phone, "Hi, Francine." He listened for a moment and replied, "Right. We're on the way. Send Jones and Mayberry over, will you?" Lamar stowed his cell phone in his shirt pocket. He turned on the lights and siren and spun the car around.

"What happened?" asked Johnny.

"Smoke's coming from the Cricket Bar."

Johnny frowned and remarked, "It's Friday night. Should be a pretty good crowd in there."

"And your point is?"

"If there was a fire, wouldn't they be a little more specific. I mean smoke could mean a lot of things."

"That's why I'm going to check it out first. No need to send the fire department if it's just a burnt pot of chili."

"I guess you're right, Sheriff."

Lamar pulled up in front of the police station. Johnny inquired, "You don't want me to go with you?"

"It's late. No sense in two of us going out there."

Johnny suggested, "I guess I'll write up the reports for today's mess."

"Thanks, Johnny. I'll check in on you later."

Johnny got out and closed the door. "Be careful, Sheriff. I don't want anything to happen to you."

"I'll be fine, Johnny. You worry about them reports." Lamar pulled away from the police station and drove down the highway.

Johnny shook his head and remarked, "Maybe someday I'll figure him out." He unlocked the door and entered the police station.

⸻ ┄┄◆┄┄ ⸻

Lamar steered his vehicle into the parking lot and immediately saw the smoke billowing out one of the windows. He remarked, "That don't look so bad."

A short distance away, one of the mutants gorged on the organs of an elderly man. It saw the headlights from the sheriff's car and hid behind a pickup truck. Lamar got out of the vehicle and scanned the area. He saw Vega and Kroll across the parking lot with one of the females on the hood of the Lexus. He wasn't sure from that distance who they were or what was happening. "Hey, what are you doing?"

Kroll and Vega were angered by the interruption. Kroll retreated cautiously toward the trees. Vega finished implanting the egg inside the woman's womb and retracted her tongue. Kroll informed Vega, "I'll take care of him."

Vega chided, "No, you fool!"

Kroll disregarded her warning and rushed at the sheriff. Lamar unholstered his .357 Magnum pistol and warned, "Stop right there or I'll shoot!" Suddenly, he realized it wasn't a person but a creature coming at him. He fired twice.

The first shot struck Kroll in the shoulder and staggered him. The second shot caught him in the left eye. The bullet penetrated his skull and entered his brain. He fell to the ground unconscious. Vega saw Kroll fall and howled a blood-curdling scream.

Lamar looked down at Kroll and uttered, "What the hell are you?" He hurried toward the Lexus and shouted at Vega, "Don't move or you'll join your friend!"

◆┄┄┄

One of the mutants charged at Lamar from behind the pickup truck. Lamar glanced over just as it rammed its shoulder into his side. He tumbled across the ground and lost his gun. Lamar retreated toward his SUV when the mutant lunged at him again. The two fell to the ground together.

Lamar shoved the mutant off and tried to crawl away. The mutant grabbed his ankles and clung to him. He saw his gun lying inches from the mutant's head. He turned over and sat up. The mutant loosened its grasp on him and bit into his right knee. Lamar groaned in pain and kicked at the mutant's head until it let go of his knee. He desperately grabbed for his pistol but when he turned on his side, he stared into the face of the mutant. It raised its giant fist to pummel him, but Lamar pointed his gun into the mutant's face and fired. The mutant let out a pained howl and rolled over dead.

Lamar wiped blood and pieces of the mutant's flesh from his face and arms. He crawled to his knees and noticed Vega kneeling by Kroll's motionless body. Vega lifted Kroll and carried him into the trees before Lamar could get off a shot.

Lamar went to the Lexus to investigate. He saw the partially eaten man inside the car and his female companion in the back seat. He saw another woman on the hood of the car and a third was dead on the ground in her own vomit. "What the hell is happening here?"

He approached the woman on the hood and heaved nauseously. Blood streamed off the hood of the car and pooled on the ground. The bare bone of the woman's right leg sickened him even more. He felt her wrist for a pulse but there was none. He shivered as he contemplated what to do with her.

Next, he approached the woman in the back seat and checked for her pulse. She was still alive. Lamar noticed teal fluid dripping from between her legs. Her facial features changed slightly, giving her a ghoulish look. The teal fluid turned to a trickle of red blood.

Lamar uttered, "Forgive me, Lord, but this ain't covered in the good book." He aimed his pistol at the woman's stomach and fired. The shot tore a gaping hole in her midsection. Blood splashed across his face and arms, nauseating him. He hurried around the car to the other woman and shot her in the mid-section, too. He shouted toward the woods, "I'll get you yet, you bitches! By God's will, I'll get you." Lamar fell to the ground and sobbed.

••••◆

Another police car pulled into the lot and stopped near the pickup truck. Officer Jones spotted the half-eaten body of the old man on the ground. He and Mayberry got out of the vehicle with their pistols drawn. They approached the body and examined it.

Mayberry complained, "Oh, man! I'm gonna hurl."

Jones replied, "What kind of creature could do this to a man?"

Lamar got to his feet and approached the officers. Jones bellowed, "What in God's name is going on here, Sheriff?"

Lamar replied somberly, "I wish I knew. I really wish I knew."

Mayberry suggested, "How about we check out the inside of the bar?"

Lamar scanned the parking lot for any more of the creatures but saw none. "Go ahead but be careful."

Jones and Mayberry approached the entrance to the bar. Lamar sat inside his vehicle and picked up the radio's mike.

The remaining mutant rushed out from behind the truck and leaped onto Mayberry. It tore into his neck and shoulder before he could react. Jones fired his pistol twice into the creature's head. The mutant stood up unsteadily and stared at him. It stepped toward him and then fell face first into the asphalt surface.

Jones saw the blood pumping from the severed artery in Mayberry's neck. He knew by the severity of the wound that it was too late for his partner so he tried to console him. Mayberry shook for several seconds and gagged. Jones uttered sadly, "It's alright, buddy. It's alright."

Mayberry looked up at him briefly and then passed. Jones cried hysterically as he cradled Mayberry against him. He knelt with his back to the creature.

Lamar heard the commotion and hurried toward his men. The mutant got up and staggered toward Jones.

Lamar shouted, "Jonesy!" Jones looked back while on his knees and screamed in fright as the mutant drew closer.

Lamar aimed his pistol at the mutant and fired. The shot struck the creature in its side and sent it sprawling across the ground. Jones set his dead partner down on the ground and approached the creature. The mutant got up on its knees and reached for Jones. He aimed his pistol shakily at the mutant's head and fired three shots. The mutant fell to the ground and breathed gruffly.

Lamar stood over the creature and fired a single shot into the side of its head. The creature hissed loudly and died. Jones asked feebly, "Is this all of them?"

Lamar rolled the mutant over and replied despondently, "No. At least one got away." He examined it and saw many of the same changes that affected Bo Davis. After pondering over the corpses, Lamar blurted, "Shit! The gates of hell have broken open!"

"What are these things, Sheriff?" asked Jones, frightened.

"If I didn't know better, I'd say it's the devil coming to collect his due."

"So, what do we do about it?"

"Call Bradford and Scott to help get this mess cleaned up. Put 'em all inside the bar for now."

"Shall I call the coroner?"

"No, I'll take care of that." Lamar entered the bar and saw the carnage across the floor. The corpses were torn up and scattered about. Several of them lay in pools of blood while others' entrails lay sloppily across the wooden floor from gutted midsections. He grew nauseous from the smoke and grabbed a fire extinguisher from its glass cabinet. After extinguishing the smoldering flames, he threw the extinguisher at the bottles behind the bar in disgust. He was a broken man. His world was going to hell at a time when he turned his back on God over what seemed to be petty issues now. He prayed, "Lord, if you believe in giving second chances, I'll make it worth your while. My big ass will be in church every Sunday." Lamar left the bar and climbed into his vehicle.

Another patrol car pulled up with Bradford and Scott inside. Bradford shouted, "What's going on, Sheriff?"

"Give Jonesy a hand cleaning up. He'll fill you in."

Lamar drove off and headed back to the police station. He shook with fear and nearly wet himself as he considered what just took place. He uttered tearfully, "I shot two women! Women! What the hell is happening to me?" He pounded the steering wheel with his fist several times in anger and turned his vehicle east onto another highway. As he drove, he pondered, *Maybe I can get a job as a security guard in a mall somewhere — anywhere but here.*

Then he noticed tail lights ahead and slowed down. The driver's-side door was open but no one was in sight. He parked beside the vehicle and got out, armed with his pistol and a flashlight. A pool of blood lay on the ground by the open door and the driver's seat was shredded with bloodstains over the seat, dashboard and windshield.

Lamar thought, *Get back in the car and leave. This can only get worse.* Behind the trees, one mutant stuffed entrails from a young woman's corpse into his mouth. He heard the sheriff walk around the vehicle and crept toward him.

Lamar thought to himself, *That's it. I'm out of here.* He retreated toward his vehicle but the the mutant lunged at him. Lamar was startled and fumbled with his gun before getting his finger on the trigger. The creature was five feet away when Lamar raised his pistol and fired at the mutant's chest, leaving a gaping hole as a souvenir. The mutant stumbled and fell at Lamar's feet. He fired another shot in the back of its head to make sure it was dead.

⬥

Grimwold, Pam and Shurek hid with two mutants in an alley around the corner from a bus station. They watched as three passengers waited on benches near the curb. Shurek questioned Grimwold indignantly, "What are you waiting for? Are you afraid of a few humans?"

Grimwold looked repulsively at Shurek. He explained with a tone of disgust, "Others are coming. We don't want to scare them off. Do we?"

Shurek replied sarcastically, "Just wondering."

A bus pulled up in front of the station and opened its front doors. The bus driver exited and unlocked the cargo bay door. Seven passengers on the bus assembled their things and stepped out, one by one.

Pam suggested to Grimwold, "Now's a good time to attack."

The five of them rushed toward the bus. The mutants tackled the bus driver and gorged on his flesh. Shurek grabbed a young couple and battered them to the ground, leaving them badly shaken and bloody. The other passengers hurried back onto the bus in a panic.

One man tried to close the door but Grimwold blocked it with his arm. His tongue whisked out and wrapped around the man's neck. In one fluid motion, it pulled the man backwards against his chest. His appendages tore through the man's shirt and into his spine. The man quivered briefly, and then fell face-first into the driver's seat unconscious.

Shurek mounted the woman from behind and injected her with his appendages. His tongue looped around and slipped into her mouth. He generated a lump of DNA compound and inserted it inside the woman's throat. Once finished, he slammed the man against the side of the bus. He pressed himself against the man's back and injected his hormone into him.

Pam slid past Grimwold and stalked the remaining passengers as they huddled in the rear of the bus. They were hysterical as they pushed against each other like cattle. Pam grabbed passengers at random and shoved them into Grimwold's waiting arms. Grimwold tossed the first two out to the mutants but took the others for himself. He injected them with his appendages and pumped his hormone into them.

Pam grabbed the last two passengers, a man and woman, and held them out for Grimwold to see. "Why don't we take a little time to play with our new friends?" she suggested.

Grimwold answered, "Very well. Pick one."

Pam studied the man and decided to keep him. She shoved the sobbing woman to Grimwold. He didn't bother with the hormone but immediately plunged his tongue into her mouth. She gagged and coughed until she nearly passed out. Grimwold retracted his tongue until her breathing returned to normal. He knelt down and inserted his tongue under her dress and probed between her legs, finally reaching up to her womb. With one claw, he held her firmly against the wall by her throat. With the other, he balanced himself on the floor. The woman was horrified and slid into shock. She looked like a rag doll in his clutches. Grimwold repeatedly penetrated her until his tongue shot out of her abdomen. He howled with twisted pleasure as blood dripped off his face and arms.

Pam shoved the man against the bathroom door and gripped his shoulder with one clawed hand. Her tongue slid out and lapped at his neck. The man pleaded, "Please don't kill me."

Pam unbuttoned his shirt and licked his chest with her tongue. It slid down the man's belly and under his belt. The man closed his eyes and shuddered in fear. She retracted her tongue and asked playfully, "Don't you like that?"

The man was horrified and pleaded, "Please don't touch me."

Pam taunted him, "How about a kiss for the girl of your dreams?" She attempted to kiss him but he turned away from her. She became annoyed and suggested, "I can see you're not a lady's man. Perhaps I can help you get over that."

Pam took the man's belt off and unbuttoned his pants. She tugged at them until they slid down to his ankles. She licked his face and reached into his boxer shorts with her clawed hand. The man panicked and cried out, "Don't touch me, you horrible monster!"

Pam rubbed against him and teased, "Too bad. I could have enjoyed this." She looked pained as her appendages emerged for the first time. She moaned and pulled the man close enough for them to sadistically cut into his chest but not penetrate it. Pam's claw formed a fist inside the man's shorts as she grabbed his penis and testicles.

The man struggled desperately and shouted, "You bitch!"

Pam shook her head in disappointment at the man. "Don't you know how to talk to a female?"

He looked at her pathetically and cried. She ripped his genitals out of his shorts and dropped the stringy heap of flesh into her mouth. She swallowed and belched. "Ah, that was almost as good as the first time I had one of those in my mouth. Of course, that was a real man, not a groveling mouse like you." She released her hold on the man and let him fall to his knees. When she turned to walk away, he cried out "Screw you, bitch!"

Pam stopped and calmly turned around. She swung her powerful arm at his head and decapitated him. His head bounced off the window and landed on the floor at her feet. She picked up the head and stared at it.

Grimwold enjoyed watching her. He waited anxiously for her response. She looked disappointedly at him and complained, "Some men just don't know when to shut up." Pam plucked out the eyes from the head and swallowed them.

Grimwold was pleased by her behavior. He commented, "Perhaps you and I do have something in common."

"Be careful what you wish for, Grimwold," Pam warned. "I'm beginning to like this."

They exited the bus together, stepping over unconscious, mutating bodies. Grimwold suggested, "Let's go inside the building and look for more of these pathetic creatures."

◆····

Pam felt satisfied with her newfound strength and enjoyed exercising her superiority over human males. Despite her alien transmutation, she still vaguely remembered that the men in her life disrespected her.

They entered the bus terminal and saw a dozen bodies lying about the terminal. Shurek was across the lobby from them, pressed against a woman from behind. His appendages were firmly implanted in her spine. Drool streamed out of his mouth and soaked the back of the woman's sweater. He shook as he strained to pump every ounce of his hormone into her.

Grimwold remarked, "He'll sleep for a week after this."

Pam kidded, "Perhaps he should have saved some for us."

"Not Shurek. His greed will be his downfall."

Pam inquired, "What happens if he injects too much hormone into her?"

Suddenly the woman's abdomen exploded. Her eyes shot out of their sockets and a mixture of blood and hormone streamed from her eye sockets, nose, mouth and ears.

Shurek dropped the woman to the ground and walked toward them. He drunkenly challenged Grimwold, "Is there a problem?"

Grimwold taunted him, "Like you're in shape to do anything about it."

Pam stepped between them and interceded, "That's enough, boys. It's been a good night so far."

Shurek looked around proudly at his conquests. The bodies already showed signs of mutating. He muttered exhaustedly to Pam, "Perhaps I'll leave the rest for you and what's his face." Shurek staggered from the terminal and disappeared into the night.

Grimwold explained, "That's the problem with Shurek. All he ever cares about is himself. Then he wonders why we hate him."

Pam mentioned, "I'm still hungry. Let's find more fresh meat." Grimwold snorted with delight and followed her out of the terminal.

The two mutants chewed up bodies near the bus and ate the innards. Pam quipped, "They sure enjoy eating, don't they?"

"That's one drawback with any species that mutates on hormone alone. They become unstable predators."

Pam replied, "That works well so long as we have food for them."

"Yes, it does, but at some time, we'll have to get rid of them."

"Oh, well. So be it."

CHAPTER V

BODY COUNTS

J oe pulled into his driveway and parked his truck. He thought about what happened to Bo Davis and Bob Schultz. Nothing about it made any sense. He changed his focus to Suzie and pondered, *Maybe I should call her. What if she and the girls are in danger?* He looked at his watch and grumbled, "Eleven o'clock. She's gonna kill me." Joe retrieved the phone from his pants pocket and dialed Suzie's number. He waited anxiously for her to pick up.

Suzie lay asleep on the table inside the spaceship. She mutated somewhat but still retained many of her human features. Her phone rang and played the refrain from Janet Jackson's "Black Cat". She awoke and sat up. The foam she lay on felt awkward and annoyed her so she ripped a chunk of it and tossed it across the room. She crooned, "Ah, much better."

Suzie pulled the phone from her sweat pants pocket and eyed the display with disdain. She said aloud to no one in particular, "Sorry, Honey. Suzie's got a lot of important things to take care of. I'll deal with you later." She closed the phone and deposited it inside her stretched sweat pants. The star-shaped programming device fell off of her head onto the table.

Suzie wandered around the main deck and studied the ship's controls. Everything looked familiar to her even though she had never seen it before. She felt an air of confidence that she had a destiny to rule. She felt free since she didn't have the girls to worry about and she didn't care what Joe thought anymore. Her womb exhibited movement from time to time as the alien egg adapted to her changing body. She placed her hands over her belly and proudly declared, "Now I'll have my baby, with or without Joe as a father."

Suzie recognized a Sporatin from her programming and activated it. She located a finger port on the right side of the base and inserted one of her bony fingers inside it. The Sporatin was a pink, translucent life form that lived in its own solution inside a glass tank. It had a soul of its own and was basically a bio-computer. She quivered as an electrode penetrated her finger and contacted a nerve ending. An alien face appeared on the Sporatin and spoke to her in the alien dialect, "Welcome, Serena Luna. I am Pitherus. What can I do for you?"

Suzie asked in mild surprise, "How do you know my alien name, Pitherus?"

"It is in your destiny. Many races await your arrival."

"When am I supposed to arrive and where?"

"It is too soon to tell. You must fulfill the first part of your destiny here on Earth before you can further your destiny."

Suzie requested, "I want the recordings of any conversations on this ship since it began its journey to Earth."

"At what speed would you like the playback?"

"Fast forward through my mind. I want to know everything that Shurek, Grimwold and Kroll have planned."

"Yes, Serena Luna."

The Sporatin fed all the ship's recordings into Suzie's mind through her finger. Suzie saw how the three aliens killed a young male and his family because he witnessed a crime they committed. The murder was recorded on a camera and they became fugitives of their law.

Suzie asked, "How will they overtake the human population, Pitherus?"

Pitherus responded, "They will create many mutants and turn them loose upon the population. The mutants will eventually rebel and kill their superiors."

Suzie asked, "Do they know this?"

"They did not ask. They only seek ways to take control, not to maintain it."

"Interesting. They don't know what they reap."

"You are perceptive, Serena Luna."

"And you are very helpful, my friend. Can I count on your loyalty?"

"I am bound to support the destiny of our races. You are part of that destiny."

"Does Shurek know that?"

"Shurek is ignorant of many truths. He only knows greed."

"Excellent. You and I will talk more about this 'destiny' thing. That's all for now." Suzie chuckled to herself. *Serena Luna - I like that.* She felt the electrode retract from her finger and terminate its connection to her.

━━━━━━━ ‣‧◆‧‣ ━━━━━━━

Lamar parked his SUV in front of the police station and rushed inside. He slammed the door and fell to the ground, holding his pistol against his chest while he sobbed. He blubbered, "Oh, Mamma, you were so right. The wrath of the Lord is upon us."

Johnny walked into the front office with a cup of coffee in his hand. He saw the sheriff on the floor, leaning against the door. Lamar's behavior surprised him and he asked kiddingly, "What the hell ails you, man? I've never seen you like this." He offered the sheriff a hand to get up. Lamar pushed it away and staggered to his feet. He walked somberly to his desk and sat down.

Johnny pulled up a chair and sat across from him. He waited patiently for the sheriff's response. Lamar looked up with saddened eyes and said, "I think it's the end of the world, Johnny."

"You haven't been drinking, have you, Sheriff?"

"I've seen the devil and his succubae. They're here in our town."

Johnny put down his cup of coffee and offered, "Why don't I give you a lift home? I'm sure you'll feel better after a good night's sleep."

Lamar exclaimed, "No friggin' way! I'm staying right here."

A man's voice sounded desperately from the radio on the counter and interrupted their conversation. "Watkins, are you there? Pick up fast!"

Johnny complained as he got out of the chair, "Now what could be bothering Hayes tonight?"

Lamar replied frantically, "It's those creatures! They're all over."

Johnny answered the call, "This is Watkins. What's the problem, Hayes?"

Officer Hayes' cruiser was parked outside the bus terminal. He stood outside the car with the radio mike in his hand. The half-eaten corpses on the ground horrified him as he searched up and down the street.

◆••••

Jimmy Hayes was twenty-four, about two-forty with blond hair and blue eyes. He wasn't afraid of much in this world and it bothered Johnny more so that his friend was rattled. Hayes blurted, "I'm outside the bus terminal and there are bodies all over the place!"

Johnny responded, "Settle down, Hayes. What's going on out there?"

"It looks like a Halloween scene out here! I think some kind of animal did this."

"I'll send backup," Johnny replied. "Don't leave your vehicle."

Pam crept up behind the cruiser. Hayes continued hysterically, "There's something else that's weird here, too. I think there's a ..." Hayes turned and saw Pam approaching. Pam's muscular body was large for a woman and her jaws protruded forward in a ghastly manner. She lunged at Hayes with her clawed hands hungrily reaching for him. Hayes scurried into the cruiser and tried to close the door.

Pam blocked it and said, "Uh-uh. Mommy's here." She grabbed him by his shoulders and opened her elongated mouth wide. Hayes screamed madly as he wrestled with her. Pam's tongue lapped against his face before it wrapped around his head like a snake.

Johnny's voice sounded over the radio, "Hayes! Come in, Hayes! What's happening?"

With one quick jerk, Pam's tongue yanked Hayes' head into her mouth. She gnawed on it hungrily like a piece of candy. Hayes' headless body quivered as Pam savored her treat.

Johnny screamed, "Jimmy, answer me!"

Lamar put a hand on Johnny's shoulder and said, "Whatever those things are, we can't stop them."

Johnny was shaken by his friend's fate. He shouted at Lamar, "We're not going to hide here all night while our friends die out there! We have to stop these things now."

"They're not from this world, Johnny."

"So friggin' what! Let's get an APB out and go after these sons-of-bitches with everything we have."

Johnny dialed the combination to the gun safe and opened it, while Lamar looked on passively. He took out a rifle, shotgun, and several boxes of ammo. He laid them on the desk in front of the sheriff and glared at him.

Lamar responded, "Is there something you want to say to me, boy?"

Johnny leaned on the desk and stared down the sheriff. "As a matter of fact, there is. Since you first got here, I put up with your crap and why? Because I looked up to you. I thought you were tough and I thought I could learn from you. There are defenseless people counting on us to protect them and you want to cower like a little girl in the corner."

Lamar was embarrassed and looked down in shame. He asked humbly, "Are you done?"

"No, I'm not! I'm going out there and kill as many of those things as I can. Now you can sit here and feel sorry for yourself or you can issue the APB and get your ass out there and help me." Johnny picked up the weapons and ammo. He paused and waited for the sheriff's response.

Lamar stared at him for a moment and then picked up the radio mike. "Attention all units. This is Sheriff Whittington. We have a situation at the bus terminal. All units report at the location, armed with intent to kill. This is not a joke. I want you armed with intent to kill." Lamar opened the drawer and took out a box of ammo. He removed his .357 Magnum from the holster and loaded it.

Johnny quipped, "Now that's more like it."

Lamar looked up at him sourly and muttered, "Johnny, shut up."

Johnny was relieved that Lamar regained his composure and recovered his attitude. He knew he needed the sheriff to watch his back if they were going to end this threat.

Lamar followed Johnny out to the police SUV. Johnny stowed the weapons in the back seat of the vehicle and heard a series of grunts nearby. He scanned the trees carefully and shouted, "Who's out there?"

Lamar warned him, "Get in the truck, Johnny."

Johnny reached inside the truck and retrieved the shotgun. He loaded both barrels and aimed the gun toward the trees. Lamar again warned, "Get in the truck, Johnny. You don't know what we're dealing with."

Johnny ignored him and shouted again, "This is the last time I'm askin'. Who's out there?"

One of the mutants rushed from the trees at him. Johnny exclaimed, "Holy shit!" He aimed and fired. The shot struck the mutant in the shoulder. It tumbled and got back up. Johnny approached the mutant and calmly pointed the gun at its head. He pulled the trigger and blew half the face off of the creature. It rolled across the ground in pain, clutching at its face. Johnny unholstered his pistol and aimed at the creature's head. He fired a round into its forehead. The mutant gasped and died.

Another mutant rushed from the trees from a different direction away from Johnny's view. Johnny stowed his pistol and reloaded the shotgun. Lamar saw the creature and quickly climbed out of the SUV. He aimed his pistol at the creature and shouted, "Look out, Johnny!"

Johnny turned as he fumbled with the second shell. His eyes widened in fright. Lamar fired and blew a chunk of brown flesh from the mutant's neck. It staggered sideways, with a gaping wound in its neck. Brown fluid oozed from the wound and the mutant fell to the ground dead.

Johnny breathed a sigh of relief and thanked the sheriff. Lamar didn't reply but stared blankly at the dead creatures.

Johnny asked, "Are you okay?"

After another moment, Lamar replied, "Hell, no. I nearly shit myself three times tonight." Johnny chuckled at him.

Lamar remarked arrogantly, "You thought I was nuts, didn't you? Well take another look, sonny boy. If that ain't one of the devil's disciples, then I don't know what is."

Johnny examined one of the dead mutants and surmised aloud, "This thing used to be human."

Lamar replied, "Yeah, like Bo Davis was. How do you explain that?"

"Beats me. Something is causing them to change."

"Well, old Kaz better come up with an answer for this before everybody starts changing into these things." The two men retreated with their weapons drawn to the SUV and climbed inside.

Lamar noticed a sedan parked in the trees across from the police station. He remembered seeing it in front of the police station earlier when Agents Cox and Melendez dropped in on him.

"That's odd."

"What's that, Sheriff?"

"Oh, nothing."

Johnny drove the vehicle away from the police station. He asked, "How many of these things do you think there are?"

Lamar put his window down and spat. "I don't know but it seems that more of 'em keep turning up."

"Any idea how to stop them?"

"There must be someone or something behind this. It's like killing a snake. You have to cut the head off to stop it."

Johnny suggested, "Maybe it's a virus or something."

"No, it's much more than that."

"I can't believe it's the devil's doing. There's got to be a rational explanation."

Lamar replied, "There is and I think our federal agents know something about it."

"Why wouldn't they tell us if they knew something?"

Their SUV turned down the main street and proceeded toward the bus terminal.

"I saw a movie once. In this movie, a virus infected a lot of people. The government didn't want a panic on their hands so they secretly quarantined the area. When the time came, they annihilated everyone inside that area to eradicate the virus."

Johnny laughed and commented, "That's science fiction stuff, Sheriff. That ain't real."

"Johnny, you've seen them things. They're real."

"What if they were aliens?"

Lamar looked at Johnny sternly and countered, "What if they're the leading edge of an invasion? Or what if this is the devil's doing? Either scenario is bigger than we can handle."

"So, what do we do about it?"

"We do what we can and keep it between us. Don't say nothing to them agents about anything we see or do. I'll handle them."

"No problem, Sheriff. Those guys make me nervous anyway."

Lamar kidded, "Is that why you called them 'spooks'?"

Johnny chuckled. "Well, Sheriff, it's good to see your sense of humor showing again."

"Thanks for the wake-up call."

"I did rather enjoy giving it to you for a change."

"Johnny."

"I know – shut up."

Their SUV pulled up on the sidewalk and crept toward the bus terminal. Half-eaten corpses littered the area. Johnny complained, "We're gonna have to walk. There's too many bodies in the way."

Lamar smirked and replied, "Drive over 'em. They're already dead."

"But, Sheriff!"

Lamar glared at Johnny and reminded him, "This isn't normal, what's happening around here. The rules have changed." Johnny looked uncomfortable as he drove over the first half-eaten corpse. A short distance from them, Hayes' cruiser was parked but he was nowhere in sight.

Johnny peered out the window at the bloody remains of a woman. "Man, this is messed up."

Lamar replied, "My big ass is gonna be in church on Sunday if we get out of this mess." The two men looked at each other uneasily.

Lamar ordered, "Stop the vehicle. There's Hayes' cruiser." Johnny stopped behind the bus and put the vehicle in 'park'.

"You know, the first creature I saw was doing something evil to this one woman," Lamar revealed. "The creature escaped and I had to shoot the woman and its companion."

"What do you mean 'its companion'?"

"Well, to the best of my recollection, there's three kinds of them things: aliens, human-like aliens; and humans degenerated into monsters."

"And what about this one you were talking about?"

"This one was like a human alien and I think it was banging the woman."

Johnny laughed at him. "What did you say, Sheriff?"

Lamar was embarrassed and got emotional. "It was banging her! It had a long tube coming out of its mouth and it went right up where the sun doesn't shine. I mean it was having some kind of sex with the woman."

Johnny was shocked. "And she was alive?"

"I think it drugged her up or something. She was pretty spaced out."

"And you killed her? That's like murder, Sheriff!"

"I had to. What if that woman got pregnant and spawned more of them things?"

"And the companion? You killed it, too?"

"No, the other creature carried it off. This thing definitely looked like an alien."

"Oh, shit! How are we gonna explain this?"

"It's not murder, Johnny. It's more like a lawman's exorcism. This shit ain't covered by the law and there's no lawyer in the world that would press a case like this."

"Gosh, I hope you're right." A mutant emerged from the terminal and crept toward Johnny's window.

Johnny spotted Hayes' cruiser. "I'm going to check it out."

Lamar warned him, "If he's there, you're not gonna like what you find."

Johnny grabbed the door handle and was about to open the door when the face of the mutant slammed against the window. Saliva splashed against the glass and streamed down. Johnny howled, "Holy shit!"

The mutant raised its arm to smash the window. Lamar quickly got out of the SUV. He leaned across the roof and shot the mutant twice in the head. It stared briefly and then fell to the ground. Johnny leaned back in his seat and breathed a sigh of relief.

Lamar leaned in and informed him, "That's one of them degenerates I told you about."

Johnny uttered, "Just friggin' great."

"You alright, boy?"

"No, I think I shit my pants."

Lamar chuckled and commented, "I don't think it'll be the last time."

Johnny got out of the SUV and scanned the area. He said, "Looks safe, sheriff."

Lamar searched for any movement and replied, "Make it quick. I don't like this one bit."

Johnny rushed to the vehicle.

Pam was in the back seat of the cruiser, eating Jimmy Hayes' entrails. She held out a length of his intestines and eyed it meticulously before eating it.

Johnny hurriedly stepped over the half-eaten carcasses and approached the cruiser. He noticed the driver's-side seat was back and wondered, *Maybe Hayes is in there?*

Johnny got closer and saw Hayes' legs on the seat. "Hayes, are you okay?" He leaned inside the cruiser and was horrified at the remains of his friend.

Pam looked up and hissed at him. She grabbed him by the collar and pulled him toward her. Her tongue shot out and lapped Johnny's face. Johnny screamed and struggled to get free.

Pam taunted, "Welcome to the party. I'm always up for a fresh bite." Johnny tried desperately to pull his arm inside the vehicle and use his pistol.

Lamar heard Johnny's scream and rushed to the cruiser. He smashed the window on the back door and reached inside. He grabbed Pam by her tongue and placed his pistol against her head. She was surprised by the sudden appearance of Lamar.

Lamar said sarcastically, "Smile, Sweetie. I got some head candy for ya'." He fired the .357 into her head and splattered green and brown brain matter across the passenger-side windows.

Pam retracted her tongue and her eyes grew wide. She muttered, "You dick." She released her hold on Johnny and fell over sideways. Johnny broke down into tears as he backed away from the cruiser.

Lamar reached in again and pulled her toward him. He took a switchblade out of his pocket and opened it.

Johnny asked tearfully, "What are you doing?"

"Collecting a souvenir." Lamar grabbed Pam's tongue and yanked on it until it extended about two feet. He cut it off and pushed her back on her side. He fired another shot into her head.

Johnny was startled and asked, "What the hell'd you do that for?"

"Because she called me a dick. Nobody does that and gets away with it."

Johnny fell to his knees and cried, "This is sick! This is so friggin' sick."

Lamar reminded him sympathetically, "Hayes is gone, Johnny. Let it go."

Johnny stared at the vehicle and uttered hysterically, "Look what she did to him. She was eating his guts!"

"If we don't get out of here, we might be next."

"Maybe that was the last one."

"I wish it were, Johnny. I wish it were."

The two men returned to the SUV. Lamar offered, "I'll drive. You sit back and take it easy." Johnny clung tightly to his pistol and stared at Hayes' cruiser.

Lamar tossed the tongue on the dashboard. He started the SUV and looked at the terminal. He saw something moving through the glass windows that made up the front wall. "Those sons-of-bitches. There's more of 'em, Johnny." Lamar opened the door and got out with his pistol drawn.

"Where you going, Sheriff?"

Lamar reloaded his pistol and replied, "I can't let any of those things live."

"But what if there's too many of them?"

"Then we're dead anyway."

Lamar hurried to the terminal and burst through the door. He saw eight mutants eating corpses. "Damn you, you spawn of Satan!" The mutants looked up and rushed at him.

Lamar took aim and fired at them, one at a time. Nine more of the mutants approached from a side hallway. Lamar exclaimed frantically, "Fuck me, Agnes!" He fired the last round from his pistol and turned to run.

Johnny burst through the door, armed with the shotgun. He fired two scatter shots and wounded five of them. They staggered backwards and fell dead. The others resumed their attack.

Johnny handed his pistol to Lamar and reloaded the shotgun. The two men fired until they killed the last of the mutants.

⋅⋅◆◆◆⋅⋅

Grimwold approached Hayes' cruiser and examined Pam's dead body. He snarled and punched the roof with his fists until the windshield exploded.

Lamar and Johnny heard the glass shatter and rushed out of the terminal. Grimwold saw them and dashed down the alley. Lamar aimed his pistol and fired at him. Grimwold felt a burst of pain in his shoulder and fell to the ground. He hissed and wriggled behind a dumpster. After pausing for a moment, he regained his composure. Lamar hurried into the alley with Johnny a short distance behind with the shotgun.

Grimwold heard them and scrambled to his feet. He raced away before they could find him. When he tripped over trashcans in his haste, Lamar heard the noise and muttered, "He's too far away. We'll never catch him now."

Johnny noticed wet blotches of brown on the dumpster under the streetlight. "Hey, Sheriff, I think you hit him."

Lamar studied the blotch and commented sarcastically, "Brown blood. Makes you wonder." He scanned the alley one more time and said, "Let's get out of here. I'm sure we'll see him again."

They left the alley and passed the cruiser. Lamar took notice of the broken window.

Johnny asked, "What is it?"

"We pissed him off."

"How, by killing all those creatures?"

"No, by killing the one in Hayes' car. That's one of the human-like aliens. He is pissed because we killed his mate, I'll bet."

"But if she was human once, how'd she get like that?" questioned Johnny.

"Don't know yet, but I'll bet he has a tongue like hers and those other creatures don't."

"Can we leave now?"

"What's the matter? Lamar kidded. "You scared?"

"No, I have to go to the bathroom pretty bad."

"You can use the rest room in the bus terminal." Johnny looked worried.

The two men entered the bus terminal. Never before had they seen so many dead bodies mutilated. At first it was shocking, but soon they became numb to it. When they reached the restroom, Lamar reloaded his .357 and kicked open the door. The restroom looked empty. The doors to each of the five stalls were partially open. Lamar knelt down and looked underneath the stalls. There was no sign of the creatures so he went to the urinal and relieved himself.

Johnny pushed the door open and inquired, "Is it safe?"

Lamar tugged the zipper up on his pants. "Sure is. Have at it."

Johnny set the shotgun down against the wall and unbuckled his pants. He entered one of the stalls and closed the door.

Lamar kidded, "Don't die in there."

"Stick around. I'm sure you're used to hanging out in shit holes."

Lamar laughed at him. "I'll wait outside."

Johnny dropped his trousers and sat down on the toilet. He placed his head in his hands and rubbed his eyes. A mutant stood on the toilet in the stall next to him. He was the last one that Grimwold injected with his hormone so he looked more like a zombie than a mutant. It peered over the top of the stall at Johnny and waited patiently. Drool streamed down its chin and its cheeks pulsed from the transformation.

Johnny finished and got to his feet. He bent over and pulled his trousers up. The mutant reached down and grabbed him around the neck. It struggled to pull him up when Johnny hooked his feet under the stall door. He grabbed at the creature's eyes and desperately gouged at them. Johnny screamed, "Sheriff, help!"

Lamar heard him out in the hall and chuckled. "Must be one hell of a shit that boy's taking."

Johnny's feet slipped off the door and he kicked at the walls. He screamed again, "Sheriff!"

Lamar complained, "I'm gonna knock him out if he's screwing around!" He kicked open the restroom door and said, "What the hell is …?"

Lamar saw the mutant and exclaimed, "Son of a bitch! Where'd you come from?"

Johnny pushed desperately at the mutant's chin with his hands. Its mouth was open as it strained to reach Johnny's arm. Gray saliva with an acrid stench streamed down the side of the stall and pooled on the floor.

Lamar grabbed the shotgun and approached the stall. He aimed at the mutant's head. The mutant hissed at him and bared its teeth. He promptly shoved the barrel in its mouth and pulled the trigger. The blast splattered the back of the mutant's head and neck all over the wall. Pieces of flesh and blood spattered on Johnny. He fell down on the ground next to the toilet and sobbed as he wiped the pieces of blood and flesh off of his shoulders and arms.

Lamar asked impatiently, "Are you coming out or what?"

Johnny got up and opened the stall door, screaming sarcastically, "I thought you said it was clear?"

"I figured you were taking a megaturd. I didn't want to interrupt."

Johnny walked to the door while rubbing his neck. Then Lamar put his hand on his shoulder and asked, "Where you going?"

Johnny was confused by his concern and replied, "Out to the truck. Why?"

"Didn't your mamma teach you anything about hygiene? Flush the damn toilet and wash your hands."

Johnny cried, "I almost got killed and you're worried about hygiene!"

"Same thing as making sure you wear clean underwear," Lamar remarked cynically. "Never want to get killed with soiled shorts." He blocked the doorway until Johnny flushed the toilet and washed his hands.

Johnny complained, "Boy, I can see you've got your swagger back."

"The more we kill these things, the better I like our odds." The two men exited the restroom.

Johnny took the shotgun back from Lamar and reloaded it. Lamar took note of his attitude and asked, "What's the matter?"

"The humanoid was right. You're a real dick, Whittington."

Lamar laughed. "I'm sorry, Johnny. It is funny when you think about it."

"Would you be laughing if I was dead or injured?"

"Hell no. I'd have to replace the best damn deputy in the state."

"You really mean that, Sheriff?"

"Of course, you knucklehead."

Lamar rubbed Johnny's head and walked around the SUV to the driver's-side. He climbed inside the truck and started it. Johnny paused and scanned the area for more creatures.

Grimwold rose from the back seat floor. His tongue lashed out and coiled around Lamar's neck. Needles sprouted from Grimwold's tongue and pierced his throat. He grabbed Lamar by the hair and pulled his head back. Glaring into his eyes, he warned in his alien dialect, "You'll pay for killing my mate. You'll pay dearly." Lamar tried to scream but he faded into a trance.

Johnny leaned inside the SUV to lay the gun down and saw Grimwold. "I'll kill you, you bastard!" he shouted. When he raised the shotgun, Grimwold quickly yanked it away from him and bolted from the SUV.

Johnny drew his pistol and fired three shots at the fleeing alien. Two of the shots struck Grimwold in the thigh and back. Despite the pain, Grimwold continued around the corner and down the alley.

Johnny pulled Lamar over to the passenger seat. "Sheriff, say something!" he pleaded. "Come on, Sheriff. Don't die on me." Johnny felt

Lamar's pulse growing weaker. He hurried in the driver's-side and drove off toward the hospital.

Lamar grew ashen and his breathing weakened. Johnny took out his phone and dialed Joe Beauchamp's number. He waited anxiously for Joe to answer.

Joe was asleep in bed when the phone rang. After the fourth ring, Joe rolled over and faced the clock. It displayed 'twelve-thirty'. He mumbled, "You've got to be kidding me"

Joe answered the phone with an attitude, "Beauchamp. What?"

Johnny babbled frantically, "Dr. Beauchamp, it's Deputy Watkins! An alien attacked Sheriff Whittington and he's been poisoned."

Joe sat up on the edge of the bed. "What do you mean he was attacked by an alien?"

"It was an alien, I think. It tried to choke him."

"Alright. I'll meet you at the hospital." Joe hung up and complained, "One lousy week a year I get a vacation and all this has to happen."

Johnny hollered on the radio, "All units respond. This is Delta-5." He waited anxiously but there was no reply. Johnny shouted, "Damn it, somebody say something!"

C H A P T E R V I

THE MONSTER WITHIN

Inside the space ship, Suzie pondered what her first move would be. She approached the control panel and pressed several buttons. The star-shaped programming device educated her on alien technology and communications so she was able to operate the equipment. She activated the monitor and sent out a homing signal.

The alien leader, Jasper, appeared on the monitor. He asked in his alien tongue, "Who are you?"

Suzie mentioned calmly, "I know you've got implants that allow you to understand and speak my language."

"I see you've been programmed. Who are you?"

"It doesn't matter who I am. I have an offer for you."

Jasper challenged, "And why should I listen to you?"

"Because you need me to stop Shurek from ruining your plans."

"Why would you do that? You've been turned?"

Suzie changed to her human self then reverted back to her alien shape.

Jasper laughed at her and commented, "That's a nice trick but he still controls you."

Suzie remarked smugly, "No he doesn't. He screwed that up."

"You'll have to prove yourself to me. I don't trust you."

"I'm sure I can arrange a token of my loyalty. I'll be in touch."

Suzie turned off the monitor and snickered. "He'll be begging for mercy one day." She lay down on the table and closed her eyes.

Shurek entered the ship looking drained of strength. He treaded slowly into the cargo bay and announced sadistically in his language, "Ah, it's time my pet for you to do my bidding." He lifted the layer of flesh that covered the cavity in his chest and removed his worm. It quivered and glistened in the light as he admired it. "Do your thing my little one."

As he lowered the worm onto Suzie's upper lip, he noticed that the homing beacon was activated on the control console. He shouted, "What's this treachery? Where are you, Grimwold?" When the worm crept near Suzie's lips, she bit it in half and chewed it up. Shurek screamed and held his claws against the sides of his head. He felt the worm's pain.

Suzie sat up and spit the remains of the worm on the floor at Shurek's feet. She asked sarcastically, "Did you lose something?"

Shurek lunged at Suzie but she stepped aside and shoved him into the console. She taunted him, "Nice try, loser."

Shurek stood up and grabbed at Suzie but she gripped his throat first and squeezed. She changed into her human form, then back to her alien form. "What do you think of your woman now, Shurek?"

Shurek was stunned by her strength. He struggled to free himself from her grip but in his weakened state, he was no match for her. Suzie released him and dropped him to the floor. She ordered, "You've got an interpreter in you. Answer my question – what do you think of your woman now?"

Shurek massaged his throat and replied hoarsely, "You'll ruin everything."

Suzie saw his throat flex as he prepared to strike at her with his tongue. She rammed her shoulder into his midsection and gripped his throat again. Her claws punctured the thick leathery layer of skin on his neck.

Shurek gasped. "What do you want from me?"

"You killed my daughters. You have to pay for that."

He pleaded, "Please don't kill me."

"Not yet. I need you alive - for now." Suzie released one of her claws from his throat and tore open her sweatshirt. She lifted the fleshy flap over a small opening in her chest. Inside were a number of small worms hanging from the top of her cavity.

Shurek saw them and was horrified. "But how? How did you …?"

Suzie retrieved one of the worms and held it in front of Shurek's face. "Didn't you ever study the female anatomy of your race? It seems that we were meant to be the superior gender in your world."

Suzie pressed against his throat with one claw until his eyes rolled back in his head. With the other, she placed the worm on his snout. Shurek grew weak and lost his ability to struggle. The worm slithered into his nose and disappeared. He shuddered and gagged. White fluid streamed from his nasal passages over his lips. Suzie enjoyed her new found superiority as she now had control of him.

Vega carried Kroll into the spaceship and stood quietly at the entrance. She was surprised to see Suzie manhandle Shurek so easily. Suzie released her hold on his throat and let him fall to the ground. Shurek's breathing slowly returned to normal. "You're ruining everything," he cried. "These plans took a long time to develop."

"Forget your plans. You're my bitch now and the only plan is going to be my plan." She approached the monitor and turned it on.

Shurek lunged at her, shouting "No!"

Suzie turned and swung her arm at his throat. The clothesline effect leveled Shurek and knocked him senseless. "I see I'll have to teach you obedience, Shurek," she remarked arrogantly.

"You'll never control me!" he shouted.

Suzie communicated with the worm and inflicted severe pain to Shurek's brain. He screamed and shook violently across the floor as he covered his ears with his claws. Suzie grinned sadistically at him all the while.

Vega retreated from the doorway and stepped outside the hatch. She didn't know whether or not she wanted to be part of Suzie's plot - yet. She set Kroll down on the ground next to the hatch and examined the wound to his head. The bullet was lodged deep inside of Kroll's brain and he was in a coma. Vega reached into her cavity and removed a worm. She whispered, "You have to help me save him. The metal object has to come out." When Vega placed the worm on the wound, it slithered inside Kroll's head and disappeared. She sat next to him and focused on the worm's progress to save his life.

Suzie finally ended the pain and returned to the Sporatin. She accessed the finger port with her claw and waited for Pitherus to appear on screen.

Shurek was stunned that she understood and could successfully access the creature's conscience. Pitherus' image appeared on the Sporatin and greeted her, "Welcome back, Serena Luna."

Suzie replied proudly, "Thank you, Pitherus. I have Shurek here with me. What would happen to him if I turned him over to his people?"

Pitherus chuckled. "His limbs and tongue would be removed and he'd be placed in a cerebrium until he expired."

"I like your sense of humor, Pitherus. Where did that come from?"

"I was programmed by the Elders a long time ago and I am expected to represent them in both mind and spirit."

"They were very wise."

Shurek stood up behind Suzie and asked, "What did you call her, Pitherus?"

"Serena Luna. She is our destiny."

"She is not our destiny! She is an aberration of a transmutation."

Pitherus warned, "You should show respect, Shurek. She is our future."

Shurek retreated away from Suzie toward the entrance. "No she's not! I'll kill her first." He raced out of the cargo bay.

Suzie laughed at him and uttered, "Pussy!"

Pitherus inquired, "If he is a problem, we can summon others to vanquish him."

"No, Pitherus, that won't be necessary. He is much more valuable as he is."

"But he disrespects you."

"And that will be his downfall. That is all for now."

Pitherus image faded and Suzie's clawed finger released from the port. She laughed sadistically as she walked out of the cargo bay. When she exited the ship, she was surprised to see Vega and Kroll. "Why do you cower out here when your home is inside the ship?"

Vega answered, "We did not wish to interrupt your meeting with Shurek."

"That was no meeting. I was helping Shurek fulfill his destiny. He just doesn't know it."

"Where do we fit into your plans?"

"Are you with me or against me?" Suzie questioned.

"Should we be against you?" countered Vega.

"Of course not. We are one family."

"Then we are with you."

Suzie knelt down next to Kroll and asked, "What happened to him, Jane?"

Vega looked baffled and answered, "I'm not Jane. I am Vega. A projectile struck Kroll and lodged in his brain."

"I can help him. Take him inside and set him on the table." Suzie then announced, "I am Serena Luna, chosen by the Elders to fulfill our destiny. You must trust me."

"Alright, Serna Luna. I will." Vega lifted Kroll and carried him inside the ship. "Why did you call me 'Jane'?"

"In your human life, you were my friend Jane."

Vega tried to recall but had no recollection. She asked, "And who were you?"

"I was Suzie," she replied as the two stared at each other. Each attempted to recall the memories of those times. "I see you care about Kroll. You always wanted someone to care for."

"He does care about me. I have to help him."

"Does he control you?"

"You mean through a worm? No."

"Interesting," Suzie remarked, curious.

"He trusted me and I trust him."

"Sounds like Earthly qualities to me."

"No, just companionship. I assume Shurek is your companion."

Suzie laughed and replied, "Hardly. He is a degenerate criminal. His actions could lead to disaster for our future."

"And you can save it?"

"Yes, I can."

"What do you require of us?"

"When Kroll is healed, you will turn as many humans as possible and gather them in a cave at the base of the mountain. We will need to battle the humans for control of the area without advertising our presence."

"I understand. What about Shurek?"

"I control him through my worm."

Vega was surprised and commented, "That's impressive!"

"Why don't you rest for now? I have to take care of some things." Suzie left them alone and walked outside the ship. She focused on Shurek and sent waves of pain into his brain.

Shurek was climbing the side of the mountain when the pain occurred. He clutched his head between his claws and howled. Telepathically, Suzie warned him, "Obey my commands and I'll show you mercy."

Shurek fell to his knees and wailed until the pain stopped. He shouted, "Never!"

Suzie instructed him, "You will turn humans and assemble them in a cave at the base of the mountain. Vega and Kroll will do the same."

"What's so special about your plan? I should be leading us to victory."

"You're sloppy, Shurek. Just do as I tell you and try not to draw any more attention than necessary." Suzie ended her communication with Shurek and returned to the ship.

Shurek snarled and slammed his head against the rock in an effort to disable the worm. Suzie felt the effect on the worm but it remained unharmed. She thought, *Killing Shurek will be so sweet.*

Vega slept on the floor against the side of the table. Above her, Kroll laid motionless. Suzie entered and eyed the two. She reached under her torn sweatshirt into her chest cavity for another worm and held it in front of Vega's nose. The worm slithered into Vega's left nasal passage and excavated its way to her frontal lobe.

Vega coughed and jarred herself awake. She covered her pug-shaped nose with her claws and moaned, "What have you done, Serena?"

Suzie replied, "It's for your own good."

Vega snorted and spit thick plugs of mucous on the floor. She shook her head spastically and shouted, "You said you were my friend. Why did you do this?"

Suzie answered calmly, "I can't afford not to have your loyalty."

Vega bent over Kroll and laid her head against his chest. She sobbed from the initial pain. When she raised her head, she informed Suzie, "You just lost my loyalty."

"Then I no longer need you." Suzie focused on Vega's worm and inflicted intense pain to her brain.

Vega screamed and lunged at Suzie. The two wrestled briefly until Suzie gripped the layer of flesh that protected Vega's worm cavity.

Suzie warned, "Quit now or I'll ruin you, Vega." Vega paused as she considered the consequences and, maybe later, another attempt on Suzie's life.

Kroll's eyes opened and he sat up. Neither Suzie nor Vega took notice. Kroll slid off the table and balanced himself against it. He summoned all his strength and whipped his tongue around Suzie's neck.

Suzie was stunned by the surprise assault and released her hold on Vega. She turned and tore Kroll's tongue out of his throat. He shuddered and convulsed until Suzie ripped his throat open.

Vega cried out, "No, Kroll!" Kroll's eyes rolled back in his head and he fell to the floor dead. "This isn't over!" she shouted and left the ship.

Suzie remarked arrogantly, "It never is, is it?"

Vega cried as she ran through the woods. Suzie's voice filled her head and reminded her, "It didn't have to be this way."

Vega paused near a stream and picked up a rock. She smashed her forehead repeatedly with the rock until she damaged the worm. Suzie felt the pain that the worm experienced and became enraged. She stormed about the ship, throwing things about.

Brown blood seeped from Vega's nose and dripped down the side of her face. She felt relief since she knew she damaged or killed Suzie's worm. Suzie tried to inflict pain to Vega but she couldn't. The worm was too badly damaged. She spoke through the worm and chastised her, "That was stupid, Vega. Now I have to kill you. What a pity?"

Vega laughed and thought, *If that's all she can do is talk to me then I'm free to do as I please.* She continued through the woods and down the mountain, knowing that she needed to find allies fast. Perhaps she could find Grimwold. At least then she wouldn't be alone.

When she reached the road on the side of the mountain, she saw the headlights from a truck approach. She leaped from the trees and grabbed onto the rear gate. After some effort, she pulled herself over the gate and lay down on the flatbed. The truck driver continued on his way, unaware of his alien passenger.

Suzie activated the monitor and initiated the homing signal. Jasper's face appeared on the monitor. He asked, "What do you want now? I'm very busy."

"My name is Serena Luna. Who are you?"

"I am Jasper, commander of our fleet in the solar system."

"Well, Jasper, it's time to talk," Suzie informed him.

"Has Shurek put you up to this?"

"I told you before, he can't control me."

Jasper inquired, "How did that happen?"

"For one, he didn't inject his hormone directly into my spine. Very little entered my nervous system, thanks to his incompetence. He did insert DNA compound into me which, without the hormone present, gave me many of your advanced attributes."

Jasper chided, "But Shurek will use the worm to control you."

"No, he won't. I've inserted one of my worms inside him. I can manipulate him at will."

"I see," said Jasper with renewed interest. "And what do you want out of this?"

"I know you plan to take over the planet. I want to lead the invasion and rule on your behalf."

Jasper laughed at her and asked, "Why would I agree to that?"

"Your clumsy oafs have already made humans aware of your presence. I can squash that and prepare a ground force discretely."

"That would make things much smoother. How much fighting capability do the humans have to repel an invasion?"

"You can't fight them in a war," Suzie warned him. "You won't stand a chance."

"I see. And I can count on you to take care of matters?"

"Of course. The programming was incomplete and I still have my human faculties. I'll make sure that no one ever remembers what happened here."

"Ah, you are an advanced hybrid of sorts."

"And an aggressive one at that. Don't cross me and things will go very nicely for you."

"Very well. I believe we have common grounds for a deal. I traced your homing signal and I'll check in on your progress from time to time."

Suzie remarked, "I'd be disappointed if you didn't."

"Well, good luck, Serena Luna."

"Thank you."

The screen went blank and Suzie eyed Kroll's corpse. She groaned, "Why doesn't anyone ever listen around here?" She approached a circular hatch about three feet in diameter with a handwheel on it. She opened the hatch and studied the controls above it. There was a green knob and two slide bars. Inside the hatch was a horizontal tube-shaped chamber.

Suzie picked up Kroll and shoved him inside the chamber. She closed the hatch and pressed the green knob. The knob flashed several times until she raised the left slide bar. Intense lasers increased in power and incinerated Kroll's body as the slide bar was raised. The green knob flashed again when the incineration was complete.

Suzie lowered the left slide bar and raised the right slide bar. A small opening in the bottom of the chamber created a vacuum, which increased when the slide bar was raised. The ashes from Kroll's body were sucked through the opening into a bin where it blended in with other incinerated bio-waste. Another laser scanned the tube for any remaining residue. When the tube was clear, the suction stopped and the green knob flashed.

Suzie lowered the slide bar to its original position, which now shut down the vacuum. She muttered to herself, "Nice knowing you, Kroll." She returned to her table and rested on it.

⋅⋅◆◆◆⋅⋅

Joe stopped at the gas station. He was pumping gas into the tank when he glanced over at a truck. As he looked closer, he noticed no one was inside it. *That's odd,* he thought. He finished pumping the gas and restored the hose on the pump.

Vega crept up behind Joe's pickup truck and hid. Joe walked over to the truck and peered inside. He saw the driver lying across the seat, torn to shreds. "What the hell?" he blurted.

Vega climbed onto the back of Joe's pickup truck and lay flat. Joe rushed back to his truck and drove away. He attempted to call Suzie.

Suzie frowned as the phone disturbed her rest. She transformed into her human shape and retrieved it from her raggedy sweatpants. She looked at the display and saw Joe's number. "Sorry, baby," she uttered to herself. "I'm not in the mood to talk." She pondered and continued, "Although I do think we need to rethink our family situation." Suzie then burst into laughter.

Joe's voice silenced her as he left his message. "Suzie, it's me. There are dangerous creatures loose in the area. Call me as soon as you can. I think you and the girls should get out of there as soon as possible."

Suzie thought, *How considerate? Where were you when I was raising the girls by myself, you selfish bastard.* She put away the phone and departed the spaceship.

Chapter VII

Wreaking Havoc

The police SUV skidded to a stop near the entrance to the hospital emergency room. Johnny leaped out of the vehicle and burst through the emergency room door. "Someone help me! I have an injured man out here."

Two nurses entered the hallway. The first nurse, Joann, had dark hair propped up in a bun and was in her late forties. Sally, the other nurse, had short, blond hair and in her mid- twenties.

Joann asked, "What's wrong, sir?"

Sally interrupted, "That's Johnny Watkins, the deputy."

Johnny stammered, "The sheriff was poisoned by an alien."

Joann put her hands on her hips and chided, "If this is a joke, Deputy, it's not funny."

Johnny shouted, "Get a friggin' gurney and get your ass out here, now!"

Sally grabbed a gurney and replied eagerly, "I'm coming, Johnny."

"Thanks, Sally." Johnny guided the front end of the gurney through the door and out to the SUV. Lamar was unconscious with his head tilted back. His neck was swollen and marked with dark spots.

Johnny lifted him from the vehicle and set him over the gurney. Sally lifted Lamar's legs up and together they rolled him on his back.

Sally inquired, "So what did happen to the sheriff?"

"I know this is hard to believe but this alien creature with a long tongue tried to choke the sheriff to death."

Sally glanced at Lamar's neck and winced. "It does look pretty bad."

Joann opened the door for them and stood back.

Sally volunteered, "I'll get Dr. Edmunds."

Joann suggested, "Tell him that it's the sheriff. He ought to get out here right quick." Sally disappeared around the corner into another hallway.

Johnny and Joann pushed the gurney into the first examining room. Johnny asked, "Why's Edmunds have an interest in the sheriff?"

Joann checked the sheriff's blood pressure, and then explained, "Sheriff's had it in for him for a few years now. Doc was drinking one night and the sheriff pulled him over. He said a few things that he shouldn't have and the sheriff never got over it. Doc's got a pile of citations for all kinds of stuff and it keeps getting bigger." Joann monitored the sheriff's blood pressure a second time.

Johnny asked, "What is it?"

"Eighty-eight over sixty-four. It's really low but it seems to be rising."

"Will he be alright?"

"I don't know yet. We'll take some blood and send it up to the lab. Luckily, two of the techs are in tonight for inspection readiness." Joann opened a drawer and took out a syringe. She removed the cap from the needle and inspected it.

<hr>

Inside the doctors' lounge, two mutants fed on Dr. Edmunds' body. Sally opened the door to the lounge and saw them tearing out his entrails. She screamed and burst into tears. The mutants looked up at her with anxious eyes as blood pooled on the tile floor and pieces of flesh spilled from their mouths. Sally ran frantically from the lounge and hurried down the hall. "Johnny, help me!"

Johnny heard Sally's cries and emphatically instructed Joann, "Stay here with the sheriff until I get back. Don't go outside. I repeat, do not go outside." He drew his pistol and stepped into the hall.

Sally raced toward him, followed by the two mutants. Johnny ordered, "Get down, Sally." Sally ducked her head and moved toward the wall.

Johnny carefully aimed at the closest mutant and fired two shots. The first struck the mutant in the forehead. The second shot penetrated its eye. The mutant fell to the ground dead. The second mutant tumbled over the dead one but grabbed for Sally's ankle. Johnny took her arm and pulled her aside. He fired three shots at the creature. Two rounds entered its head and the third round struck the artery in its neck, killing it. Joann peered into the hallway and was mortified.

Sally cried hysterically and hugged Johnny. "Oh, Johnny! It was horrible! They were eating Doc Edmunds."

When Johnny embraced her, Sally wiped her tears from her eyes and asked, "What are those things?"

Johnny looked callously at the dead creatures and replied, "They're not the ones that poisoned the sheriff."

Joann responded uneasily, "You mean there's more?"

"Oh yeah, and I'm sure they are nearby. They travel in packs."

Joe Beauchamp entered the ER and saw the creatures on the floor. "What the hell's going on?"

Johnny pointed into the examining room and explained, "Sheriff's been poisoned. He's in there."

Joe browsed at the dead creatures. "What about these things?"

"You tell me."

Joe instructed him, "Watch the hall in case there's any more of those things around."

The phone in the examining room rang. Joann answered it. She looked horrified and exclaimed aloud, "Those creatures are trying to get into the lab on the second floor."

Joe checked the sheriff's pulse and said, "He's not going anywhere. Where's the lab from here?"

Joann instructed him, "Take the stairs at the end of the hall to the second floor. When you get off, go to your right. It's the third door down."

Joe asked Johnny, "You got any more guns?"

"Sure do. I'll be right back." Johnny exited the emergency room and went to the SUV. He searched the area around the vehicle and saw nothing, although he had an eerie feeling that he was being watched. He reached inside the SUV and grabbed the shotgun and two boxes of shells. He shut the door and hustled back inside the hospital.

Joe loaded the shotgun and dumped the remainder of the shells into his pants pockets. "Would one of you girls show me the way?" he asked.

Sally volunteered, "I will. Just promise me you'll kill them before they kill us."

"I'll do my best."

Joann told the caller, "They're coming up to help you. Hold on."

Joe and Sally entered the stairwell and crept up the steps. They paused at the second-floor entrance when they heard the mutants beating on the lab door.

Joe asked Sally, "How far is it to the lab door?"

"About thirty feet."

"You open the door and I'll go through." Joe stood nervously with the shotgun pointed up at the ceiling.

Sally yanked the door open and Joe rushed through. He shouted at the mutants, "Hey, scuzzballs!" The mutants saw him and one raced toward him.

Sally urged him, "Shoot it!"

Joe knelt down and aimed at the creature. He fired once and tore a hole in the mutant's chest. It clutched at the wound briefly and fell to the ground dead. The second one rushed at him.

Joe aimed and fired a second shot. The blast wounded the mutant in the shoulder and knocked it down. He reached into his pocket and fumbled for two more rounds. In his haste, he dropped them to the floor. The mutant got up and snarled at Joe.

Sally picked up the rounds and shoved them into Joe's hand. She pleaded, "Load it and shoot that thing, will you please?"

When the mutant lunged at Joe, he swung the gun at the creature's head and stunned it. The creature's momentum shoved him against the wall. Joe couldn't raise the gun so he fired at the mutant's knee.

The blast sent the mutant to the ground. It wrapped its arms around Joe's waist and pulled the shotgun from his hands.

Joe shouted, "Get the gun, Sally!" Sally reluctantly picked it up and stared at them.

The mutant crawled on top of Joe as he struggled to get loose. He grabbed the creature's lower jaw with both hands and held it back. "Shoot it, Sally!"

Sally sobbed. "I can't. I'll hit you."

The mutant slapped Joe across the side of the head and cut him with its claws. Joe screamed, "Shoot it, Sally!"

Sally was terrified. She approached the creature and pointed the gun at its head. The mutant paused from its attack on Joe, staring at her with sinister eyes. Sally pulled the trigger and blew its face off. The mutant shrieked and fell to the floor. It covered its face and shook violently. The kick from the gun knocked Sally against the wall and on her ass. She lay in tears on her side, clutching her shoulder.

Joe scurried to his feet and picked up the shotgun. He fired another shot into the mutant's chest and killed it. Sally looked pitifully at Joe and cried. He helped her to her feet and put his arm around her to comfort her.

"Let's get the lab techs out of here in case more of those creatures are around." Sally nodded in agreement. Joe reloaded the shotgun and followed her to the lab door.

Sally called out, "Rachel! Maria! It's Sally. Are you in there?"

A woman cried out, "Are they gone?"

"They're dead. You can come out now."

Inside the lab, Joe and Sally heard desks sliding across the floor. Finally, the door opened and two women in their early twenties warily stepped out.

Maria asked, "Are there anymore?"

Joe replied, "I certainly hope not. Let's get back downstairs."

Sally asked the girls, "Do you have the results from Sheriff Whittington's blood work? It's important."

Rachel answered, "I just finished with it when those things chased Maria down the hall." Rachel hurried back into the lab and returned with a small scroll of chart paper.

Joe instructed the girls, "Go ahead down the stairs. I want to make sure if there are any more of those things, they can't follow us." He heard snarling from around the corner and muttered, "Oh, shit! That answers my question."

Four mutants charged around the corner toward him. Joe slammed the stairwell door shut and propped the shotgun between the door and the wall. The mutants rammed the door repeatedly and beat on it but it wouldn't budge. Joe eyed the shotgun one more time until he was comfortable it wouldn't move. He hurried down the stairs to the emergency room.

Vega sent two mutants toward the main hospital entrance. As she peered from the bushes at the emergency room entrance, a familiar voice startled her. "I see we both have the same intentions."

Vega turned and took a defensive position. Grimwold patiently awaited her response. "Where's your better half, Grimwold?"

"Dead. That feeble specimen of a human inside the building killed her."

Vega taunted, "What? You didn't protect her! I suspected that you were a coward when it came right down to it." Grimwold reached for her throat but buckled over in pain, clutching at his shoulder and back.

Vega chided, "So, you're also a cripple. I could finish you off easily if I wanted to."

Grimwold knew she was right and chose the diplomatic approach. He explained, "I have no quarrel with you. I want my revenge against the uniformed human who did this to me."

Vega considered how she could use this to her advantage and responded, "Very well. I have a plan."

Grimwold informed her, "I have four mutants nearby. They'll be here soon. We can use them."

"The humans are gathered by the entrance. I want you and the mutants up on the second floor. There should be easy pickings for even a cripple like you."

Grimwold snarled but kept his composure. "So, what will you do?"

"I'll distract them on the main floor. I'll flush them up the stairs toward you and the other mutants."

Grimwold queried suspiciously, "All by yourself?"

"Of course. They've never seen one of us before – only the mutants."

"How do we get in?"

Vega pointed around the corner and answered, "There's a glass door marked 'entrance'. That's the main lobby. When you enter, you'll see metal doors. Press the 'up' arrow and wait for them to open. Once you enter, press '2'."

"I don't like this. Are you trying to trick me?"

"Of course not, you fool. It's a lift that the humans use to go up to higher tiers of their buildings."

Grimwold reluctantly replied, "Fine. But if this is a trap, you'll pay for your treachery."

"My mutants are already up there, you fool! Stop playing games!"

Vega took two steps toward the building when Grimwold responded, "We'll take care of it."

Vega whispered to herself, "I thought you would."

When Grimwold left her, Vega stepped back in the trees.

Joe returned to the examining room and inspected Lamar's neck. Rachel opened the scroll of chart paper and informed them, "His blood work isn't consistent with anything we check for although there were small quantities of opiates."

Joe complained, "It's a shame we don't have one of these creatures to study how they did this to Whittington."

Johnny overheard him and revealed, "Sheriff Whittington cut off one of their tongues. It's in the truck."

Joe replied exitedly, "Well, go get it! That might be the clue we were looking for."

Vega climbed up a tree and jumped onto the roof of the emergency room. She scaled the rainspout to a second-floor window and kicked in the glass. Once inside, she saw two bloody corpses on the beds. *Ah, my pets have been busy.*

Vega went into the hall where her mutants beat on a locked door. Satisfied, she went in the other direction and found another stairwell. She descended the stairwell to the first floor and entered the Intensive Care Unit.

Three nurses hid in one of the rooms behind the curtains. One of them peered out and saw Vega. She panicked and screamed. Vega stormed into the room and blocked the doorway to prevent their escape.

An old man laid in the bed with tubes and wires hooked up to him. He opened his eyes and saw Vega. He immediately went into cardiac arrest. The monitor alarmed and the indicator flat-lined.

Vega ripped the power cord out of the wall and silenced the equipment. She grabbed the nearest nurse; a young, Hispanic woman. She kept her eyes on the others as she held the woman by the back of the neck in a firm grip and ripped the woman's uniform off with her other claw. The nurse cried hysterically as she stood helplessly in her lace bra and thong. Vega's appendages emerged and quivered excitedly. She made the woman face her coworkers and wrapped her muscular arms around her.

The woman's eyes bulged wide as Vega pressed against her from behind and her appendages bore into the woman's back. Vega moaned lustily until she finished injecting her hormone into the woman. She tossed the woman on top of the dead man on the bed. The woman lay unconscious with her eyes open and faced the other nurses.

Vega's tongue emerged from her mouth and wiggled as she approached the second nurse, an elderly woman. The nurse picked up three long Q-tips from the table as Vega gripped her throat. The nurse stabbed at Vega's eye with the Q-tips and injured her. Vega ripped the woman's arm off. She shoved the woman against the wall and beat her unmercifully with it until the woman fell to the floor dead.

The last nurse, also an older woman, attempted to run past Vega to the door. Vega's tongue shot out and wrapped around the nurse's throat. She pulled the woman back and pushed her onto the floor on her back. The nurse struggled to scream but Vega's tongue kept enough pressure on her throat that she couldn't. Vega chose not to use the numbing agent from her tongue, but slowly tortured the woman. She ripped open the woman's uniform and used one of her sharp claws to slice open the woman's abdomen. The nurse lay helplessly with a wide-eyed look of horror. Vega gripped the nurse's throat with her claw and retracted her tongue. She then forced her tongue into the nurse's mouth. The nurse struggled desperately as Vega tugged and pulled the nurse's tongue from her throat and swallowed it. She looked like the devil with a nightmarish grin across her mutated face. The nurse's eyes darkened and puffed from her fright. Vega reached inside the woman's abdomen and gently lifted her intestines above her body for her to see. The nurse no longer struggled but stared in shock.

Vega's tongue lapped at the nurse's lips and pressed into her mouth. She moved her tongue in and out until she lubricated the woman's throat with her fluids. As she inserted her tongue further into the nurse's throat, it sucked up anything that obstructed its path. Soon the tongue burst through the nurse's stomach, spraying stomach acid over the two of them. Vega gleefully retracted her tongue.

Tears streamed from the nurse's eyes as the acid left red welts on her skin. Vega was unaffected by the acid and feasted on the nurse's intestines. The nurse died with her eyes open in a fixated horrible stare.

⁕

Johnny crept warily out to the truck. He scanned the area but saw no sign of the creatures. He leaned inside the passenger-side door and took the tongue from the dashboard. Before he pulled away, one of the mutants opened the driver's-side door and lunged for him. Johnny shrieked and fell backward on the ground. The mutant crawled across the seat toward him.

Johnny retreated from the vehicle. The mutant climbed out of the SUV and charged at him. Johnny aimed his pistol at the mutant's head and fired. The mutant clutched at its mouth but continued toward him. Johnny fired again and struck the creature in the eye. The creature fell to its knees and, after a short gasp, it fell to the ground dead. He hurried back inside the hospital with the tongue in hand.

Joe returned to the examination room and saw the tongue in Johnny's hand. "Let me see it!" Johnny handed the pink piece of flesh to Joe and followed him over to the counter.

Joe requested, "Can you get a hold of Sam Berman?"

"Sure. What for?"

"I want his expertise in figuring out how to stop these things."

Johnny took out his phone and dialed Sam's number.

⁕

Sam and his girlfriend Alicia were parked outside her apartment in his red Corvette. As they kissed, Sam unbuttoned Alicia's blouse. Alicia teased, "Is this going somewhere?"

"I certainly hope so."

Alicia complained disappointedly, "But you promised to take me to the after-hours club."

Sam reached under her blouse and massaged her breasts. Alicia pushed him away and persisted, "You didn't answer me, Sam."

He became annoyed and relented, "Alright, we'll go. I don't know what the big hurry is." His phone rang and surprised him. He reached into his pants pocket and fumbled for the phone.

Alicia urged him, "Don't answer it. We're going to be late."

Sam looked at the display and replied, "It's Deputy Watkins. I have to take this." Alicia frowned and buttoned her blouse. With her arms folded, she stared out the window.

Sam answered the phone, "Sam Berman."

Johnny sounded excited as he spoke. "Sam, it's Johnny Watkins! We've got a real crisis and we need your help!"

"Slow down, Johnny. What's going on?"

"Sheriff Whittington was poisoned by an alien and they're mutating humans into killer creatures and …"

Sam grew impatient and interrupted, "Hold on a minute. Where are you now?"

"At the hospital. These things are all over the place!"

Sam asked, "What do you need me for?"

"Dr. Beauchamp requested your assistance. We've got corpses here and he wants to find out what they are."

Sam held the phone to his chest and muttered, "Shit. This can't be happening." He got back on the phone. "I'm on the way. I'll be there in fifteen."

"Thanks, Sam."

Sam closed the phone and stowed it in his pants pocket. Alicia moaned, "I'm going home. I can't believe you did this to me, Sam."

Sam pleaded, "Come on, Sweetheart. We'll be there ten minutes and I promise we'll go to the club right after."

"I promised my friends we'd be there by twelve-thirty. It's already one o'clock."

Sam begged, "Come on, Honey. We'll be there by one forty-five." He gently stroked the inside of Alicia's thighs and kissed her lips.

Alicia pushed him away again and warned, "If we're not there by one forty-five, I'm leaving."

"That's my girl." He started the car and raced toward the hospital.

Alicia asked, "How come they're calling you at this hour? I thought you only worked days."

"I do. Every now and then something comes up that can't wait until morning. This is one of those times."

Alicia fixed her eyes upon him and inquired, "Are you really going to leave your wife for me?"

Sam looked uncomfortable and hesitated as he searched for the right words. Alicia noticed and became angry. She warned, "Look, Sam, I don't plan on being your whore every time you get an urge to pop an asshole. I want a commitment from you."

Sam held Alicia's hand and explained, "I'm going to leave her. I just don't want to hurt the kids."

"Well, that's not my problem."

"I know, Alicia, but I have to come up with a smart way to handle this. Besides, you know what alimony and child support cost?"

Alicia unbuttoned her blouse and opened it, exposing her perky breasts. She smiled coyly and asked, "Aren't I worth it?"

Sam looked at them and nearly drove off the road. He breathed a sigh of relief as he returned to his lane. "Of course, you are. I'm just trying to do this the smart way."

Alicia buttoned her blouse and looked out the window with a bored expression.

⋯✦⋯

Joe Beauchamp studied the marks on Sheriff Whittington's neck while Joann checked his blood pressure again. She announced, "One hundred over seventy."

Joe replied, "Whatever he was injected with seems to be wearing off." He examined the back of Lamar's neck as well.

Joann asked, "What are you looking for?"

"For starters, whatever did this to the sheriff wrapped itself around his neck and compressed it before sedating him. See the contusions."

Joann looked closer. "What do you think this creature was trying to do to the sheriff?"

"It may have been preparing him for something else."

Joann covered her mouth and looked nauseous. She commented, "I don't even want to know."

Joe looked around and noticed that Maria and Rachel were missing. "Where's your friends, Joann?"

Joann looked surprised. "I guess they took off. I haven't seen them in the last twenty minutes."

"Well, they're on their own. We have enough to worry about."

Lamar's breathing became regular and the color returned to his face. Joe informed everyone, "The sheriff's going to be fine. He just needs a little time to recoup."

Sally and Johnny watched from the doorway. Johnny exclaimed, "That's great news, Doc!"

Joe asked, "What do we do about our friends upstairs?"

Johnny was at a loss to make a decision. "Gee, Doc, I really don't know what we should do."

"We've got to kill those things – every one of them."

"But they can't get to us right now, can they?"

"Deputy, if they get loose, then what?"

Lamar's eyes fluttered and he sighed deeply. He muttered, "What in the hell are you two bickering about?"

Johnny's eyes lit up with joy. "Sheriff, you're okay!"

Lamar sat up on the edge of the gurney. "Of course I am, you boob. Now where are those friggin' alien assholes?"

Joe replied, "Second floor. There's at least five of them."

Grimwold stepped into the room and challenged Johnny, "You and I have unfinished business."

Lamar shouted, "Not so fast. This is my world and you're not welcome here!"

Grimwold's tongue shot toward Johnny. Lamar anticipated it and drew his pistol. He fired three quick shots into the side of Grimwold's jaw. The tongue dropped limply to Grimwold's chest and his eyes rolled back in his head. He dropped lifelessly to the floor.

Lamar declared confidently, "I've got some payback for the rest of those creeps, too." He checked his pistol for rounds and stormed out of the examining room. Johnny checked his pistol and hurried after him. Meanwhile, Joe examined Grimwold's corpse.

Sam and Alicia entered the emergency room lobby just as Joann and Sally walked out of the examining room and nearly collided with them. Joann screamed and fell against the wall. Sally shrieked. Sam shouted, "What the hell is wrong with you people!"

Joann yelled, "You scared the hell out of us!"

Joe pleaded, "Stop it – all of you!" He suggested to Joann and Sally, "You'd better keep an eye on the front door. If you see any of those things, holler."

Sam inquired, "What's all the hubbub about? It's one o'clock in the morning."

Joe stepped aside so Sam could see Grimwold's corpse on the floor.

Sam was amazed and remarked, "What the hell is that thing?"

"This one is an alien. The others used to be human."

Sam approached the corpse and examined it. He uttered, "Where in the hell did these things come from?" The sounds from a series of gunshots startled everyone.

Joe explained, "Sheriff Whittington and Deputy Watkins are hunting the others upstairs."

Sam replied, "I see. So, we have our first alien encounter."

Joe picked up the tongue from the counter and held it out for Sam to see. "This is their modus operandi."

Alicia stood impatiently in the doorway with her arms folded. "Sammy, is this going to take long?"

Sam took the tongue from Joe and looked back at her disappointedly. "I'm sorry, Alicia. This is very important and we could all be in danger."

Alicia rolled her eyes and muttered, "Yeah, right." She left the examining room and went to the lobby. The doors were chained shut by the Sheriff and Deputy Watkins so Alicia felt safe. She took out her phone and checked for messages. Vega peered around the corner at her.

Alicia stowed her phone inside her pocketbook. Vega crept up behind her with her tongue stretching hungrily toward her. Alicia sensed someone behind her and froze. Vega wrapped her muscular arms around Alicia and pulled her tightly against her chest. Her tongue whipped around the front of Alicia's face and penetrated her mouth. She chose not to numb the throat of the girlfriend of her philandering husband, but to let her suffer instead. Alicia struggled to scream but Vega's tongue slid further down her throat.

Vega's appendages injected hormone into Alicia's back. Alicia quivered and spasmed violently. Her eyes rolled back as she struggled to breath.

Vega heaved and strained to produce a large lump of DNA compound in her tubular tongue. She rocked against Alicia's back as she injected more hormone into her and pushed the DNA compound into her throat. Alicia became limp as Vega retracted her tongue from her throat. She tossed her over her shoulder and carried her to the door. With one swing of her arm, she knocked the glass out and left the hospital.

Joe heard the sound of breaking glass and announced without hesitation, "We're leaving as soon as the sheriff gets back." He grabbed the shotgun and reloaded it.

Joann asked him sarcastically, "Where are we going at this hour of the night?"

"The morgue. We're taking the corpses for a late-night autopsy."

Lamar and Johnny entered the emergency room looking pleased with themselves. Lamar announced proudly, "We finished off the alien garbage."

Joe responded, "Good. We need to get to the morgue and dissect these things."

"Anyone call Kaz to tell him we're coming?" asked Johnny.

"Not yet." Lamar took out his phone and made the call.

Kaz groaned as the phone rang next to his bed. He reluctantly answered it, "George K. What?

Lamar informed him, "We need you at the morgue, pronto."

Kaz sat up attentively and replied, "Sheriff, I didn't know it was you. What's going on?"

"We've got a fresh alien corpse for you to look at. See you there."

Kaz hung up the phone and rubbed his eyes. "Here we go again."

Johnny backed the police SUV up to the emergency room doors while the men pushed a gurney with Grimwold's body outside the emergency room. Vega waited nearby and eavesdropped on to their conversation. Alicia lay unconscious on the ground next to her, still mutating.

Johnny got out of the vehicle and scanned the area for any sign of the aliens or mutants. After they loaded Grimwold's body into the back of the vehicle, Lamar closed the hatch and instructed them, "Everyone follow in a single file in case we run into any more of these things."

Joe asked Sam, "Would you mind riding with me? I'd like to discuss some things with you."

"I'm sure the nurses wouldn't mind taking my car."

Joann's eyes lit up with excitement and she poked Sally excitedly. "Of course. I'd love to drive your 'Vette."

Sam tossed his keys to Joann and pleaded, "Don't get any marks on it, please."

"Don't worry, Sam. It'll be fine."

Sam felt uneasy about letting the girls drive his car as he followed Joe to his pickup truck. He looked around for Alicia but there was no sign of her. "Alicia, where are you?" he shouted.

Lamar warned, "We don't have time for this, Sam."

Sam rushed inside the emergency room and called, "Alicia! Where are you?" He reached the lobby and found Alicia's phone on the ground. He noticed that the door was smashed and the glass broken outward. Sam muttered, "What a waste of a good piece of ass."

<hr>

Joann and Sally got into the Corvette and buckled their seatbelts. Joann asked, "Do you know what I'm thinking, Sally?"

"No, what?"

"If these things are real aliens, then this area's gonna be surrounded by the military and we're gonna be slaughtered like sheep."

Sally looked panicked. "What should we do?"

Joann suggested, "How about Vegas, baby?"

Sally smiled and replied, "I like it! What about Sam's car?"

"He may not live long enough to miss it."

"Then let's go."

"When they take the expressway east, we'll go west. They'll never know we left."

Sally teased, "Joann, you're evil."

"Damn right and we'll live longer for it."

———◆———

Sam returned to the parking lot.

Lamar chided, "You didn't find her, did you?"

"No. She was taken out the lobby door."

"If there's no more distractions, then let's get out of here."

Chapter VIII

THE NEW ORDER

Agents Cox and Melendez pushed through the trees and bushes on Graham's Mountain. Agent Cox whispered, "Mother says that an object disappeared under their radar around here."

Agent Melendez inquired, "Could they have crashed?"

"No. This is a scouting party for a potential invasion. We have to find out what their weaknesses are."

Agent Cox saw the dim glow from the space ship's hatch. He peered past several trees. "I see it!" The two agents drew their pistols and crept toward the space ship.

Suzie lurked in the trees behind them and thought, *How convenient? I can use two federal agents under my direction.* She crept toward them in her human form. The two men gazed in awe as they entered the ship.

Cox mentioned excitedly, "We're the first humans to see a real alien ship let alone step foot on it. I wonder what the aliens look like."

Melendez replied, "I don't see anyone. It could be a trap."

Cox studied the control panel while Melendez stepped down the stairs to the cargo bay.

Suzie stepped inside the ship and slid inside a small cabinet. She closed the door and latched it. Agent Cox heard the latch click and approached the cabinet. Suzie stretched her tattered sweatshirt down her left shoulder, revealing most of her cleavage. Cox turned the latch with his gun pointed at the cabinet. He unlocked the door and backed away while opening it.

Suzie pleaded, "Please don't shoot me! I've been stuck here since yesterday."

Cox ordered her, "Get out slowly and keep your hands where I can see them."

Suzie crawled out from the cabinet and stood up. She held her hands out and innocently replied, "Thank goodness you've come. I don't know how long I could have held out in there."

Suzie's shapely figure and her partially exposed left breast enamored agent Cox. He approached the stairs while watching Suzie and called out, "See anything, Melendez?"

Melendez shouted back, "It's deserted down here. I'm checking out some equipment."

"I'll cover you from up here. Be careful."

Melendez replied, "I'll be fine."

Cox turned his attention to Suzie and asked, "Have you seen them?"

"Oh, yes!" she exclaimed convincingly. "They're horrible."

"Can you close the hatch?"

Suzie looked at the controls and pointed at the wall next to the hatch. "They placed their hands on that red square to close it." Cox approached the hatch and placed his hand on the square. It flickered twice and the hatch closed.

Cox looked relieved. "At least we're safe in here for now."

Suzie nestled up to Cox and seductively ran her hands underneath his suit. "Thank you so much for rescuing me. I was ready to give up."

Cox massaged her shoulders and subtly slid her sweatshirt further down, exposing her entire breast. When she nibbled at his neck, he massaged her nipple. He kissed her cheek and lifted her chin so he could reach her lips. She willingly obliged and returned his advances. As soon as they embraced in a passionate kiss, Suzie changed shape and her tongue pressed into his throat. Cox quickly succumbed as she pumped her DNA compound into him. His knees weakened and buckled as Suzie retracted her tongue from inside him. She set him down on the ground and slid her clawed hand into her chest cavity. Suzie removed a quivering gray worm and placed it on Cox's upper lip. The worm slithered into Cox's left nostril and ate its way into his frontal lobe. Suzie lifted him into a sitting position against the wall. She transformed into her human self and descended the stairs to the cargo bay.

Melendez sat on the stainless-steel crate and studied an odd control device for a storage container. Suzie tugged the sweatshirt up slightly to cover up her cleavage and descended the stairs. She called, "Agent Melendez, your partner figured out the controls for the ship. Can you come up?"

Melendez Melendez drew his pistol. "Who the hell are you?"

Susie looked frightened and answered, "He rescued me from a locked cabinet. I was a prisoner here."

Melendez stormed past her to the stairs. Suzie hurried after him and followed him up the steps to the control room. Cox staggered to his feet and rubbed his eyes. A small stream of blood trickled from his nose. He wiped it away with the sleeve of his coat, leaving a smear across his cheek.

Melendez grabbed him by the arm to support him. "What happened? What did she do to you?"

Suzie communicated through her worm to Cox, "You bumped your head and fell."

Cox chuckled at Melendez and answered, "I'm fine. I tripped and fell on my face."

Suzie suggested to Melendez, "Why don't we go back downstairs and I'll brief you on what I saw?"

"And I should trust you?"

Suzie walked toward the stairs and smiled coyly. "Suit yourself. I'll be down there if you change your mind."

Melendez looked back at Cox and waited for his response. Cox chuckled. "She's just a mixed-up ET seeker. Even thinks they're coming to save mankind."

"Oh, really."

"Yeah. I wouldn't mind getting a piece of her but she doesn't think I'm her type."

"I see. And you tripped on your own I assume."

"Well, I overstepped my bounds a little. She got a quick swing and caught me with an elbow."

Melendez laughed and replied, "Now that I can believe." He followed Suzie down the steps. She lay on the table with her sweatshirt tugged seductively low across her cleavage. Melendez eyed her and pondered how to approach her. Suzie reached for him and beckoned, "Agent Melendez, you seem like a gentleman. I like gentlemen."

Melendez stood next to the table with his arms crossed and eyed her breasts. Suzie ran her hand up the inside of his pant leg to his crotch and massaged it gently. He remarked callously, "I guess you don't take no for an answer."

Suzie took off her sweatshirt and slid her sweat pants low enough to get a rise out of him. "Make love to me," she seductively requested. "The ship's secure and no one can get in."

Melendez looked about uneasily and responded, "Making love in an alien space ship just doesn't do it for me, Honey."

Suzie turned on her side and unbuckled Melendez' pants. She reached inside his boxer shorts and stroked him slowly. Melendez closed his eyes and took a deep breath. "Feeling anything yet, Agent Melendez?" she asked.

"I'm starting to," he admitted and then kissed her passionately. He slid one hand into her sweatpants and placed the other behind her head. Suzie interrupted the kiss and asked, "Can I share something with you?".

"Of course," Melendez replied with feigned interest. He continued to massage her as he sucked hungrily at her breasts. Suzie took his head in her hands and gently pulled him toward her. She stared with an evil grin on her face. "What devilish thoughts are going through that pretty little head of yours?" he asked, now fully under her influence.

"Just this," she replied coldly. Suzie transformed into her alien form and her tongue latched onto Melendez' mouth. He struggled to pull away but her tongue probed its way inside his mouth. She closed her powerful legs on his hand and pulled his face closer to hers as her tongue worked its way down into his digestive tract. A lump of DNA compound formed inside her tubular tongue and slithered into his mouth. She reached under the flap of protective flesh on her chest and retrieved another of her worms. This one was larger than the others and appeared much more active.

Melendez's eyes bulged as his body absorbed the alien DNA. He shuddered as Suzie held him firmly with her legs and hand. Using her free hand, she held the worm in front of Melendez, nose. The worm stretched eagerly toward his nostrils and nearly leaped from Suzie's clawed hand onto his cheek. Her eyes bulged fiendishly as the worm disappeared inside

Melendez's right nostril. She retracted her tongue and turned back into her human form. Melendez fell to the floor with a glazed look in his eyes. Suzie stood up and stared at Melendez' boxer shorts. She rubbed her breasts in circular strokes and moved her left hand down inside her pants. She masturbated and leaned back on the table.

Agent Cox descended the stairs and approached her. She looked over at him and inquired, "What took you so long?" She knelt on the floor as Cox approached her. She caressed his genitals and indulged in carnal pleasures. Melendez awakened and eyed the two. Suzie remarked coyly, "There's always room for one more." Melendez removed the remainder of his clothes and joined them.

⸺⸺⸺ ✦ ⸺⸺⸺

The Corvette lagged further behind the police SUV and Joe Beauchamp's truck. Joann quipped, "We'll be in Vegas in time for a late breakfast."

Sally replied disappointedly, "It's a shame we couldn't bring Deputy Watkins with us. I'd really like for him to put me in handcuffs and have his way with me."

"I wonder how he'd handle both of us."

"Joann, that's dirty!"

"And what's wrong with that?"

"I never joined in a threesome with another woman before."

"I'm sure you and I would have a lot of fun." Joann gently rubbed the back of Sally's neck.

The trucks turned onto the eastbound ramp and entered the expressway. Joann grinned as she pressed down on the accelerator. The Corvette raced toward the westbound ramp.

Joann shouted, "Here we go!" The girls' hair flowed wildly in the wind as the Corvette reached one hundred miles per hour. The car rounded the bend and slowed. The road ahead of them was blocked by a tractor trailer.

Joann uttered nervously, "What the hell is this all about?"

Sally suggested, "Maybe we should go back."

"No, they might just be broken down."

When the Corvette drew closer, Joann recognized four dark sedans alongside it. Several federal agents in black uniforms and suits stood in a line with automatic weapons pointed at them.

Sally panicked and shouted, "I told you we should have gone back! They're gonna kill us." Joann punched Sally in the side of the face and attempted to run down the men. Sally slid down the seat, dazed by the punch.

The agents opened fire and riddled the Corvette with bullet holes. Joann was struck several times in the shoulder and neck. Broken glass struck her face and embedded into her skin. She was covered with blood and slumped against the steering wheel. The Corvette swerved and slammed against the railing. The engine idled eerily as the men approached. Six creatures darted from the trees and attacked them. The sounds of gunfire and screams shattered the still night.

Sally awoke and sat up. She was terrified when she saw Joann's bloody corpse. One of the creatures threw an agent onto the hood and tore his insides out with its claw.

Sally reached over and opened the driver's-side door. She pushed Joann out onto the road and pulled the door shut. As she slid into the driver's seat, the mutant saw her. Sally alertly shoved the car into reverse, knocking the creature off balance and to the ground. She sped back toward town, grateful to be alive. The creatures killed the remaining agents and disappeared into the trees.

··✦✦✦··

Joe drove his pickup truck into the morgue parking lot. He immediately noticed Kaz's car by the main entrance and parked next to it. Lamar and Johnny parked on the other side of Kaz's car at a sharp angle in case they needed to leave in a hurry.

Sam got out of Joe's truck and looked anxiously toward the street. Joe stepped out and, noticing the missing Corvette, he asked, "You don't really think they'd hurt your car, do you?"

"No, but I sure don't see them coming. Do you?"

"Give them a few minutes. I'm sure they're close behind."

Lamar and Johnny opened the rear gate on the police SUV and dragged Grimwold's corpse out of the vehicle and onto the ground. Lamar complained, "It would be nice if you boys gave us a hand. These aliens are heavy." Sam and Joe reluctantly joined then and together the four men carried the dead alien into the morgue.

Kaz greeted them in the lobby with a gurney and offered, "There's hot coffee in the kitchen."

Lamar remarked, "I could use a pot or two. I'm beat."

Sam and Joe pushed the gurney and followed Kaz into one of the lab rooms. Lamar and his deputy entered the kitchen and each poured a cup of coffee. Lamar drank his down quickly while Johnny sipped gingerly from the hot brew.

Johnny quipped, "You thirsty, Sheriff?"

"A little." Lamar filled his cup again and walked out of the kitchen.

Inside the lab, Kaz and Sam did a cursory examination of the corpse. They laid out the necessary tools for the autopsy and set up a tape recorder on the counter nearby.

Lamar entered the room and inquired, "Is there a place we can rest for a bit while you boys do your work?"

"On the second floor, there's a TV and two couches," answered Kaz. "I'll call you when we have an idea who or what our alien friend is."

Sam suggested to Joe, "Why don't you get some rest, too? I'll help George out for a while."

"Thanks, Sam."

"Oh, and let me know when my car shows up."

"Will do." Joe followed Lamar and Johnny down the hall to the stairs.

⋯◆⋯

Suzie linked to the Sporatin with her finger through the port and waited as the creature connected with her. "Greetings, Serena Luna."

"Hello, Pitherus."

Pitherus noticed that Serena Luna (Suzie) was in human form and nude while the two agents lay asleep on the floor. Pitherus remarked, "I see you're exploring your sexuality."

"Oh, yes, and it's wonderful."

"You've secured some valuable allies for your cause."

"They're going to clean up some loose ends for me."

"And you've chosen to keep them in their human form."

"Yes. I can't risk anyone seeing them in any other form."

"Very smart. What can I do for you?"

"I'm concerned about the ship. Is there a way to hide it to erase any evidence of our presence here?"

Pitherus pondered for a moment and then replied, "If we shut down all systems, we can activate the ship's reflective field."

"What will that do to the ship?"

"Basically, it creates a three-dimensional field around it that reflects certain color schemes. In this case, the scenery around the ship will be reflected and nothing else."

"Can the ship be detected by instruments?"

"Only if any of its systems are powered up."

"Will that affect your habitat?"

"Yes, it will. I'll only survive a short while without having my nutrients replenished."

Serena Luna grew concerned and said, "We can't let that happen."

"My mission is to serve you. If you must shield the ship, then I accept that fate."

"Have you always had this form?"

"No. In this shape, I can bond mentally with my lieges."

"So, you are more of a spiritual entity?"

"In a sense."

"Can I offer my body to you as a host?"

"I don't know. If there's time, I can study the potential consequences of such a move."

"I have some work to do and I'll be back. We'll figure something out."

"Thank you, Serena Luna."

Suzie removed her finger from the port and stared down at the naked agents. She mentally stimulated the worms on their frontal lobes and woke them. The two men nestled against her and caressed her. Suzie became aroused but reluctantly pushed them away. "Come on, boys. We're on a timetable."

Melendez reminded her, "We're here for you, Serena Luna."

"I know and here's the deal. I want you to dispose of as much evidence as possible. I don't want anything left that proves we exist." The two agents listened obediently as they dressed.

Suzie continued, "You have to keep the authorities out of our business."

Cox assured her, "We won't disappoint you."

"I know you won't. Now go back to town and take care of business." The two men left the ship.

Suzie dressed in her ragged sweat suit and departed the ship as well. She was anxious to complete an inner circle of guardians to watch her back and execute her plans.

The moon shone brightly over the campsite as the night haze dissipated. Suzie washed in a nearby stream and returned to her vehicle. She opened a suitcase and removed a clean sweat suit. A strange feeling swept over her when she glanced at the blood-soaked tents. She knew and understood what happened to her daughters but the emotional attachment was severed somehow. When she finally dismissed the concern, she dressed and climbed into her SUV. Her next destination was in town. Suzie glanced at the time on the stereo display and sighed. "One-fifteen. I hope it's not too late to find new subjects."

Forty-five minutes later, Suzie steered the SUV down a seedy street lined with dark, dilapidated shops and a small corner bar. She spotted three hookers standing across the street from the bar and thought, *What better prospects than this? No one will recognize their faces.*

The three hookers conversed until the SUV parked across from them. They eyed the vehicle enthusiastically, hoping for a late-night client. Peaches, a young, blonde-haired girl with a petite body, wore leopard skin pants and a red, satin blouse. She unequivocally informed the other girls, "This one's mine, baby."

Sugar, a young, ebony-skinned woman with long dark hair, braided in cornrows, wore a black leather mini-skirt, a white blouse and no bra. She challenged, "Says who?"

Tasha, the third hooker, was an older brunette, wearing a red sundress and flip-flops with bright red lipstick. She warned, "Chill out before you scare them away."

Suzie lowered the window and stared at the hookers. Sugar remarked disappointedly, "I think it's a she."

Peaches suggested, "It could be a cop."

Tasha advised, "Let me handle this. I'll find out if she's a cop."

Suzie grew impatient and hollered to them, "Hey, you girls looking for some work?"

Tasha strutted toward her and asked, "What's a soccer mom like you doing out at one in the morning?"

"How about an introduction first? I'm Suzie."

"I'm Tasha. You didn't answer my question."

"I look at it as a career change."

"I don't get it."

Suzie reached out the window and ran her left hand into Tasha's dress. She gently caressed her breast, much to Tasha's surprise. Suzie placed her right hand behind her neck and nudged her closer. With a seductive smile, Suzie then kissed her hungrily.

Tasha was surprised but turned on by the innocence Suzie presented. She returned her kiss with even more passion. Tasha then asked, "What's in it for us?"

"Why don't you get in and we'll discuss it?"

Tasha hurried around the vehicle and got in the passenger-side. Suzie eagerly pulled Tasha to her and pressed against her. Her emotions raced as she felt an overwhelming desire to dominate. She pressed her moist lips against Tasha's and lapped her tongue against her new friend's mouth. Suddenly, she felt the alien in her take over and she became Serena Luna. Her tongue grew and rounded as she thrust it down Tasha's throat.

Tasha's eyes widened with horror as Serena Luna held her in her sordid kiss. A small lump formed inside Serena Luna's tongue and grew. She strained and forced the lump of DNA compound down her victim's throat. Tasha struggled briefly and then passed out.

Serena Luna removed a worm from her chest cavity and placed it inside Tasha's right nostril. Blood trickled from Tasha's nose as the worm disappeared from sight. Serena Luna transformed into Suzie and laid Tasha gently against the passenger door.

An occasional car passed by and disappeared down the otherwise lonely street. Sugar and Peaches watched from across the street with envy. Sugar complained, "I knew Tasha would screw us over. That woman's all over her."

Peaches suggested, "Let's cross the street to the other corner. I can't watch this."

Sugar remarked, "Satch is going to come by soon. He'll be pissed at us for not doing some business."

Peaches asked, "Did you ever make it with a woman, Sugar?"

"No, only johns. Have you?"

"Yeah, a few times. It's a nice change of pace."

Suzie gazed at the two hookers from her vehicle and pondered her options. She called out, "Hey, Blondie! You want in?" Peaches looked surprised.

Sugar suggested, "Maybe Tash is looking out for you."

"I'll get you involved. Don't worry, Sugar," Peaches promised and then hurried to the SUV. Sugar grew uneasy and stood with her back against the boarded-up window of an old butcher shop. The temperature felt about ten degrees cooler when Peaches left her alone.

Suzie stepped out of the vehicle and extended her arms to Peaches. "Welcome to my party. I'm Suzie."

Peaches was excited as Suzie embraced her in a friendly hug. She introduced herself and then looked inside the SUV. Tasha moaned gently as she gazed blankly out the window.

Suzie urged her, "Go in the back seat. Tash wants to watch us."

"Is she alright?"

"Of course. She's just a little overwhelmed being with another woman."

Peaches climbed into the back seat, followed by Suzie. Peaches asked, "How do you want to do this?"

Suzie gazed into her eyes and whispered, "Slowly. I want to enjoy every part of your body as if we were one." She removed her sweatshirt, revealing her supple breasts.

Peaches stroked each breast and crooned, "Ooh, baby. This is gonna be nice."

Peaches placed one hand in Suzie's sweatpants and the other behind Suzie's head. She sealed her mouth across Suzie's lips and kissed her. Suzie transformed into her alien form and slid her tubular tongue down Peaches' throat. She took a liking to Peaches and tried to make the transition pleasurable. Peaches eyes widened as soon as Suzie's tongue grew and elongated. She reached her hand down into Peaches' leopard skin pants and gently stroked her.

Suzie, now Serena Luna, eased her tongue forward and back until it reached Peaches' digestive tract. She strained until a large lump of DNA clotted in her tongue and made its way inside Peaches. Serena Luna transformed back into Suzie as soon as the lump was deposited. She continued to kiss Peaches and massage her. Peaches laid in a hallucinogenic trance. Part of her was in a euphoric state while the rest of her was numbed from the DNA insertion.

Suzie whispered to her, "You'll be my special one." She retracted her hand from Peaches' pants and licked her fingers lustily. "Ah, the scent of youth." Suzie transformed into Serena Luna and removed a worm from her cavity. She chose a small one and inserted it into Peaches' left nostril.

Serena Luna transformed back and explained softly, "I chose a small one so it doesn't hurt so much. You'll understand later why I had to do this."

Peaches stared blankly at her as blood streamed from her nose. She shook briefly and gasped. Suzie held Peaches close to her and comforted her. "Don't fight it, Sweetie. You'll be fine. I'll take care of you."

Peaches became still and closed her eyes. Suzie licked the blood from her nose and mouth, and then rested her against the door. She leaned over Tasha's shoulder and whispered, "How are you doing, my pretty friend?" Tasha grunted and heaved but gave no other acknowledgement. Suzie stroked Tasha's dark hair back from her eyes and assured her, "You'll feel much better in a little while."

Contented with her progress, Suzie leaned out the window and shouted to Sugar, "Hey, girl! Want to join the party?"

Sugar walked toward the SUV and complained, "It's about time. I thought you forgot all about me."

"No, no. We were warming up the party for you. Come on in." Suzie opened the door and welcomed Sugar with a kiss.

Sugar remarked as she climbed in, "I'm glad to see a woman like you has no color barriers."

"Of course not. I love all of you girls the same."

Sugar closed the door and noticed her two friends looked dazed. She chided, "Don't tell me you gave them smack. They've been clean for over a year."

Suzie placed her arms around Sugar and said calmly, "No drugs. Only my love." She unbuttoned Sugar's blouse as she kissed her. Each time, her emotions grew stronger and harder to control. She lapped at Sugar's breasts and eagerly slid her hand under Sugar's skirt.

Sugar moaned and uttered, "Oh, wow, A perverted soccer mom! Who would have thought?"

Suzie leaned down between Sugar's legs and indulged herself. Sugar stretched her legs up in the air, one over the front seat and the other across the back seat. Her foot lay just behind Peaches' head. She moaned and, in her euphoria, kicked Peaches in the head. Peaches didn't respond.

Sugar grew concerned and pushed Suzie's head out from under her skirt. Suzie was surprised and asked, "What's wrong?"

"What did you do to my friends?"

"They're fine. Trust me." Suzie leaned forward to kiss Sugar but she resisted. Sugar warned, "Don't come any closer until you tell me what you did to them."

Suzie looked annoyed and informed her, "I'll do one better – I'll show you." She transformed into Serena Luna and shot her tongue into Sugar's mouth before she could let out a sound. Her emotions ran wild and a larger lump of DNA compound formed inside her tongue. She realized that the more aroused she became, the larger the lump of DNA compound she could produce.

Sugar's eyes bulged as she tried to fight off Serena Luna. Serena Luna rubbed her alien breasts against Sugar's as she reached into her cavity for another worm. She realized she only had one left. Serena held the worm up for Sugar to see and inserted it into one of her nostrils. Being close to the worm as it entered Sugar aroused her to an incredible climax. Sugar's eyes rolled back as she panicked. The lump passed from Serena Luna's tongue and was deposited into her digestive tract. She retracted her tongue and transformed back into Suzie.

Sugar whimpered weakly, "Why?"

Suzie grabbed her by the back of the neck and kissed her passionately. Sugar became motionless as the DNA compound dissipated throughout her body. When Suzie regained her composure, she realized she was losing control. *What's happening to me?* She thought frantically.

Suzie looked at Sugar with her blouse open and her large breasts visible. Then she peered at Peaches with her leopard-skin pants half way down her hips. She placed her hands to her head and uttered, "I've got to get control of myself. This is insane."

Suzie climbed into the front seat and started the SUV. As she rushed back to Graham's Mountain, she felt her womb stir and realized it must be the baby, Shurek's baby, affecting her this way. Anger filled her as she considered what to do about it. She recalled her discussion with Pitherus and how it needed a host to survive outside the chamber.

Suzie exclaimed, "That's it! This won't be Shurek's child; it will be mine. Pitherus will live." She accelerated up the mountainous road that led to the campsite.

Shurek led a group of twenty mutated humans through the woods to a cave. Once inside, Shurek announced, "You will be my army. We must defeat the traitors before we start our conquest of the planet. The time will come soon when you will fight for me. I'm counting on you." The mutants grunted loudly and waved their fists in the air.

Shurek walked to the entrance of the cave alone and thought, *I have a surprise for you, Serena Luna. The next time we meet will be your last.*

Suzie escorted the hookers inside the space ship and paused at the open hatch to read Shurek's thoughts. She responded telepathically, *Don't worry, Shurek. I have a surprise for you as well. I hope you didn't count on being a father.*

Shurek was stunned when he remembered that his egg was implanted inside of Suzie. Hoping to affect her maternal instincts, he replied, *Why would you kill an innocent baby?*

Suzie was amused by his lame attempt. *I didn't say I would kill it; I'll just make sure it won't be yours.*

Shurek became angry and screamed, "What do you mean by that? Show yourself to me!"

All in due time. Your days are numbered, Shurek.

The mutants watched in confusion as Shurek howled crazily and slammed his head against the wall of the cave.

Suzie smiled at the night sky and entered the space ship. She closed the hatch and proceeded to the Sporatin. The three hookers stood by and waited for Suzie to give them orders.

Suzie looked at them with pride and explained, "You are my inner circle. If you do my bidding, I promise I'll take care of you."

The three women replied in unison, "We will serve you, Serena Luna."

Suzie corrected them, "In my human form, I am Suzie Beauchamp. Only in my alien form will you address me as Serena Luna." The women nodded in agreement.

Suzie placed her finger in the socket of the Sporatin's tank and waited for Pitherus to respond. She was pleased when the alien's image appeared in the translucent solution. She felt at ease with the innocent white face that appeared almost ghostly.

Pitherus glanced at the three women behind Suzie and greeted her, "Hello, Serena Luna. I see you have company."

"Yes, Pitherus, these are my chosen body guards."

"They certainly don't look the role."

"Ah, but they are tactically ideal. No one would suspect them."

"That is true, but who will protect you?"

Suzie replied proudly, "The humans."

"And you have a plan for this, of course."

"Yes, and a solution to your well-being if we camouflage the ship."

Pitherus read her thoughts and smiled at her. "I would be honored to become your child."

"Now how do we perform the transfer?"

Pitherus explained, "The egg must be accessed externally."

"Will it survive the extraction?"

"If my instructions are followed exactly."

"What instruments are required to do this?"

"None. It will be done by hand. When would you like to begin?"

Suzie replied confidently, "Right now. Time is of the essence."

"Then lie on the table and relax. Have one of your friends link to me. She will be my interface to you."

Suzie requested that Tasha be her link to the sporatin during the extraction.

Tasha stepped forward and replied, "Of course, I will." Suzie removed her finger from the socket and laid on the steel table.

Tasha approached the tank and placed her finger in the socket, located in the base. She shuddered as Pitherus scanned her body and mind. Pitherus instructed her, "You have the same physiology as Serena Luna. I will give you detailed instructions and you will relay them to the others."

Tasha responded, "I will do whatever Serena Luna requires of me."

Suzie requested, "I'd like for Peaches to handle the egg. She and I have a special relationship."

Pitherus reminded them, "This is going to be painful and it will require care at every step."

Suzie revealed, "I will open my mind to Shurek. I want him to know what I'm doing to him and let him feel my pain."

Pitherus replied, "He is sure to be incensed to the point of madness. This is truly a most brutal punishment for him."

"Then let the fun begin."

"I want you to close your eyes and focus on controlling your emotions," instructed Pitherus. "This is critical."

Suzie breathed deeply and closed her eyes. "I will control myself," she repeated several times.

Pitherus instructed Peaches, "You will reach inside Serena's womb and gently pull the egg just outside of her body."

Peaches asked uneasily, "Won't that hurt her?"

"This isn't a human egg. Do it slowly and gently."

Sugar inquired, "What's my role in this?"

"You will remove me from the tank and place me on the table by the egg. I will complete the transition into the egg. After that, the egg must be reinserted into the womb. I can only survive a short time outside of the tank so you must not waste time in moving me to the table."

Sugar replied, "You'll be fine, Pitherus."

"Then let's begin. Remove the cover off of my tank."

Sugar reached up and unscrewed the round cover from the tank. It was made of a lightweight plastic and spun easily. She set it on the counter nearby.

Pitherus' body sprouted tentacles like a jellyfish and latched on to the top of the tank. It lifted itself off the bottom of the tank and hovered about halfway to the top. Pitherus continued, "Remove the egg from the womb."

Shurek left the cave and proceeded down the mountainside. He considered how he would get his revenge on Suzie until she interrupted his thoughts. *Well, Shurek, it's that time.*

Shurek placed both hands on the sides of his head and shouted, "No, no, no! This can't be happening."

Suzie warned him, "You're going to feel pain and anguish that you never knew. I just want you to know that I thought long and hard about a suitable way to repay you for what you've done to my life."

"Leave me alone!" Shurek shouted. He banged his head repeatedly against a tree in an attempt to get Suzie out of his head, but to no avail.

Suzie focused on the egg extraction and controlling her emotions. Peaches removed Suzie's sweatpants and tossed them on the floor. She parted her legs and reached into Suzie's uterus. It was awkward at first but after twisting her hand and pushing, she reached the egg. Suzie felt incredible pangs from within her and, despite her best efforts, trembled.

Shurek rolled spastically around the ground, clutching at his head and gut. He shouted every curse he knew from his alien dialect as he felt her pains.

Peaches announced, "I've got it."

Pitherus asked, "What do you feel?"

She answered, "It's connected by a lot of roots to the womb."

"Ease it out slowly."

Peaches gently pulled her arm out of Suzie's uterus until the egg was visible.

Tears streamed down Suzie's cheeks as she felt spasm after spasm of horrific pain shooting through her body. She fought back the urge to quiver while her insides felt as though they were torn out.

A few miles away, Shurek looked like a rabid animal, ramming his head violently against anything he could find. Saliva streamed from his mouth as he howled and moaned vociferously.

Pitherus announced to Sugar, "It is time. Lift me out of the tank."

She reached over the top of the tank and grasped pairs of tentacles. Pitherus slid over the top of the glass as Sugar tugged on the tentacles. Pitherus squealed as she lowered him from the top of the tank. He rapped his tentacles around Sugar's head and pulled himself onto her.

Sugar staggered backward in horror as four of Pitherus' tentacles penetrated her chest and neck. His gelatinous body covered her like a blob of jelly. She became still and stood calmly with the creature covering her head.

Tasha nervously jerked her hand from the socket in the base of the tank and severed her finger. She cried out as blood dripped steadily and pooled on the floor.

Peaches wrapped her arms around Tasha in fear and backed away from Pitherus. The egg lay partially exposed between Suzie's legs.

Pitherus shouted at them, "Finish removing the egg before it's too late!"

Peaches cried out, "What have you done to Sugar?"

"She'll be fine. She's keeping me alive, you fools!"

Peaches reluctantly returned to the table and manipulated the egg from Suzie onto the table. It was deep luminous pink with the visible shape of the infant alien inside it. Tan roots were enmeshed around it and trailed from inside Suzie's uterus.

Peaches blurted frantically, "There – it's out!" She backed away fearfully. Tasha bandaged her hand where the finger was torn away.

Sugar approached the table and knelt in front of it. Four of Pitherus' tentacles slithered toward the egg. Tiny razors emerged from the ends of two of the tentacles and carefully cut slits in either side of the egg. Red clouds appeared in the fluids.

Suzie convulsed and gasped frantically.

Pitherus ordered the girls, "Hold her down!" Tasha and Peaches each grabbed one of Suzie's arms and held her down on the table.

One of the tentacles attached directly to the infant's brain while the other attached to the heart. Pitherus warned in a shaky voice, "Close your eyes, quickly."

The girls obeyed and pressed down on Suzie's shoulders for additional support. Suzie heaved violently as her eyes rolled back in her head, revealing only the whites of her eyes. Her tongue ejected in alien form into the air and stretched desperately toward the ceiling. She could no longer control herself and screamed hysterically. The second pair of tentacles glowed brightly as pulses of flashing matter shot through the tentacles into the infant alien. Suzie's screams became ear-shattering. The girls cried as their eardrums throbbed.

When the pulses stopped and the flashing ceased, Suzie calmed down and regained her composure. The tentacles fell limp on the table. Sugar removed the dead mass from her head and set it on the edge of the table. She tugged on the tentacles until they retracted from her body.

Peaches asked, "What do we do now?"

Sugar instructed her, "Insert the egg into Suzie's womb." She then pulled the tentacles delicately from the egg and tossed the dead creature back into the tank.

Peaches cupped her hand under the egg and pushed it between Suzie's legs until it slid inside her.

Suzie arched her back and moaned for a brief moment as Peaches restored the egg inside Suzie's uterus. The roots tightened as they reattached and secured the egg in place. Peaches pulled her hand out from inside Suzie and backed away from the table. Blood and mucous liquids dripped from her arm and hand onto the floor.

Exhausted from the procedure, Suzie slept. Sugar's face was marked with numerous cuts in her skin and her blouse was stained where blood flowed from her wounds. She instructed the girls, "We are to clean up and await further orders. Serena Luna will need time to heal."

✦

Shurek laid on the ground, facing the night sky. He breathed irregularly and swore, "I will have my day with you, Serena Luna. I swear I will." Shurek then passed out from the pain.

Chapter IX
VENGEANCE

Agents Cox and Melendez stood in the emergency room as several men in white suits and gloves removed the corpses from the building and placed them inside a large biohazard truck.

Agent Cox spoke to his superior on his phone, "The cleanup is almost finished. You'll make sure the valley is quarantined?" He listened for a moment and replied, "Good, I don't want to take any chances of these things escaping." Agent Cox put away his phone and informed Agent Melendez, "Everything's going just like we expected. No one gets in or out of the valley without my okay."

"Serena Luna will be pleased."

Melendez asked curiously, "How do we handle Mother?"

"Mother is under the impression that local authorities are annihilating alien invaders. All we need to do is provide one body for study."

"And what body did you have in mind?"

"I believe we'll give them one of the mutants' corpses. That's all they need to know about."

"Imagine this; we're going to rule the world through Serena Luna."

Cox replied somberly, "For some reason, I doubt it'll be at all what we expect."

"But, if anything, Serena Luna is one hell of a lay."

"That she is." The two men chuckled sadistically.

Sam washed his face over the sink and groaned, "I've got to get some sleep, George. I can't stay awake."

Kaz removed Grimwold's brain from his skull and set it in a stainless-steel tray on the table. "Get some rest. When you wake up, I'll have everything laid out for your analysis."

"Thanks. I appreciate it." Sam laid on a gurney nearby and fell asleep.

Kaz continued his dissection of the brain.

••••••

The three men slept until it was nearly noon. Lamar woke first and stared out the window at the wet streets. He mumbled to himself, "Looks like a shitty day to handle a shitty problem." He poked at Johnny a few times until he woke up.

Johnny asked wearily, "What's the matter, Sheriff?"

"We've got to meet with the feds. Let's go."

"Oh, alright."

Joe sat up on the couch and looked at his watch. "Oh, shit! I've got to try Suzie." He took out his phone and called her. Lamar and Johnny paused by the door to the stairs. Lamar asked, "How many kids you got, Joe?"

"Two daughters - they're both with her."

Joe waited anxiously for Suzie to answer. After several rings he became teary-eyed.

Lamar suggested, "Give me an hour and we'll help you look for your family."

"Thanks, Sheriff." Joe dialed the phone again and waited. He still had no answer. Dejectedly, he stowed it in his pants pocket.

Lamar placed his hand on Joe's shoulder and instructed him, "Come with us. We'll find them." The three of them descended the stairs to the first floor.

Downstairs in the lab, Kaz leaned back against the wall, stretched his arms and yawned.

Lamar poked his head in and said, "I've got to meet with the feds and I'm taking the doc with me."

Kaz replied, "Good luck."

"I'll need it. These guys don't know when to quit." Lamar left the lab.

Kaz looked over at Sam as he slept. "He's got the right idea." He leaned against the counter and stared at the eyes from Grimwold's skull. "Damn, he's one ugly dude."

Greta filed her nails and watched The Oprah Winfrey Show on a small TV atop the file cabinet.

Lamar entered the lobby and teased, "At ease, Greta. We're just passing through."

"You're welcome to stay – all three of you."

Lamar opened the outside door and kidded, "You're too much woman for me."

Johnny said politely, "Have a good morning, Greta."

"You, too, Johnny."

Hoping to avoid her attention, Joe kept his head down and followed Johnny closely through the door.

Greta called out, "Hey, Dr. Beauchamp, I'll be here if you need me."

Joe replied dryly, "I'm sure you will." He quickly closed the door behind him and breathed a sigh of relief.

Lamar asked, "What's the matter, Doc. She make you nervous?"

"Just a little, Sheriff."

Johnny laughed at them. "You guys are funny."

Lamar advised him, "Save it, Johnny. There's nothing funny about meeting the Feds. I've got to give them some answers."

Johnny knew he was right. This could turn badly for them without the right answers.

✦✦✦

Vega and Alicia stood behind the hearse and watched the doors to the morgue. Alicia's face had grown larger and her skin turned leathery and brown. Her body was no longer petite but muscular and manly. "Why don't we go in after them?" Alicia asked, curious.

"You keep your mouth shut and do as I tell you."

Alicia mimicked Vega. Vega turned and slapped her across the face. Alicia muttered, "Damn, you've got bigger balls than your husband."

Vega remarked, "We're going to take care of that problem, shortly."

Sheriff Whittington, Deputy Watkins and Joe Beauchamp exited the morgue and climbed into the SUV.

Vega remarked, "That's why we waited. I want to enjoy our little reunion."

The SUV drove out of the parking lot and turned onto the highway.

Vega grabbed Alicia by the arm. "Come on. We're going to pay Sammy boy a visit."

The two of them walked brazenly to the doors, unconcerned about being spotted in daylight. Vega opened the door and entered the lobby. Greta stopped filing her nails and looked up scornfully. She chided Vega, "Halloween's not for another couple of months. Beat it, Geek."

Alicia entered and stood next to Vega. Greta chuckled derisively at the pair and said, "You Goth chicks really take your act seriously, don't you?"

Vega reached over the desk and grabbed Greta by the throat. She lifted her up in the air and threw her against the wall. Greta's head slammed hard and she fell to the ground motionless.

Vega snarled, "I'll show you Halloween, you bitch!" She walked through the doorway to the hall beyond the lobby.

Alicia looked down at Greta and muttered, "Damn, woman! You've been served!" She hurried after Vega.

Greta rubbed the back of her head. Her hand grew wet with blood from her matted hair. "Those bitches!" she groaned.

Vega opened the door to the first room. She peered in and saw Kaz looking over several of Grimwold's organs. She scanned the room and saw Sam sleeping a short distance away on the gurney.

Alicia waited anxiously behind her and whispered, "Is he in there?"

Vega glared back and ordered, "You just stay here and make sure neither one gets out." Vega entered the room and approached Sam.

Kaz was unaware of the mutants' presence and laid Grimwold's tongue out on the waxed paper covering the counter. He spoke aloud for the recorder, "Well look at this! The tongue is tied to quite a few functions of the body, including the reproductive system."

Vega flipped the gurney over and sent Sam sprawling across the floor. Sam leaped up and was stunned. Kaz spun around in the chair and was horrified. He tried to escape through the doorway.

Alicia queried him cynically, "Going somewhere, Mr. Magoo?" She caught him around the midsection and hurled him into the corner of a steel cabinet. Kaz fell to the ground, nearly unconscious. Blood streamed from a cut on the back of his head and pooled where his face lay against the tile floor. "I didn't think so."

Sam stared at Vega for a brief moment, shuddering. "Jane, is that you?"

"Not anymore." Vega cornered Sam and informed him, "Oh, faithful husband of mine, I have something of yours."

She gestured for Alicia to join her. Alicia complained, "Thanks for coming to my rescue, Sammy. You're quite a man."

Sam flattened against the wall and cowered in fear. "Jane. Alicia. What happened to you?"

Vega queried, "Did you really think you could handle two women, Sam?"

Sam babbled, "I still love you, Jane. I had issues to deal with."

Alicia chided, "What issues? Dating a younger woman while your wife suffered at home?"

Sam replied pathetically, "It's not like that at all."

Kaz staggered to his feet and hobbled toward the door.

Vega caught him from behind and said playfully, "Not so fast, Magoo." She bit sloppily into his throat and greedily slurped his blood. She uttered drunkenly, "Ah, I love the taste of blood when it's served at room temperature." She then gnawed on the tender flesh around Kaz's throat. He stared upward with a vacant look in his eyes as the last breath of life left his body.

Alicia grabbed Sam by his arms and lifted him up in the air. Sam pleaded, "Please put me down, Alicia. I'll find a way to cure you, I swear."

"Maybe I don't want to be cured. Maybe there's nothing wrong with me."

Vega playfully asked Alicia, "Now what would you do to your husband if he was naughty?"

Alicia grinned deviously and replied, "Perhaps what he wants most. Give him two women." They snickered together.

Sam begged between sobs, "Please let me go. I'll do anything you want."

Vega responded coldly, "Of course you will." Her tongue emerged and forced its way into Sam's mouth.

Sam struggled but Alicia held him forcefully against the wall. Vega's tongue slithered down into Sam's throat. He heaved and gagged as he shook from fright. His pants became wet as he urinated.

Alicia noticed the urine pool under his feet and groaned, "I can't believe I looked up to you. You're nothing but a coward."

A round lump emerged from Vega's mouth through her tongue as she strained incredibly. Alicia laughed as she recognized the lump as an egg, not DNA compound. "Oh, Vega, this is great!"

Vega's eyes widened and rolled back as she forced the egg forward into Sam's mouth. Once inside, she easily manipulated it down to his digestive tract. She retracted her tongue and mocked, "Now you'll know what I went through for you when I gave birth to your child."

Sam heaved and spasmed as the egg spread roots throughout his digestive tract and attached to his organs. Vega held him firmly by the shoulder. "Your turn, Alicia. Anything you want to give to our man?"

Alicia released her hold on Sam's arms and declared, "As a matter of fact there is." She turned away and coughed violently. Thick, pink mucous spewed from her mouth onto the floor. She proudly displayed her new tongue, which emerged from her mouth and hovered in front of her before retracting. Alicia continued, "Sammy boy, I want you to know how I felt all those times I tried to make you happy." Sam's eyes were puffy and wide. He tried to speak but could only gasp.

Alicia unbuttoned Sam's pants and slid them down to his ankles. She chuckled as she tore his boxers off and tossed them away.

Her tongue extended from her mouth and slithered across Sam's belly to his back. It dropped down to his thigh and quickly plunged into his rectum. Sam lurched and moaned as tears poured down his cheeks.

Vega howled in laughter as Alicia worked her tongue in and out of Sam. Each time, he convulsed and shook like a puppet. Blood streamed down his thigh and stained his pants around his ankles.

Sam's head tilted sideways as he despondently waited for the torture to end.

When Alicia retracted her tongue, she noticed the blood trickling from his rectum down to his pants and chided, "That's nothing to worry about, huh, Sammy. Like you said to me, it's nothing that won't heal."

Greta entered the room with a baseball bat. She saw Kaz's bloody body lying on the floor and became enraged. She rushed at Vega and smashed the bat against the side of her head. The bat shattered and the barrel shot across the floor.

Vega doubled over in pain and clutched at her ear. She yelled, "You should have stayed away, bitch!"

Alicia leaped at Greta from behind. Greta turned and shoved the broken bat handle into her throat. Alicia fell to her knees, grasping at her torn throat. Greta grabbed her by the back of the neck and drove the bat handle into her throat three more times until a gaping wound oozed rust-colored blood all over her chest.

Vega's tongue darted out of her mouth and wrapped around Greta's knees. She tugged and sent Greta sprawling to the floor. Still dazed from the impact to her head, Greta struggled to her knees, ready to resume the battle. Vega retracted her tongue and whipped it toward Greta's mouth. She tried unsuccessfully to force Greta's mouth open. Greta grabbed at Vega's neck with one hand and shoved the bat handle through her lower jaw and tongue. Vega moaned and fell to her knees.

Greta stated proudly, "It's you two bitches that got served." But then Vega shoved her clawed hand into Greta's chest and clutched her heart. Greta became wide-eyed with fright.

Vega blurted with a slur, "You lose, bitch." She ripped Greta's heart from her chest and dropped it to the floor. The two of them fell over dead.

Sam sobbed and crawled across the floor to the cabinet drawers. His pants were still around his ankles and a stream of blood trailed from his rectum. He coughed and chunks of mucous and blood spurted on the floor. His chest pulsed where the egg grew to its gestating size, creating painful pressure on his stomach and surrounding organs.

Sam opened the middle drawer and took out a scalpel. He looked at Jane (Vega) and Alicia once more and then cut his wrists, one at a time. He cried aloud as the blood seeped from his wounds. He stabbed himself in the abdomen repeatedly until he passed out and expired.

The station was a small, one floor pre-fab consisting of a dozen cubicles and a kitchenette. Usually, two or three police vehicles could be seen in or around the station, but today there was only the black sedan that belonged to agents Melendez and Cox.

The police SUV parked in front by the main entrance. Lamar complained to Johnny, "Damn. The spooks are already here."

Johnny inquired, "When did you get a sense of humor, Sheriff?"

"I guess a man can be pushed to a point where he has nothing to lose. I reached that point and I'm not afraid anymore." They stood by the vehicle and waited for Joe.

Johnny offered, "Want me to go get some doughnuts, Sheriff?"

Lamar replied dryly, "Nah, it's their turn to treat." Johnny chuckled.

Joe's truck pulled up and parked. He stared out the window in a tired daze before exiting. The three of them reluctantly approached the front door. Lamar suggested to Joe, "You might want to wait out here. I have to give the feds a little song and dance about our situation."

"That's fine, Sheriff." Joe took out his phone and tried to contact Suzie again.

Lamar and Johnny entered the police station. Agents Melendez and Cox sat quietly with their hands folded on their laps. Each one's eyes looked dark and tired. Lamar couldn't resist an opening shot and teased, "You boys look like you've been out all night. Have a good time?"

Agent Melendez replied, "You're hardly in a position to joke, Sheriff."

"Lighten up. We've got our hands full and humor's the only thing keeping my sanity." Johnny stared at him in disbelief. He always got chided by the sheriff for making humor.

Agent Cox stood face-to-face with Lamar and demanded some answers. Lamar pushed him away and taunted, "I've got some gum that'll help with that halitosis."

Johnny tried to stifle his laughter but with little success. Cox sat down and glared at Lamar. Agent Melendez questioned impatiently, "Are you going to talk to us or do we need to take action?"

Lamar sat down behind his desk. "Come on guys, I'm kidding around."

Melendez warned, "We're not."

"Alright, here's what we know. There have been several killings in the area and all I can tell you is that there's a strange pack of animals doing it."

Melendez looked at Cox, suspicious. Johnny grew nervous by their silence and suggested, "How about I make some coffee?" He entered the kitchenette.

Melendez inquired, "What actions are you taking to control the situation?"

Lamar grew uneasy as he realized they were about to take away his authority. "I placed a call with the governor about sending in the state police or the National Guard to contain these creatures and exterminate them. I'm waiting for a call back."

Cox replied, "We've arranged for the valley to be quarantined until we fully ascertained the situation."

Lamar said dejectedly, "Then I guess you know what's happening around here."

"Yes, we do. We've already arranged for a decon team to clean up the bus terminal and the hospital. That's why you need to tell us what you know."

Lamar leaned forward and placed both arms on his desk. He asked, "Do you know anything about these creatures?"

Melendez answered, "Probably as much as you."

"Then you know what we're up against."

Cox asked, "Can you handle it?"

"So far. If you're backing me up on this and cleaning up the mess, I'll keep you up to date on everything from here on out."

"We'd greatly appreciate that."

"How about a number I can call you guys on?"

Melendez handed him his card and suggested, "Don't lose this one."

Lamar reached inside his drawer and took out two cards. He handed one to each of the agents. Cox and Melendez got out of their chairs and shook hands with Lamar.

Melendez looked relieved. "I'm glad you've come to realize we're on the same side."

"Well, some things take time to understand. Obviously, this is a very unusual situation that requires mutual cooperation between us."

"Good luck," said Cox. "We're counting on you." The two agents left the office. Lamar leaned back in his chair and let out a long sigh of relief.

Johnny returned with two cups of coffee and set them down on Lamar's desk. "Everything okay, boss?"

"I guess so. I'd better make a call to the governor."

"For?"

"For some help. We're gonna need it." Lamar picked up the phone and dialed the governor's number.

Johnny sat down and sipped from his coffee. He mumbled, "It's gonna be a long day, ain't it?"

"Sure is." Lamar's eyes widened and he spoke enthusiastically, "Good morning, Governor. I'm sorry to bother you but I need your help in an urgent matter." Lamar stood up and paced the floor. He explained to the governor, "We have a very serious animal problem and we can't control it." Lamar peered out the side window and noticed the black sedan still parked nearby. He continued, "No, sir. I don't recommend you come down. What I do need is thirty or forty shooters – staties or guardsmen, I don't care."

Johnny opened his wallet and stared at pictures of his parents and a close female friend. He pondered, *Maybe I ought to make time for family if we get out of this.*

Lamar replied enthusiastically, "Yes, governor. I'll await your call." He stowed his phone and informed Johnny, "The governor agreed to get us some help."

Johnny responded, "Hallelujah!"

Lamar teased, "What's the matter? You afraid of a few aliens, boy?"

Johnny replied playfully, "Like you aren't, Sheriff." The two exited the police station.

⋯⋯◆◆◆⋯⋯

Shurek stood inside the cave in front of twenty mutants. Torches lined the walls of the cave, outlining their shapes and sizes. He shouted,

"Tonight we will hunt the she-devil and end this treason!" The mutants grunted and waved their claws in the air.

Suzie awakened inside the ship and heard Shurek's words. She felt her womb and knew that the transformation was a success. She focused on Shurek and entered his mind. *Shurek, you bring your army with you to the campsite tomorrow night. I'll be waiting.*

Shurek became obsessed when he heard her voice inside his head. He faced the woods outside the cave and screamed, "I'll kill you! You'll suffer like my child did. I swear it!" The mutants backed away in fear of him. They didn't understand who he was shouting at.

Telepathically, Suzie taunted, *I don't suppose you'd be bold enough to fight me one on one, would you?*

Shurek uttered, "I'll enjoy eating the flesh from your body and your offspring."

Suzie teased, *You would harm Pitherus, a former Sporatin? That's terrible.*

Shurek was stunned by her words. He mumbled to himself, "Pitherus – inside of her?" To harm a Sporatin is punishable by a horrible fate on his planet. But, then again, he wasn't on his planet. He still grew concerned over this latest development.

Suzie responded, *That's right, Shurek. Pitherus and I are one. We will achieve our destiny and you will play your role.*

Shurek lost control and shouted, "I will fight you. I'll kill you both!" He turned to his mutant army and announced, "Tomorrow, we will have our revenge! In the meantime, we will feed." Shurek and his creatures stormed through the forest and down the mountainside.

Suzie taunted, *You can't do anything in the daylight, you fool.*

Shurek replied telepathically, *I'm going to blow our cover wide open. They'll know all about us when I'm finished.*

"Then so be it," she concluded. "You will still lose."

Chapter X
Suzie's Return

Peaches, Sugar and Tasha stood next to Suzie as she slid off the table. Suzie put on her sweat pants and shirt. She placed her hands gently on Sugar's cheeks and kissed her forehead. "I won't forget what you've done for me. Every time I look at you and see the scars on your face, I'll remember that you received them in service to me. Thank you."

Sugar bowed and replied, "You are welcome, Serena Luna."

Suzie took Tasha's wounded hand in hers and kissed her forehead. "Every time I see your hand without one digit, I will remember that you gave it in service to me as well. I thank you for your loyalty."

Tasha replied humbly, "I am honored to serve you, Serena Luna."

Peaches looked down at the ground in shame. Suzie asked, "What is wrong?"

Peaches replied, "I gave nothing in service to you, my queen. I am ashamed."

"Ah, but you did. I trusted you with my offspring and the Sporatin. You executed the transition perfectly. For that I can never repay you." Peaches looked relieved.

Suzie hugged her and pressed Peaches' head against her bosom. "As I told you before, my child; you are special."

Suzie turned to the others and reminded them, "The three of you are my inner circle. I will care for you as my own children and your loyalty will be rewarded in time. Now, I must prepare for Shurek's disposal."

Tasha asked, "What do you require of us, my queen?"

"You will go to Clearview Hospital in the next town and await my arrival. We must be ready for Pitherus' arrival into the world as my offspring. Take whatever actions are required to control the premises."

Tasha replied, "We'll be ready."

Suzie instructed them, "If you encounter any law enforcement groups, avoid them. I need the three of you alive and well." The three girls left Suzie alone and departed the ship.

Suzie put on her socks and sneakers while she studied the control panels. She approached the controls and shut down every system in the ship. As soon as the protective field activated around the ship and disguised it, she departed as well.

Once outside, Suzie took her phone from her pants pocket and called Joe. She tightened her facial muscles and forced tears from her eyes as she waited for Joe to pick up.

Joe leaned on the driver's-side door with his elbow and mourned the loss of his family. He was convinced there was no way the girls could survive against these terrible creatures. When his phone rang, he reached across the center console for it. When he noticed Suzie's number on the display, he grabbed the phone and answered it. "Suzie, is that you?"

Suzie pretended to weep and said, "Joe, thank goodness it's you."

"Suzie, are you alright?"

Suzie sobbed, "Oh, Joe, it was horrible. These terrible creatures attacked us. I ran for my life to escape them."

Joe asked frantically, "What about Dee Dee and Sarah? Are they okay?"

"The creatures …! They were on us before we could help the children."

"I'm coming for you. Where are you now?"

"No, Joe. It's too dangerous. They'll kill you, too."

"I don't care. You're all I have left."

"Joe, these aliens will stop at nothing to kill me. I've seen too much."

Joe grew curious and inquired, "What did you see, Suzie?"

"They can do things to people and make them into monsters."

"But, why didn't you call me sooner. I could have helped you."

"You wouldn't understand, Joe. You weren't here."

Joe became more confused. "That doesn't make sense. What wouldn't I understand – that creatures attacked you? I have a gun. I could have helped hunt them down at least."

Suzie blurted, "It all happened so quickly. We had no place to run and then I lost the phone in the grass. Oh, it was terrible, Joe."

"Look, I'm leaving the police station now. I'll meet you at the campsite. Can you be there?"

"Yes, I can. Thank you, Sweetie."

Joe stowed the phone and started the truck.

Lamar and Johnny noticed Joe's excitement and approached him. Joe exclaimed, "Suzie called, Sheriff! She's alive!"

Lamar looked at Johnny suspiciously and then back at Joe. He ordered, "Get in my truck. We'll find her." Joe shut his truck down and hurried into the police SUV.

Lamar leaned against the roof of the vehicle and pondered, *How could Joe's wife be alive after all this time?*

Johnny opened the door and placed one leg inside the SUV. He paused when he noticed Lamar's hesitation. "You okay, Sheriff?"

Lamar, with his gaze fixed away from the vehicle, replied, "Yeah. Get inside." Johnny climbed in and waited.

Joe questioned Johnny, "What's he waiting for? We've got to get my wife out of there before those creatures get to her."

Johnny turned around and patted Joe on the arm. "I understand how you feel," he said sympathetically. "We just can't barge into the woods without taking precautions against these things. It could jeopardize all of us if we're not prepared."

Joe became annoyed and opened the door. "If you guys aren't taking me, then I'll go myself."

Lamar climbed inside the vehicle and closed the door. "Relax, Joe. We'll get there soon enough."

They closed their doors and Lamar started the vehicle. He looked in the rear-view mirror and noticed the black sedan with the two federal agents was gone. He rolled the window down and remarked nonchalantly to Johnny, "You see our buddies from the Bureau over there earlier?"

"Yeah. Where'd they go?"

"I wonder."

Joe urged them, "Come on, already! She could be in danger!"

Lamar drove the vehicle onto the main road toward the highway. Curious, Johnny asked, "What's on your mind, Sheriff?"

"Joe, did your wife give any indication of how many alien creatures there are?"

"No. She only mentioned that they swarmed on them and she had no time to help the others."

Lamar requested, "See if you can raise any other units, Johnny."

Johnny looked gravely at Lamar and asked, "You sound as if they're all dead?"

"Hell, I think most of the town is dead," he responded, irritable.

Joe inquired uneasily, "How could they have spread so fast?"

"It's not the speed; it's the way they did it without being detected," explained Lamar.

Johnny called on the radio, "All units report in. This is Deputy Watkins." They waited uneasily but heard no response.

Lamar steered the vehicle off the ramp and proceeded onto the highway. He contemplated aloud, "So they took out our units as well. Hmm." Then his phone rang, interrupting his thoughts. He answered the phone, "Good afternoon, Governor." Lamar listened intently for several seconds and replied, "I understand. Nineteen hundred." Lamar set the phone down and informed them, "The governor is sending in fifty Army Guardsmen tomorrow afternoon. They'll be armed and competent for battle."

Joe asked, "What are they going to do?"

"Help us kill those sons-of-bitches out there."

Johnny remarked, "I'm surprised we don't have reporters swarming all over the place."

"The governor already knew we had a situation. He's says they're trying to suppress it from public knowledge in any way possible."

Johnny asked, "So the reporters are banned?"

"Not likely. I think we've been quarantined."

"So, they're afraid these creatures could spread all over the country?"

"I don't know. I have my suspicions about how and why this is going on, though."

"Are you going to tell me or what?" Johnny asked impatiently.

Lamar glared at him and complained, "Don't you ever shut up?"

The police SUV raced up the two-lane road toward Graham's Mountain. Lamar looked in the rear-view mirror and noticed the anxiety in Joe's face. He inquired, "Did your wife say anything about the other women?"

Joe replied stoically, "She mentioned that they couldn't help the children."

"Is she in danger?"

Joe became angry and sniped, "Now what the hell do you think?"

"It's important, Joe. Is she in danger?"

Joe recalled the conversation. "She did say the aliens would stop at nothing to kill her. She saw too much."

Lamar pondered and mimicked, "She saw too much."

Joe remarked sarcastically, "You don't believe her. I guess she's conspiring with the aliens to take over the planet. Gee, Sheriff, you are a smart one."

"Give it a rest, Joe. I'm just trying to do my job."

A black sedan returned to the campsite with two vans. Six men got out and quickly surveyed the remains of Suzie's friends and daughters. Two men opened the rear panel of the trucks and each pulled out a pair of canvas bags.

Suzie emerged from the trees and joined the two agents. Melendez greeted her, "Good day, Serena Luna."

Suzie chastised him, "It's Suzie when I take this shape."

"Yes, Suzie."

Cox was amused and added, "It's a pleasure to see you so soon."

Suzie smiled coyly and replied, "Likewise. How is the cleanup going?"

"Quite well. This is the last stop."

Melendez inquired, "There are still a few humans in the town who are ignorant of their situation. Should we take care of them?"

"Not yet. Let's deal with the issues at hand, first. Some men are coming up to take me back to town and I want this area cleaned up quickly."

"Do you want us to obstruct them?"

"Not at all. This is an essential part of our plan. I'm counting on them to eliminate Shurek's army, no matter how big it is."

Cox asked curiously, "Why can't we do it?"

Suzie placed a hand on his shoulder and explained, "Because, dear, I want them to think they've eradicated the alien presence and there is no chance of a cover-up. That clears the way for us to freely execute our own operation without interference."

"Ah, now I see. You are wise, Suzie."

Suzie remarked arrogantly, "That's why I'm in charge and Shurek isn't." She strutted away into the trees.

Melendez remarked, "She certainly is." They chuckled deviously and joined the other men in cleaning up the remains.

————— ·•••••• —————

The SUV rode up the trail and approached the campsite.

Joe questioned Lamar, "Why aren't you concerned about my wife, Sheriff?"

Lamar replied, "Something isn't quite right about this."

"What, that she survived?"

"Well, yes, and the fact that she's been able to elude the creatures this long."

Joe snapped, "Thanks a lot for your sympathy."

Lamar explained, "I certainly hope she's fine and her story is legit, believe me."

"Then why make this more difficult for me?"

"You're right, Doc. I apologize."

The black sedan and two white vans pulled away from the campsite and passed them. Melendez waved to them on the way by. Lamar was surprised to see them and waved back.

Johnny remarked, "They sure got here in a hurry.

Lamar marveled, "I wonder what they're up to now."

Suzie hid in the trees near the campsite. She waited patiently as the police SUV pulled next to her vehicle and parked. *I'd better fix myself up a little,* she thought to herself.

Suzie tore the knees out of her sweat pants and rubbed a handful of dirt all over her clothes. She tossed her hair back and matted it down.

As soon as Joe appeared from inside the SUV, Suzie rushed from the trees to him. "Joe! It's really you!"

Joe embraced her and sobbed, "Oh, Suzie, I was so worried about you and the girls."

"Honey, it was horrible."

Joe scanned the campground and saw nothing of the remains of the victims. "Where did it happen?"

Suzie took him by the hand and led him to the flattened grass area where the girls were murdered. Joe broke into tears and hugged her again.

Lamar leaned against his vehicle and studied the ground around the tires on Suzie's SUV. He noticed several tracks indicating that someone drove the vehicle away and returned.

Johnny saw the intense look on Lamar's face and asked, "What's wrong, Sheriff?"

Lamar whispered, "Dust the steering wheel for prints. I'll distract them while you do it."

Johnny reached inside the police SUV for a brown case and entered Suzie's vehicle from the passenger-side. Lamar nonchalantly meandered toward Joe and Suzie. He politely asked, "Can I interrupt the two of you to ask a few questions?"

Joe replied sarcastically, "Can't you give us some time alone? This is tough enough on us."

Lamar held his hands up in understanding and respectfully walked away from them. He scanned the perimeter and noticed traces of footprints leading into the trees. He looked back to see if Suzie or Joe noticed. The two sobbed in each other's arms. Lamar drew his pistol and disappeared in the trees. The faint tracks led him to a small clearing, where he spotted a cave, partially hidden in the trees. *I'll bet that's where Reyes and Borden were killed,* he thought. *That's probably the nest.* Lamar returned back to the camp.

Suzie and Joe knelt on the ground where their daughters had perished. She held Joe in her arms and consoled him. She was immediately aware of Lamar's return and became concerned. "Sheriff, where did you go?"

Lamar approached the two of them and replied, "I thought I heard something. Must have been a deer."

"It's dangerous out there. I wouldn't go far."

"Don't worry, Missy. I wasn't planning to." Lamar looked back and saw Johnny standing in front of the police SUV. Johnny gave him a thumbs up and displayed the brown case. He climbed inside the vehicle.

Lamar suggested, "Why don't we get out of here? We can talk later."

Joe replied sadly, "There's nothing more we can do here. Let's go."

Lamar asked, "Mrs. Beauchamp, can we talk later about your ordeal?"

"Of course, Sheriff. We'll come by the station later, if that's alright."

"I'll be waiting."

Lamar went to the SUV and got in the driver's-side. He started the truck and waited patiently for Joe and Suzie to get inside her vehicle. Johnny asked, "Why'd you want the prints?"

"Because I wanted to make sure Mrs. Beauchamp was the only driver of the vehicle." Johnny looked confused but said no more.

Lamar remarked, "Doesn't seem like Mrs. Beauchamp's in a big hurry to get out of here, does it?"

"Maybe she's suffering from fright."

"Fright, my ass. Where would you hide out here if you were a predator?"

"In a cave, Sheriff."

"Exactly. What did Reyes say about finding body parts?"

"They were in a cave."

"How many caves are there on Graham's Mountain that are big enough to walk into?"

"Well, I only know of one. It's not far from here."

"That's right. And neither is the camp."

"So, we trap them in the cave and kill them, right?"

"No, Johnny, that's the worst thing we can do. Ever play poker?"

"Not really."

"Well, we're going to find a way to bluff."

"I don't get it."

"I want to make them reveal everything about themselves before we kill them."

"You mean like interrogate them?"

"Johnny, do I have to teach you everything?"

"I'm lost, Sheriff."

"You'll see when the time comes. We can't afford to let any of them slip away and I mean any of them." They watched as Joe and Suzie got in Suzie's SUV.

Joe drove as Suzie stared with a dazed look about her. He reached over and held her hand. "I was so worried about you and the girls, Suzie."

Suzie replied disinterestedly, "It was a terrible ordeal."

"I called several times but you didn't answer."

"I told you, I lost my phone during the attack. When I came back to search for the girls, I found it. That's when I called you."

Joe inquired tearfully, "What are we going to do without the girls?"

"What about a new family?" she countered immediately.

Joe responded sadly, "I couldn't imagine replacing Dee Dee and Sarah."

Suzie bit her lip in disgust and turned away from Joe. He noticed her disapproval and added, "Let's wait a little while and see. I need time to get over this."

Suzie thought back to all the time she spent with the girls while Joe was at medical school. She felt anger arise inside of her and she struggled to control herself. She said calmly, "I guess we'll deal with it when the time comes."

Joe asked, "So how did you manage to survive out there, Honey?"

Suzie answered defensively, "I'm no slacker. I stayed on my feet and kept moving."

"Relax, Suzie. I never questioned your resolve. I just asked how you did it."

"I'm sorry. It's been a bad time for me."

Joe rubbed her knee and said assuredly, "We'll get through this, I promise."

Suzie's SUV turned down the suburban street and paused at a stop sign. Suzie commented, "It sure looks deserted around here."

"Most folks are dead or hiding. I don't think you'll see anyone on the road."

Suzie was impressed with the effectiveness of the mutants and how fast they could overrun an area.

Joe pulled into the driveway and parked next to his pickup. He and Suzie got out of the SUV and walked together to the front door. He opened the door and suggested, "Why don't you go inside and relax. I need to take care of something in the garage."

"Thanks, Joe. I'll be waiting for you."

Joe went to the garage and opened the wooden door. He searched the area around him and, feeling that it was safe, he entered.

Inside, Suzie eyed the kitchen and heard Kraus growling. *I always hated that dog.* When she entered the kitchen, Kraus was ready to lunge at her. The two instinctively rushed at each other. Suzie grabbed the dog by the neck and slammed him to the ground. The dog whimpered and crawled a short distance away. "Oh, no you don't," she uttered. Like a wild animal, she leaped on top of the injured dog and snapped his neck in half. "Some watchdog you were" she mocked. After opening the sliding glass door, she dragged the dog's carcass onto the back steps.

Joe unlocked his gun vault and opened the door. He browsed over his collection and decided to take a Colt .45 Diamond back with him.

Suzie knelt on the back step and held the dog's head in her arms. She did her best to look distraught. Joe entered the kitchen and saw his dog lying motionless in Suzie's arms. He blurted, "What happened to Kraus?"

Suzie answered calmly, "I found him on the back step like this. His neck is broken." She moved the dog's head back and forth, demonstrating her assessment. Joe stroked the dead dog's head and sobbed. Suzie became annoyed and thought, *He cared more for that damn dog than he did for his real family.*

Joe stood up and went to the living room. He sat on the couch and covered his face with his hands, then cried. Suzie cradled him in her arms and said soothingly, "It's alright, Joe. We'll get through this."

Joe replied sadly, "I don't think we'll ever get over this."

"Yes, we will." She rocked him until he fell asleep. Suzie slipped into the bathroom. She turned on the shower until the water was scalding hot. *Now that's more like it.* Suzie removed her clothes and stared at the mirror. She became Serena Luna and commented proudly to herself, "I am one bad bitch. Look at me." She grinned through her sharp teeth and then stepped into the shower. The hot water didn't bother her in the least. Her appendages extended from her chest and stretched out. Her whole body relaxed as she took in the moist heat.

Lamar sat at his desk inside the police station and tapped his fingers rhythmically against the wood. He took out a notepad and pencil from the top desk drawer.

Johnny pulled up a chair and sat next to him. He kidded, "You changing careers, Sheriff? Looks like you're ready to write a book."

"I wish. Some things just don't add up." He drew a square with a circle inside it, then another circle four inches away. He pointed to the square and explained, "This is Graham's Mountain and the inner circle is the campsite. The outer circle is the town."

Johnny slid the chair closer and watched attentively. Lamar drew two lines from the inner circle to the outer circle and said, "Everything started on the mountain right around that campsite. If these things are alien, then there must be a ship up there." He drew two arced lines from the inner circle to the outer circle and continued, "The attacks spread outward to town. If the alien creatures return to their ship at night, then why go into town and make such a scene?"

Johnny answered, "Maybe they were hungry."

"No, I think there's more to it. They're building an army."

"For what, Sheriff?"

"To invade, you boob!" Lamar pounded his fist on the table and exclaimed, "It's too friggin' simple!"

"But isn't that good?" questioned Johnny.

"I'm worried. What if we wipe them out and create a bigger problem?"

Baffled, Johnny remarked, "I don't see how that could happen. It's like having rodents in your house and you get rid of them. That's a good thing."

"But what if the rodents are keeping something worse away?"

"You keep talking in riddles, Sheriff."

"I'm worried about Beauchamp's wife. Something's not right about her." Lamar drew a stick person and a crude alien. Between them he drew a stick alien. He pointed to the stick alien and said, "See that. It's our worst fear."

Johnny inquired, "We already know they create a half mutant/half human creature."

"But what if that's just one kind. Maybe they can produce a different kind. They use their tongues and those things on their chests and God knows what else."

"You think Doc's wife's an alien?"

"I hope not. If so, they can make aliens that look human."

Johnny pushed the chair away and looked concerned. "They'd be impossible to stop, wouldn't they?"

Lamar fixed his gaze on the drawing of the stick alien and inquired, "How would you contain a potential alien outbreak if you were in charge, Johnny?"

"I'd probably quarantine the area and weed them out."

"What if you couldn't? What if their very existence threatened the survival of the human race?"

Johnny replied uneasily, "You'd have to kill everything inside the quarantine."

"Exactly. Now what about our agent buddies? They don't seem too concerned about getting to the bottom of this."

"What do you think they're up to?"

Lamar rubbed his chin and contemplated aloud. "They seem to be waiting for us to make all the moves. I wonder why?"

Johnny suggested, "Maybe they think we're doing a good job of handling it."

Lamar looked disgustedly at Johnny and chided, "Now how can you say we're doing a good job of handling this? We have mounting casualties. We haven't contained the creatures yet. We sure haven't found their ship. We've done everything possible to bungle this job and they are good with that."

"Do you think this makes us expendable in a worst-case scenario?"

Lamar replied somberly, "It may already be too late. We may have been expended and don't know it yet." The phone rang, interrupting their conversation. He answered, "Sheriff Whittington speaking. Can I help you?"

He looked relieved as he listened intently. "I understand. We'll wait for him here at my office. Thank you, sir."

"Well?"

"Captain Ames will meet us here in two hours. He's flying in by helicopter. Let's go for a ride." Lamar pushed the chair back from the desk and reluctantly trod to the door.

Johnny got up and complained, "Are you going to tell me what's up?"

Lamar stopped at the door and turned toward him. "Ames is arriving with the Guardsmen. The area was quarantined but it's been broken."

"That can't be good."

"One of the blockades was taken out by the creatures during the night on highway 56."

"So, what do they want to do?"

"We're going to hit the creatures with everything we have. Every one of them must die. Then we have to hunt for any strays that might be out there."

"But there's a lot of territory out there to cover!"

"I know that. In the meantime, I want to speak with Kaz about these things. Are you coming or what?"

Johnny hurried toward the door. "Of course, I'm coming." The two of them left the station and got into their vehicle.

⁕

Shurek stood outside the cave and stared into the woods. Anger flowed through his body as he considered how many ways he could make Suzie suffer. His mutants dragged a dozen wounded humans from the woods to him. Shurek pointed to a young man and said, "He'll do."

The man pleaded, "Please don't hurt me."

Shurek pulled the man firmly against his chest. His appendages greedily extended from his chest and penetrated the man's spine. The young man struggled briefly then succumbed to the alien hormone spreading throughout his nervous system.

Suzie projected her satisfaction over the outcome of things to Shurek, interrupting his ritual. He became enraged again and released the young man from his grip. The man staggered and fell to his knees. Shurek tore his arms off in a violent fit. Blood splattered everywhere as he threw the arms into the trees and bit into the man's torso.

Telepathically, Suzie informed him, *Tomorrow evening, you and I will have our moment.*

Shurek replied, *I'm not that stupid. I know you'll have the humans hunt me and kill me.*

Nonsense. What fun would that be? she taunted. *You and I will have a special engagement.*

Shurek seethed with fury. "I'm going to enjoy devouring every piece of your flesh, Serena Luna. You underestimate me." Suzie smiled and focused her thoughts on her prior life.

Shurek shredded the torso of the man, sending pieces of his entrails across the ground. The mutants eagerly grabbed at the bits of flesh, relishing every little taste.

———— ·+·+·+·+·· ————

As Lamar drove to the morgue, Johnny remarked, "These things might be comparable to animals in the woods."

"And what makes you think that, smart guy?"

"They hunt in packs and they seem territorial."

"So, you think they're stupid?"

Johnny pondered for a moment and then explained, "Not necessarily. Maybe they have animal instincts but limited intellect."

Lamar considered his comments and elaborated, "You may be on to something. What if they have a leader, like an alpha male or female?"

"Well, Sheriff, if we kill the alpha male, another will take over."

"What if there is no other alpha male, only mutants?"

"Then the alpha male will avoid conflict to stay safe. He'll only fight if provoked."

Lamar chuckled to himself. Johnny asked, "What's so funny?"

"If Mrs. Beauchamp is telling the truth, we may be able to lure him out."

"You mean like use her for bait?"

"Uh-huh. She said the aliens want her dead."

"Now I see."

The police SUV pulled into the morgue parking lot. Lamar instructed Johnny, "We'll have to make this visit quick. When we get back, I want to make sure our guardsmen are ready to go on the attack tomorrow."

"Why not tonight?"

As they left the vehicle, Lamar explained, "I'm looking for answers from Mrs. Beauchamp and the creatures."

Johnny opened the door for Lamar and followed him inside. "I don't get it, Sheriff."

"We'll see how they react to the delay and what occurs in the meantime." Johnny was again baffled by the sheriff's logic.

The lobby was empty and bloodstains covered the floor. Lamar remarked, "This looks bad – really bad." He knelt down and studied the bloodstains. Johnny drew his pistol and approached the door to the rear hall.

Lamar warned, "Don't go back there without me." He got up and peered outside the window. There was no one in sight. The hearse was empty and sat idle.

Lamar locked the front door and drew his pistol. He marched to the rear door and kicked it open. He and Johnny burst through the door and aimed down the hall at either side. Johnny whispered, "It's too quiet in here."

"Cover me." Lamar walked down the hall to the lab. He called out, "Kaz! Sam! Anybody here?"

Lamar paused by the door and motioned for Johnny to catch up. Lamar kicked the door open and burst through.

Sam lay in a pool of blood in one corner, with both wrists slit and his boxers around his ankles. Greta and Vega lay next to each other, soaked in brown and red blood. Alicia lay a short distance away as did Kaz.

Lamar shook his head in awe, "Holy Mother of God. Will you look at this mess?"

Johnny stood behind him and grew nauseous at the sight of the bludgeoned corpses. He turned away and leaned awkwardly against the wall, vomiting.

Lamar looked back at him and complained, "You're screwing up a crime scene, you ninny."

Johnny mumbled weakly, "Sorry, Sheriff."

Lamar walked around the room and studied the position of the bodies. He tried to understand how the blood fest unfolded. When he noticed Sam's bloody rectum, he uttered in amazement, "Well, I'll be - a crime of passion."

Johnny regained some composure and hollered, "What the hell are you talking about, Sheriff?"

"Seems that Sam here was playing the field. Looks like this creature was his wife and that one was his girlfriend."

Johnny examined Alicia's corpse and remarked in surprise, "That was his girlfriend. She disappeared at the hospital last night."

Lamar explained, "Here's the problem that we have. These things infected humans and turned them into something else, but these things still acted like humans. The other mutants didn't. They were more like animals."

"What's your point?"

"We've definitely got at least two types of mutants on our hands."

"Could there be more?"

"I'm wondering. What if Mrs. Beauchamp was a third type?"

Lamar walked out of the room and headed for the lobby. Johnny felt a chill run down his spine as goose bumps formed on his arms. He anxiously left the room and followed the sheriff.

Five trucks loaded with equipment and weapons entered town and parked outside the police station. A CH-47 Chinook helicopter landed in another parking lot nearby. A tall, middle-aged officer stepped out of the helicopter followed by a large contingent of soldiers. The officer entered the police station. "Anyone here?"

After a few minutes of silence, he pulled up a chair and sat at Lamar's desk. Agents Cox and Melendez entered the room from the kitchen. Cox greeted the officer, "Good afternoon. I wondered when you guys would show up."

Captain Ames was startled and leaped out of his chair. "Who the hell are you?"

Cox extended his hand in friendship and answered, "Agents Cox and Melendez - Federal agents."

Captain Ames shook his hand and replied, "I'm sorry. You startled me. I'm Captain Ames." The three men sat down around the desk. Captain Ames asked, "Any idea what's going on here?"

Cox replied, "What have your superiors told you?"

"We're here for some kind of animal control. I was advised that these animals are of the dangerous sort."

Melendez chuckled and informed him. "These animals are alien creatures."

Captain Ames was amused. "Really. Now what kind of creatures are we actually talking about?"

"You and your men are going to exterminate a group of dangerous aliens."

Lamar and Johnny entered the station. Lamar kidded, "Well, well. It's my friendly neighborhood federal agents and you must be Captain Ames. What and who are we exterminating today?"

Captain Ames stood up and shook hands with Lamar. Johnny stepped forward and shook hands as well. "Good afternoon, Captain. I'm Deputy Watkins."

"Hello, Deputy."

Cox responded, "We were just explaining to Captain Ames what he and his men will be up against."

Lamar informed them, "I believe I have a plan."

"Enlighten us with your wisdom, Sheriff," said Melendez, amused.

"I'd be happy to. I believe Mrs. Beauchamp will help us weed out the alpha alien while the captain's men wipe out the mutant army."

Captain Ames became annoyed and complained, "Look, we've come a long way and I'm not particularly in the mood for games. What are we dealing with?"

Melendez asked, "Didn't you find it interesting why two federal agents would be involved if you were only dealing with animals?"

"It did cross my mind."

"This is no joke and we're trying to keep this from getting out to the general public."

Cox added, "Imagine the pandemonium that would break out if people knew about this."

Ames asked, "Haven't the locals noticed any of these creatures yet?"

Lamar answered calmly, "The locals are the creatures now." Ames became uneasy and stared out the window at some of his men.

Melendez suggested, "We could brief your men for you if you don't feel comfortable addressing the topic."

"No, I'll do it. When do we begin?"

Lamar suggested, "How about tomorrow night? You guys got Star-Ds for night vision?"

"Yes, we do. I thought it was strange that they issued them to us for animals."

"The creatures are holed up in a cave. We're going to lure them into the open and let your boys cut them down."

"No problem. I'll let the men grab a bite to eat and then I'll brief them."

"Thanks, Captain." Lamar looked back through the kitchen window and saw a mutant staring in at them. He drew his pistol and fired. Everyone in the room jumped in surprise. The bullet struck the creature in the forehead, killing it instantly.

"Take a look, Captain. That's what you're up against."

Captain Ames exited the station, wondering if this was someone's idea of a practical joke. He instructed four of his men to collect the corpse for inspection.

Johnny became antsy and went to the men's room. Lamar informed the agents, "We'll need Dr. Beauchamp and his wife. They need to participate if we're going to execute this."

Cox offered, "If there's any problem, let us know. We can help."

"Thank you, Agent Cox." Lamar entered the kitchen warily and glanced out the window. Four soldiers dragged the dead mutant to the front of the station. He poured a cup of coffee and accessed his phone.

⋅⋅✦✦✦⋅⋅

Joe's phone rang and startled him. With Suzie asleep next to him, he took the call in the kitchen, expecting more bad news.

"Doc, it's Sheriff Whittington."

"Hello, Sheriff. What's up?"

"Quite a bit, actually. George, Sam and Greta are dead. Sam's wife and girlfriend, as well."

"Did the creatures get them?"

"Sam's wife and girlfriend were the creatures."

"Oh, shit!"

"It was a real mess. Is your wife there?"

"Yes. She's asleep."

"Well, we need to speak with her."

"What for, Sheriff?"

"Your wife mentioned that the alien is particularly interested in killing her. She could help us lure the creatures into the open."

"You're not using Suzie for bait!"

"Why don't you let her make that decision?"

"I'm making the decision for her. She's not doing it."

Suzie entered the kitchen and asked, "What's going on, Joe?"

"Sheriff wants you to help him catch the alien."

"When?"

Joe looked surprised. "You're kidding!"

"No. We have to finish this."

Joe stared at her in disbelief. Suzie took the phone from him and said, "We'll be at the station in a while, Sheriff."

Lamar answered, "Thank you, Mrs. Beauchamp." He hung up the phone and relaxed. Everyone waited expectantly for an explanation from him.

"Well, I think Mrs. Beauchamp knows a lot more than she's revealing right now."

Agent Cox inquired, "What makes you think that?"

"Well, let's just say it's a lawman's intuition."

⋅⋅✦✦✦✦⋅⋅

Suzie hung up the phone and gazed seductively into Joe's eyes. She took his hand and led him into the bedroom. Joe paused in the doorway, shocked. "Our daughters were just murdered. How can you even think about having sex right now?"

Suzie looked hurt. "Isn't that more of a reason to start over and have another child?"

"Suzie, I can't. I just can't."

Suzie replied angrily, "You mean you won't. At least be a man about it and say 'no, I don't want any more kids with you, Suzie'."

Joe answered apologetically, "I didn't mean it that way. I'm sorry."

"Let's go. We have work to do."

"You're not seriously going to let them use you for bait, are you?"

"What do you care?"

Joe followed Suzie out of the house to her SUV and pleaded, "Don't do this, Suzie. You're all I have."

Suzie considered his reaction to his damned dog and the girls. She thought, *Of course, I'm all he's got. Now he needs me.* She grabbed Joe by both his arms and said, "Look, this has to be done. You can either support me or stay here. Make up your mind."

Joe was taken aback by her directness. He whimpered, "Alright. I'll support you."

"Good. Now get in the SUV and don't say another word about it."

Joe felt as though Suzie had become a stranger. She was cold and showed no compassion for him.

━━━━━━ ·◆◆◆◆· ━━━━━━

Shurek followed several of his creatures through a trailer park. They ripped doors off their hinges and trashed the interiors. Inside one of the trailers, a mother and her two-year-old daughter huddled together. The little girl cried briefly before the mother muffled her sounds.

Shurek paused outside the trailer and listened. He heard the brief cry and suspected that someone was inside. He crept into the trailer and scanned the interior. His curiosity moved him to approach a pile of blankets at the rear. He tossed the blankets on the table, exposing the woman and her daughter.

The woman looked up with a horrified, pathetic stare. She sobbed as she nestled her daughter against her in a vain attempt to protect her. Shurek pulled the woman to her feet by her hair.

The woman begged, "Please don't hurt us. I'll do whatever you want."

Shurek released his hold on her and stared at the young girl. He pointed at the child.

The woman cried frantically, "No, not my baby! Please."

Shurek yanked the little girl from her grasp and set her on the table in a sitting position. She cried hysterically. His tongue slithered from his mouth and pushed its way into the little girl's mouth, gagging her until she couldn't make a sound.

◆ · · ·

The woman screamed frantically, "No! Stop it!"

Shurek realized that should he fail against Suzie, he wanted some means of exacting his revenge on her. She has the sporatin in human form. If he turned the little girl, she could be the one to take down both Suzie and her child in years to come. This child would know their secrets.

The mother lunged at Shurek in desperation but he caught her by the throat and held her against the wall. He forced her to watch as he inserted his DNA compound into the young girl's throat. When he finished with the girl, he turned his attention back to the woman. He spun her around and pressed her against his chest. His appendages grappled into either side of her spine. The woman convulsed as she stared vacantly at her daughter. Tears streamed down her cheeks as her will to resist faded. The little girl stared back with a blank gaze on her face. Shurek dropped the woman on the floor and declared arrogantly, "Now, Serena Luna, we'll see who wins."

Agents Cox and Melendez exited the police station just as Suzie and Joe arrived. Cox warned Melendez, "Watch what you say? We don't want to ruin her cover."

Melendez smiled as he held the door for Suzie when she approached. "Good evening, ma'am."

Suzie nodded and smiled as she passed. Joe stopped and asked, "Are you men federal agents?"

Cox remarked, "Perhaps. Why?"

"Do you have any idea how many more of those creatures are out there?"

"Not many based on our satellite imagery. Don't sweat it, Doc." Cox and Melendez walked away to their sedan.

Joe muttered cynically, "Don't sweat it! Now why would I sweat something like this?"

Suzie sat across from Lamar and waited patiently for him to open the conversation. Joe entered and sat next to her. Lamar twiddled his thumbs and studied her facial expression.

Johnny became uneasy and offered, "Can I get anyone a cup of coffee?"

Suzie replied, "No thank you, deputy."

Sally pulled up in front of the police station in Sam's badly damaged Corvette. She rushed into the police station tearfully.

Johnny shouted, "Sally! Where were you?"

Sally sobbed, "It was terrible! Joann's dead and they tried to kill us."

"The creatures?"

"Yes, and the agents!"

Lamar stood up uneasily. "What did you say?"

"The agents blocked the road and came after us with guns. They shot up the car and killed Joann. The creatures ambushed them and killed them all." Johnny comforted her and escorted her into the kitchenette.

Lamar inquired, "Do you know something about these creatures that might help us defeat them, Mrs. Beauchamp?"

"I believe so. There is just one left and he's determined to kill me."

"Why is that?"

"I saw how he infected his victims."

"And that is?"

"They have these appendages and they inject fluid into their victims. It causes them to mutate into the horrible creatures that we've seen."

"And what about this tube of theirs?"

"What about it, Sheriff?"

I've seen it do some ungodly things."

"Such as …?"

"Such as impregnate a woman. Such as pump a blob of something down their throats. Such as numb a person's neck to the point where he can barely breathe."

"I'm not familiar with that."

"Are you sure?"

"Of course, I'm sure!"

Joe leaned forward on the table and interceded, "Look, Sheriff, she's not one of the creatures! Don't provoke her like this."

Suzie took Joe's arm and nudged him back into his seat. "It's alright, Joe. I can handle this."

Lamar asked, "Did you drive your vehicle at all after you arrived at the campsite other than today?"

Suzie suddenly realized that the sheriff was cross-examining her. "As a matter of fact, I did. I tried to escape the area but the creatures blocked the road. I returned to the site and fled into the forest on foot."

"Did you ever see the aliens' ship?"

Suzie countered, "You aren't interested in killing the aliens, are you, Sheriff?"

"Of course, I am."

"Then what else are you looking for, particularly from me?"

"Am I looking for something else?"

Joe exclaimed, "That's enough, Sheriff! I won't tolerate any more of this."

"Mrs. Beauchamp, do you think you can lure the alpha alien into the open where we can kill it?"

"I'm sure I can."

"If we kill it, does that stop the creation of mutants from humans?"

"It sure does. The mutants are basically eating machines. They have to be killed."

"Then we'll meet at the campsite at six, tomorrow evening."

"Will we hunt all the creatures down?" she asked.

"Without a doubt."

"Thank you, Sheriff." Suzie and Joe exited the police station.

Lamar muttered to himself, "And maybe we'll find out just what you are, Mrs. Beauchamp. I'm not fooled."

Johnny and Sally exited the kitchenette. Johnny informed the sheriff, "I'm going to take Sally back to my place for the night. We need to get some rest and she's been through a lot. I'll take care of the report in the morning."

"No need for a report. Be careful, you two."

Johnny drew his pistol and escorted Sally out to his jeep.

Lamar locked the door and slept in his chair. He tossed and turned as he wrestled with Suzie's story.

CHAPTER XI

EXECUTION

The next afternoon, an army convoy arrived at the campsite where the aliens first attacked Suzie and her friends. The last rays of the fading sunset slipped behind the mountains, casting an eerie mood over the area. Captain Ames ordered his men to secure the perimeter.

The police SUV pulled up nearby. Lamar climbed out and approached the officer. "You're men ready, Captain?"

"Yes, we are," Ames replied.

Suzie's SUV sped into the campsite and skidded to a stop in front of Lamar and Captain Ames. Lamar watched Joe and Suzie as they got out of the truck, studying their expressions.

Suzie inquired, "Are we ready?"

"I believe so," answered Lamar. "The creatures are hiding out in a cave not far from here. The captain's men will surround the entrance to the cave. You'll be at the forefront with Captain Ames and myself to bait them out."

Suzie shook her head in disagreement. "It won't work. The alien will escape."

Lamar thought, *The alien – so there is only one.* He grew frustrated and stared at the ground for several seconds before looking up at Suzie.

"Now look here, Ms. Beauchamp. I realize you went through a lot with these things but you're speaking in riddles as far as I'm concerned. How about we cut the chase and get to the point?"

Joe responded defensively, "That's my wife you're talking to, Sheriff!"

Suzie explained, "I need to be in another area to bait the alien out of hiding. The mutants will spread out in the woods with only a few remaining in the cave."

Lamar folded his arms and asked, "So then what? What will you do when this creature arrives and attacks you?"

"Give me a gun and I'll take care of it. I owe that son-of-a-bitch."

Lamar took his pistol from his holster and checked the magazine. It was loaded. He handed the gun to Suzie and reminded her "I expect this back when you're done." Suzie examined the gun and stowed it in the pocket of her sweatpants.

Joe was very upset and questioned Lamar, "Who's going to cover her in case she's ambushed?"

Captain Ames suggested, "We could put an ice vest on her and monitor her with night vision goggles."

Lamar asked, "Any problem with that, Mrs. Beauchamp?"

"None at all, Sheriff."

Joe reached inside his vehicle and retrieved his rifle. He kissed Suzie's cheek and assured her, "I'll watch your back, Honey."

Suzie replied unenthusiastically, "I'm sure you will." Joe became more confused by her strange behavior.

Captain Ames informed them, "I'll send in twenty of my men to the cave. The remaining men will cover them from the left and right sides of the cave."

Suzie suggested, "You might want to put about ten men on the ridge to watch their flanks. We don't know how many mutants are out there and how far out they've spread."

Captain Ames replied, "We can spare ten men up there and still cover the cave and clearing."

Suzie announced, "I'm going into the woods. He'll find me soon enough."

Lamar thought again, *He — so there's a single male alien — an alpha male.*

Captain Ames called out, "Hold on, miss." He went to one of the trucks and opened up a crate. Inside was a case with several ice vests packed in dry ice. He removed one and closed the case.

Suzie quipped, "You boys were sure prepared for this one."

"It wasn't me. My superiors determined what we needed."

Suzie thought, *My boys Cox and Melendez are on top of everything. Not bad.* She put on the ice vest and said, "Thanks, Captain. This'll help." She hurried into the trees and disappeared.

Joe looked lost as she left without even a goodbye. Lamar took notice and pondered. Captain Ames left them and ordered his men into position.

Johnny took out two rifles and handed one to Lamar. "You might need this, Sheriff."

"Thanks, Johnny."

Joe paced uneasily and then announced, "I'm going after her."

Lamar suggested, "Why don't you get yourself some field glasses and go with us? I want to see this alien for myself."

"But we saw them already."

"Yeah, but there's something special about this one."

Johnny asked, "Why the interest, Sheriff?"

"No offense to Joe, but there's something fishy about this whole situation with Mrs. Beauchamp."

Joe complained "Why do you keep treating her like an enemy? She's been through a lot."

"It's just a feeling that something isn't right. I don't know what it is." Joe glared at him.

Lamar suggested calmly, "Let's go keep an eye on your wife and make sure she's okay." The three men entered the woods with their guns pointed ahead of them.

⸺ ⬦⬦⬦ ⸺

Shurek sent four of his mutants up to the ridge and dispersed the others into the woods around the cave. He instructed four of them to remain in the rear of the cave as a distraction.

Suzie trod through soft mud alongside a pond. She removed her ice vest and tossed it into the water. "That should keep them off my trail for a while." She returned to the woods and headed for the backside of the ridge.

Shurek ascended the side of the mountain with the semi-conscious, young girl. He looked across the treetops below and thought, *Serena Luna, your time is coming.*

Suzie paused when she sensed his thoughts. *Ah, Shurek. You and I will settle our issue away from them.*

Shurek angrily ripped a pine tree branch from its trunk. He tossed it down the side of the mountain and uttered, "I'll kill you. I swear, I'll kill you." He dashed toward the ridge with the little girl over his shoulder.

Suzie pondered why he had the girl with him. He hadn't revealed any thoughts or intentions that she could read.

⸻ ·+·◆·+· ⸻

Ten of Captain Ames' men ascended the ridge. They cautiously pressed through the pine branches toward their vantage point at the top. Three mutants charged at them from the left. Six of the soldiers knelt down and fired at the creatures. Two of the soldiers turned and watched the rear from the same position. The remaining two soldiers scanned the treetops. They spotted one of the mutants above them in the trees and fired. The mutant clutched at its throat as brown blood gushed from the wound. It fell to the ground with a thud.

The other soldiers took down the attacking mutants with gunfire. They examined their victims and were appalled at what they were. One of the soldiers became panicked and uttered, "What the hell are these things? They aren't human."

A second replied, "They were human once."

The third suggested somberly, "Let's just finish our assignment and go get some beers." The soldiers continued warily to the top of the ridge.

The soldiers, led by Captain Ames, approached the cave with their rifles raised and targeted the entrance. Captain Ames eyed the area above the cave on the side of the mountain. He gestured for ten of his men to secure the cave. The remaining soldiers split into two groups. Ten took position on Captain Ames left and ten took position on his right. Both groups took cover in the trees and waited for the creatures to appear.

The mutants lay flat on the leafy forest ground, covered with branches and leaves. They waited for their opportunity to attack. The soldiers saw nothing of the creatures' images through the night vision goggles. They focused their attention on the clearing in front of the cave.

The sounds of gunfire erupted from inside the cave. The mutants saw that as their opportunity to attack. They emerged from hiding and attacked both groups of soldiers from behind. The battle was fierce as the mutants took multiple gunshot wounds before succumbing. Numerous soldiers were killed in the initial attack.

Seven soldiers emerged from the cave and joined Captain Ames' group. One of them reported, "There were only four in there, sir."

Captain Ames frowned as he realized this cave was only a distraction and maybe a trap. He ordered them to assist the group on the left and he took his group to assist those on the right.

Lamar led Johnny and Joe to the top of the hill. He spotted the ice vest beyond the trees near the pond with his night vision goggles. It was difficult to recognize at first since the pond water warmed the vest significantly. Instead of a bright blue, he saw a faint gray that was barely distinguishable. "She's down there," he whispered.

Joe gradually became accustomed to the glasses and grew panicked. "If that's her, she's not moving."

"No, she's not. The vest isn't giving off much of a glow either." Lamar hurried through the trees and descended the hill. Joe and Johnny stumbled as they attempted to keep up with him.

Lamar wallowed through the mud and waded into the pond. His first thought was that she was killed and tossed into the pond. When he reached the vest, he raised it up and uttered, "Son-of-a-bitch! We've been had."

Johnny and Joe looked confused as Lamar splashed toward them with the vest in hand. He tossed it on the ground and questioned Joe, "Can you explain what Mrs. Beauchamp was thinking that she threw this in the pond?"

Joe shook his head in bewilderment. "I don't understand it. Why would she do that?"

"Now maybe you'll understand why I have doubts about her story."

Johnny suggested, "She can't be far. Let's find her before it's too late."

Lamar stomped out of the mud and ascended the hill. Johnny mentioned sympathetically, "I'm sure there's a reason for this."

"There'd better be," complained Joe.

••••••

Suzie taunted Shurek, "Come out and face your destiny unless you're afraid?"

Shurek leaped out of the trees with the little girl and stood before Suzie. "You'll pay for what you did to my offspring. You had no right to destroy it like that."

Curious, Suzie inquired, "Is she here to defend you?"

"No, just a little insurance in case you brought friends." Shurek pushed the girl onto the ground. She lay with a vacant stare in her eyes.

Suzie changed into Serena Luna. She removed the pistol from her sweatpants and tossed it on the ground. "It was a pleasure taking away from you as you took from me."

Shurek lunged at her but Serena Luna calmly stepped aside. She struck him in the throat and sent him sprawling. Shurek shrieked and charged at her. She deflected his reach and rode him to the ground face first, before releasing her hold on him.

Shurek became enraged and dove at her leg. Serena Luna grabbed his upper jaw as he tried desperately to bite into her thigh. She punched him in the head several times with her clawed fists and dazed him. He released his hold on her and dropped to the ground.

Serena Luna jumped on his back, knee first, and slammed his head into the ground. She backed away from him as he lay motionless. She chided, "I guess all those mutants you created took away your stamina, Shurek?"

Shurek didn't respond. As she prepared to deliver a lethal blow to Shurek, she thought, *I need to be wounded to convince the humans that I'm not alien.* She rolled Shurek over and reached into his chest cavity. She pushed her claws through soft flesh into Shurek's organs.

Shurek's eyes opened and he convulsed briefly. Serena Luna pulled away and remarked, "Now that's more like it."

Shurek staggered to his feet and clutched at his chest cavity in pain. He breathed irregularly and spasmed several times. Serena Luna shook her head at him in pity." Come on, Shurek. You must have more than that. You're pathetic."

Shurek glared at her, his face tensed and distorted. Serena Luna relaxed and waited for him to make some attempt at her. "Oh, Shurek, you look so juvenile," she badgered him. "Fight like a real male."

Shurek summoned every ounce of energy in desperation that he could. He lunged at her and caught her in the upper chest. The two tumbled across the ground, wrapped in each other's arms.

Lamar emerged from the trees and saw the two combatants. He couldn't distinguish them from the distance but he knew one had to be Suzie. Joe and Johnny arrived behind him. Joe called out to her, "Suzie!"

Serena Luna saw them and panicked. She couldn't let them see her in her alien form. Shurek sensed her distraction and went on a vicious assault. He slashed and punched her, landing blow after blow to her face. Serena Luna desperately shoved her clawed hand into his cavity again and groped for his heart. Once she felt it firmly in her hand, she ripped it from Shurek's chest.

Shurek suddenly froze with a blank stare in his eyes. Serena Luna shoved him off of her and transformed back to Suzie. She held his heart in her hand and lay stunned.

Joe raced to her aid with his rifle in hand. He called out as he approached, "Suzie, are you alright?"

Suzie muttered, "I'm fine, Joe." She stood and staggered toward him. A mutant darted at her from behind.

Joe raised his rifle and targeted the mutant. Unaware of the mutant, Suzie pleaded, "Don't shoot me, Joe. I can explain."

Joe fired and placed a perfect shot in the mutant's forehead. The creature stumbled against Suzie's back and fell to the ground. Suzie was shaken and felt helpless to defend herself if Joe wanted to shoot her.

Joe questioned her, "Explain what? I'd never hurt you, Suzie." He tossed the night-vision goggles on the ground.

Suzie was rattled and tried to think of something smart to say. "I … I can explain the ice vest."

Joe looked down at the alien and at the heart in Suzie's blood-soaked hand. She dropped it on the ground and cried. Joe pushed her hair out of her eyes and asked, "Is it over now?"

◆ • • •

She answered tearfully, "Yes, it is."

Lamar and Johnny stood beside them. They looked down at Shurek's dead body and the large, blue heart on the ground nearby.

Joe kidded, "You really screwed him up."

Suzie picked up the sheriff's pistol and handed it to him. "Sorry, Sheriff, I didn't need it after all." Suddenly she felt a sharp pang in her stomach and fell to her knees. She uttered, "Oh, no! Not now."

Joe helped her to her feet and pleaded, "Sheriff, we have to help her!"

"Let's get her to the truck. We can't do anything for her out here."

As Joe lifted Suzie in his arms, Lamar offered, "Can we help you, Doc?"

"Just lead me back to the vehicles. We need to get her up to Clearview Hospital, fast."

The little girl hid behind the trees with tears streaming down her cheeks. "Mother," she cried repeatedly, but no one heard her.

Captain Ames and twenty-one surviving soldiers met Lamar's group at the edge of the campsite. He informed Lamar, "The area is secure and all the creatures have been terminated. We've confirmed that with our satellite imagery."

"That's good news, Captain. I'm impressed that you had access to the satellites' data."

"I guess Uncle Sam thought this was a big enough priority," he kidded.

"Thank Uncle Sam for me, will you?"

"Of course. We're going to collect our dead and wounded. We'll return to town to set up camp for the night. You and I will debrief in the morning."

"That'll be fine. Right now, we need to get Mrs. Beauchamp to the hospital."

"I understand. Where are you taking her?" Ames inquired.

"Clearview is the closest."

"I'll call ahead and instruct them to let you pass," Captain Ames offered.

Cox overheard and approached them. "I've already taken care of that, sir. They are expected."

Ames looked at Cox suspiciously as he returned to the other agents.

"Cox and Melendez are really on the ball," quipped Lamar cynically. "That worries me."

"Yes, they are," replied Ames suspiciously. They collected the dead and laid them in a neat row in the middle of the campsite.

Joe opened the door of the SUV for Suzie.

Lamar suggested to Joe, "Why don't I drive you to Clearview Hospital and Johnny will bring your vehicle?"

"I'd appreciate that, Sheriff."

Joe sat in the back seat with Suzie as Lamar raced down the highway. Two black sedans and an eighteen-wheeler blocked the road.

Lamar complained, "What the hell is all this about?"

Suzie instructed him, "Tell them we have authorization from Agents Cox and Melendez."

Lamar wondered what Suzie's affiliation with the two agents was. Neither she nor her husband were close enough to hear Cox inform them about the arrangements. He stopped short of the blockade and waited as two armed agents approached them. Joe suggested, "Maybe they have the town quarantined still."

Lamar added, "Or something worse." He rolled the window down and waited as the men approached from either side of the vehicle. Lamar greeted the man at his window, "Good evening. We have authorization from Agents Cox and Melendez to proceed."

The agent asked, "What's your destination?"

"Clearview Hospital."

The agent looked in the back of the vehicle and saw Suzie. "Wait here." He walked away and made a call. The second agent kept his gun targeted on Lamar.

Lamar mentioned, "I'm an officer of the law. You don't have to point that thing at me."

"Sorry. We have orders not to trust anyone."

"I see."

The first agent returned and announced, "You have clearance." He waved the eighteen-wheeler out of the way.

Lamar responded with a slight bit of sarcasm, "Thanks a lot."

As soon as the eighteen-wheeler was out of the way, Lamar raced through. To his relief, Joe asked Suzie the burning question, "How do you know federal agents?"

Suzie grimaced and wrapped her arms around her gut. She explained, "They are part of the reason I escaped."

Lamar didn't buy her response but kept to himself. Joe questioned her, "Where are you hurt?"

"My stomach. The alien drove his shoulder into my stomach and I fell against a tree."

"I can't believe you killed that creature. It was much bigger than you?"

"It has an opening in its chest. I shoved my hand through and got his heart. That was the weakness I knew I could use against it. Another reason it wanted me dead." She let out a yelp and doubled over next to Joe.

Joe cradled her in his arms. "Hold on, Honey. We're almost there."

Lamar drove up to the emergency room door and parked. He hurried to the passenger-side and opened the door for Suzie. Peaches exited the ER dressed as a nurse and warned, "You can't park there."

Lamar responded sarcastically, "This isn't a social call. We have an injured woman here."

Peaches went inside and returned with Tasha and a gurney. She looked at Suzie's pale complexion and asked, "What happened?"

Suzie answered weakly, "My insides are killing me."

"We'll get you inside and the doctor will check you out."

Joe lifted Suzie onto the gurney and the girls pushed her inside. He thanked Lamar.

Lamar replied, "Just doing my job. If there's anything that you think I ought to know about, don't hesitate to call."

"I think everything will work out, Sheriff." They shook hands and Lamar got back in his truck.

Joe entered the hospital and caught up to the nurses at the elevator. "Where are you taking her?"

"To the trauma unit."

The elevator door opened and they pushed Suzie into a private room. Joe followed and wondered what was going on. Peaches and Tasha moved Suzie onto the bed and made her comfortable. Joe grew curious as the nurses seemed to be aware of Suzie's condition and where she needed to be without an examination.

A doctor entered the room and introduced himself. "I'm Dr. Johnson. I'm going to examine you and see what's causing your pain."

Joe held Suzie's hand and reminded her, "I'm here for you, Suzie."

Suzie started "There's something I want to ..." but then erupted into a scream as pain shot through her entire body.

Tasha shouted, "It's time!"

Peaches and Tasha pulled Suzie's sweatpants off and Sugar propped up her legs. Peaches immediately assumed the role of midwife. Joe was stunned by the unfolding events. "What the hell are you doing? She's not pregnant."

Then his worst nightmare occurred as his wife gave birth to the alien infant. It looked like a beige, little monkey without a tale. Joe staggered backward until he hit the wall. Peaches cradled the infant in her arms and took it into the bathroom to wash it off.

Dr. Johnson grew frantic and hollered, "What the hell is that?" When he retreated toward the door, Sugar blocked his path, and prevented both men from escaping.

Suzie opened her mouth and shot her tongue toward the doctor. She yanked him into her grasp and inserted her tongue into his mouth. A lump of DNA compound was promptly deposited inside the doctor. His eyes rolled back and he gagged before falling to the floor next to the bed.

Suzie retracted her tongue and gazed meekly at Joe. "Honey, I meant to talk to you about this. Do you still think we can work things out?"

Joe shuddered and cried, "Stay away from me, you monster! You murdered Krauss and the girls, didn't you?"

Suzie was amused and chuckled. "No, I didn't kill the girls, you fool. I was thrilled at the chance to get rid of that damned dog, though."

"You're nothing but a sick alien whore!" he shouted.

Suzie was hurt and pleaded, "Come on, Joe. You can be like me. We'll start over and everything will be fine." Sugar and Tasha stalked Joe in an attempt to subdue him.

"Get back or I'll shoot!"

"Back off. He's not going to shoot any of us," said Suzie confidently.

"You're right. I won't shoot you, Suzie. I loved you too much."

He pointed the gun at his head and pulled the trigger. A second later, a loud blast was followed by blood and pink portions of brain matter streaming down the wall onto the tile floor. Joe's limp body fell to the ground with a thud.

Tasha replied remorsefully, "I'm sorry about your husband."

Suzie complained, "You know, men do the darndest things?"

Dr. Johnson got up off the floor and remarked, "Yes, we do." They laughed hysterically.

Peaches handed Pitherus to Suzie. She affectionately held the infant alien in her arms.

"We'd best get everything cleaned up before someone asks questions," suggested Dr. Johnson.

"That's why we picked the trauma unit. It's empty right now," said Peaches proudly.

"Good choice, girls. I knew I could count on you," Suzie complimented them.

• • ◆ • • •

Lamar and Johnny sat on the hood of the police vehicle in front of the hospital. "I just heard a gunshot!" exclaimed Lamar.

"I didn't hear anything. Relax, Sheriff."

"Yeah, maybe my nerves getting the better of me."

"I think I've had enough of this place for a while. Me and Sally are gonna take a long vacation. Maybe you should too, Sheriff."

"No, I still have unfinished business here. This ain't over yet."

A black sedan pulled up in front of them with the two agents inside. Cox leaned out the window and asked, "What next, Sheriff?"

"You tell me."

"Looks like it's over."

"Uh-huh. I guess I'll have a few days of solitude before the evacuees are returned."

"Our field team will make one more sweep through the town and then pack it in," said Melendez.

"I'm sure you'll be happy to know that we're leaving," kidded Cox.

"Yes, I am. I'm looking forward to good old, quiet Parmissing Valley the way it was. Good luck, agents."

• • • ◆

"You, too. We'll meet again, I'm sure."

The sedan slowly drove away.

"What did they mean 'we'll meet again'?" asked Johnny.

"I was thinking that same thing. Don't book that vacation just yet."

Lamar stared with a piercing gaze at the night sky and swore, "I'm going to get to the bottom of this yet."

"You mean it's not over?" asked Johnny uneasily.

What do you think?"

"We killed them all, didn't we?"

"Yes and no. There's one kind left and we have to figure her out."

"I was afraid of that," groaned Johnny.

"Why don't we take a ride up to Graham's Mountain and look around?" suggested Lamar.

"For what? It's pitch dark."

"Wait here for me. I want to ask Doc Beauchamp about something first." Lamar left the vehicle. As usual, Johnny knew the sheriff had something up his sleeve and wasn't saying.

Lamar stepped off the elevator and nearly collided with Peaches. She stepped in front of him and blocked his passage with her arm. "You can't be up here, sir. Hospital regs."

Lamar pushed her aside and informed her, "This is police business, missy. I need to talk to Doc Beauchamp for a moment."

Peaches became nervous and uttered, "Uh, Doctor Beauchamp had an accident."

Lamar eyed her suspiciously and realized that he knew her from someplace. "What could have happened to Doc Beauchamp in the last hour since I've seen him?"

"I can't talk to you right now," she replied, looking frightened. "You have to leave."

Lamar pushed her arm aside and said sternly, "I'll see for myself."

Dr. Johnson exited the room and blocked his path. "Can I help you, Sheriff?"

Lamar paused and studied the doctor's face. He seemed calm and unnerved. "I understand Doc Beauchamp had a little problem."

Dr. Johnson put his arm around Lamar's shoulders and nudged him back to the elevator.

"Doc Beauchamp became very unsettled over his wife's condition. One of our orderlies tried to subdue him and his gun discharged."

Lamar looked into the man's eyes. "And what? He shot himself?"

"No, no. Nothing like that. I told him to leave or I'd have his license pulled for his behavior."

Lamar knew something wasn't right. He pressed the button for the elevator. Dr. Johnson watched anxiously for his departure. "So, Doc is probably at home, right?" he questioned suspiciously.

"Oh, I'm sure he is," Dr. Johnson assured him. "He's had a very traumatic day."

"How about his wife, Mrs. Beauchamp?"

"She'll be fine. We're running tests to make sure there are no internal injuries to her or the baby."

The elevator doors opened. "I see. Well, take care of her," said Lamar as he stepped into the elevator.

"Thank you for understanding," replied Dr. Johnson. The doors closed and the elevator descended.

Lamar took in everything that just transpired and considered what he witnessed. Even more strange was the fact that Johnson mentioned a baby.

When he exited the hospital, he realized that whatever Suzie had become, so were the others. So were Agents Melendez and Cox. He wondered how far this had spread.

⋯⧫⋯

Tasha and Sugar stood next to Suzie adoringly with Sugar holding the infant Pitherus. Suzie sat up in bed and took her child from Sugar. She nestled him against her breast and placed her hand upon his head. She communicated telepathically with him before handing him back to Sugar.

Dr. Johnson and Peaches returned to the room. Suzie noticed the concerned expressions upon their faces. "What is it?" she asked.

"That sheriff stopped back. He wanted to see your husband," replied Dr. Johnson.

Suzie grew uneasy. "I see."

"He arrested me once last year. I don't think he recognized me but there is a chance," added Peaches.

"Did he ask about me, Doctor?" Suzie asked, curious.

"Yes, he did. I only told him that you and the baby were fine. Your husband was sent home for erratic behavior."

Suzie sat on the edge of the bed with her feet on the floor. She took her phone and called Agent Cox.

Cox's phone rang as he and Melendez sat in the sedan near the police station. "Cox speaking. This is a secured line."

"We have a problem. The sheriff may know more than we want him to," explained Suzie.

"I understand. We'll take care of it."

"I want them alive. Take them to the ship and we'll meet you there in an hour."

"No problem," replied Cox.

Suzie hung up the phone and asked innocently, "Could you take a look at my child, Doctor? He doesn't seem well."

"Of course, Serena Luna."

Sugar handed Pitherus to the doctor. Suddenly, thorny tentacles erupted from the infant's head and torso. Two penetrated the doctor's nostrils, four entered his mouth and descended into his stomach and two penetrated the arteries in his thighs. The tentacles were pink and opaque.

The women watched as a stream of blood, and pureed organs and brain were sucked through the tentacles. The doctor fell to his knees and his eyes bulged in sheer horror.

Tasha and Peaches each grabbed a shoulder to keep him from falling with the child in his arms. When Pitherus was done feeding, he retracted his tentacles and returned to a harmless child again. Sugar removed the infant from his stiff arms and Peaches shoved his empty carcass face down to the floor. He hit with a thud and lay flat.

"That's how disloyalty is rewarded. The sheriff now knows of the child and that its term was not human-like," declared Suzie angrily.

✦✦✦✦

Lamar returned to the police SUV and climbed inside. He had a smug look on his face.

"What's so funny, Sheriff?"

"Johnny, this might be the last ride for us."

"You never know. Sally and I both have roots here."

"That's not what I meant. Take us back to the station."

Johnny drove the vehicle onto the highway and sped back toward the police station.

"Are you gonna tell me what's going on, Sheriff?" Johnny asked suspiciously.

"Suzie Beauchamp is definitely one of them things."

"What did you just say?"

"There's more. Joe Beauchamp's dead. The doctor and nurse at the hospital are one of them things, too."

"How do you know all this?"

"You'll see."

"Are you okay to travel, Serena Luna?" inquired Sugar.

"I'm well enough. We must return to the ship at once. Take care of the good doctor's body, please."

As soon as the girls wrapped the doctor's corpse and disposed of it in a dumpster, they joined Suzie and exited the hospital with the infant. Suzie drove them past Parmissing Valley to Graham's Mountain in her vehicle.

Johnny parked the SUV in front of the police station and got out. Lamar stared across the street at the wooded lot. He noticed the faint outline of Melendez and Cox's black sedan.

Johnny paused at the entrance. "Now what's wrong?" he complained.

Lamar closed the SUV door and hurried inside the station. Johnny followed and slammed the front door shut. He stood in front of Lamar and glared at him. Lamar placed his finger in front of his lips for silence. He searched underneath the desk.

"I guess I'll have to process your paperwork since you're leaving, Johnny," he said, feigning his intentions.

"I guess so if you're that anxious to get rid of me."

Lamar scribbled something on a sheet of paper. "No, it's just that I'm not the sentimental type."

Johnny read the sheriff's writing: "The place is bugged. Cox and Melendez are parked in the woods across the street." He looked surprised but then caught on to Lamar's warning. "Why don't you and me grab a six-pack and go tie one on in the woods tonight? Maybe we can part ways with a little clarity about all this," suggested Johnny.

Lamar winked at him and smiled. "I guess a few beers can't hurt. It's not like there's anyone left around here that needs protectin'." He opened his desk drawer and removed a catalog of pictures. "Well, let's go before it gets any later. It's already past my bedtime."

The two men exited the police station and returned to their vehicle. As they pulled away, Lamar explained, "This is bigger than we thought. Those agents are still worried about something."

"How could they be aliens and still look human?" asked Johnny.

"I'm not sure, but we're going back up to the campsite now. I think we'll find the answers there."

"But won't those agents follow us?"

Lamar took out his .357 and loaded it. "I'm counting on it," he replied.

"You can't shoot them! They're federal agents."

Lamar stared at Johnny and reminded him, "I told you, this might be our last ride."

"You're scaring me, Sheriff."

"Shut up and drive."

Johnny grew uneasy as he focused on the road. Lamar paged through the catalog using his flashlight to see. He studied the female pictures as he turned the pages. About ten pages in, he recognized Peaches' picture. Lamar pounded the dashboard. "I knew it! I'm on to them now!" he exclaimed.

"Do I want to know what you're talking about?" asked Johnny.

"The nurse at the hospital... I knew I recognized her. We picked her up for prostitution before."

"I don't remember us locking up any nurses for prostitution, Sheriff."

"No, you butthead! She's posing as a nurse. It's Peaches Callahan. How else can Suzie Beauchamp keep her secret? She's got her own posse and there's something else."

"Well don't stop now," replied Johnny sarcastically.

"The doctor mentioned that Beauchamp and her baby were doing fine. Did she look pregnant to you?" Lamar questioned him.

"No way."

"They're aliens, Johnny. Shit's different with them."

"Alright, let's suppose your theories are correct. What are we going to do about it?"

"They've got to have a weakness. That's why Cox and Melendez are still watching us."

The SUV pulled into the campsite and parked at the edge of the woods. Lamar and Johnny got out with their pistols drawn. Lamar had a pair of night vision goggles from the earlier battle and strapped them to his head. They entered the woods and ducked down in the dense foliage.

"So how long are we going to hide out here in the dark?" inquired Johnny.

"What's wrong, boy? You nervous or something?"

Johnny shivered as he saw his breath in the chilly night air. He looked at his watch and complained, "It would be nice to get some sleep. It's three forty-five and I'm exhausted."

"I am, too, but if we don't solve this tonight, it won't matter. We'll won't have to worry about law enforcement anymore."

Johnny informed him, "I'm not looking to shoot any agents if that's what you're referring to."

"Johnny."

"I know, I know."

Lamar pulled the goggles over his eyes and gestured for Johnny to follow him. The men entered a clearing at the edge of a steep rise in the side of the mountain. Trees cluttered much of the area and a large patch of bushes and shrubbery encompassed one particular area. A small girl lay nestled at the edge of the clearing and sobbed.

Johnny glanced at Lamar. "Be careful. This has all the makings of a trap," warned Lamar.

Johnny approached the little girl. "Where's your mother?" he asked compassionately.

"The monster killed her," sobbed the child.

Johnny tried to comfort her. "You're safe now. I'll get you a blanket and warm you up as soon as we get back to the truck." The girl looked up at him with pleading eyes. Johnny's heart broke for her. "What's your name?"

"Claudia," replied the girl. A low-pitched humming sound interrupted the moment as the spaceship appeared before them.

"Well, I'll be! Will you look at that?" uttered Johnny.

"Looks like someone just turned on the power," quipped Lamar. When the hatch opened, light streamed out and flooded the clearing. He pulled off his goggles and tossed them aside.

The little girl pulled away from Johnny and ran inside the ship. Johnny called to her but she ignored him. Lamar grabbed his arm. "Let her be. Something's not right about any of this."

"I'll go in first, Sheriff."

"No, Johnny. You wait here until our friends show up. I'll go in." Johnny reluctantly obeyed as Lamar entered the ship alone.

Lights appeared down the trail as the sedan approached the campsite. Johnny spotted them at the base of the mountain. He ducked into the trees and waited.

Lamar was amazed at the inside of the ship. He noticed the shredded matting on the floor from the table and Pitherus' broken tank. On the table were two of the star-shaped programming devices. He picked one up and studied it. At the end of the retracted probes, he noticed pieces of singed hair and skin. Unsure of its function, he dropped the device back on the table and walked past the control panels. The flashing lights and strange indicators impressed him, although he had no idea what they were for. Then he realized he was being watched. He backed away from the table and spun around.

Jasper emerged from the cargo bay below. His tongue rolled from his mouth and he hissed at Lamar. Lamar aimed his gun at Jasper's head and warned, "We can do this the easy way or we can do it the hard way." Jasper eyed him suspiciously.

The black sedan arrived and parked. Cox and Melendez exited their car and searched the police SUV. "Neither of them leaves this mountain, got it?" ordered Cox.

Melendez checked his pistol. "Got it. I'll bet they're looking for the ship."

"That makes our job that much easier." The two agents entered the woods and headed north.

Johnny spotted the flashlights coming toward them and rushed in to alert Lamar. "They're coming, Sheriff!" Johnny saw the alien creature across the room from Lamar and drew his pistol.

"Don't do anything unless I say so," ordered Lamar.

"But the agents are coming."

"They're a little anxious," Lamar commented. "I thought we'd have at least an hour head start."

The two men backed away and stood on either side of the hatch. They kept their pistols trained on Jasper and waited patiently for the agents. "Don't make a sound or I'll take out both your knees, got it?" Lamar warned Jasper.

"I don't think he understands. Maybe he's not one of the smart ones," quipped Johnny.

"I'll show you who's not so smart," blurted Jasper. He raised his claws in attack mode but refrained when both men prepared to fire.

The two agents burst in and were surprised to see Jasper. Lamar and Johnny surprised them from behind and held them at gunpoint as well.

"Get over there by the alien, boys," ordered Lamar. "You can get reacquainted while we wait for the rest of the party to arrive."

Melendez and Cox walked slowly with their hands over their heads and stood next to Jasper. Jasper hissed and his tongue slithered out of his mouth.

"We'll have none of that," warned Lamar and he fired one shot into Jasper's shoulder. Jasper reeled back against the wall and clutched the wound.

"Don't make me say it again," Lamar reminded them.

"You have no idea what you're getting into, Whittington. This is bigger than you and me," Melendez warned.

"When did you turn on your own species, Melendez? Did you volunteer?"

"That harlot Beauchamp duped me and Cox. Now we're one of them and there's no going back."

"You don't say." Lamar sat on the steel table. "Is she (Suzie) the one behind all this?"

Melendez sat down on the floor and leaned against the wall of the ship. "Not originally," he answered. "She became something special and she knew it. It's her game now and let me tell you, she is more dangerous than the alien creatures that started this mess."

"Find me a woman who isn't dangerous," Lamar chided.

"Believe it or not, she's the reason the alien invasion force hasn't attacked already."

"Not for long," uttered Jasper.

Lamar raised his gun and aimed at Jasper's other shoulder. Jasper turned away defensively.

"She's doing the same damn thing the aliens would have," Lamar responded. "I don't want to become one of those things and I sure don't want them telling me what to do."

"You never know. You might like it," joked Melendez.

"Did you?" he countered.

"No, but I'm past all that."

Lamar turned his attention to Cox. "Not in a talkative mood, Coxy?"

"I always hated you, you worthless piece of ..." uttered Cox. Lamar fired a shot at Cox's knee and sent him sprawling to the ground before he could finish.

"I never liked you either. Now shut your pie hole."

Cox groaned and clutched at his shattered knee. "You son-of-a-bitch!" he cried.

"Suck it up like a man or did she take that away from you, too?"

Cox crawled over by Melendez and lay on his side, leaving a trail of brown blood across the floor.

Tasha and Sugar charged through the hatch and knocked Johnny to the ground. Sugar wrestled his pistol from him. "Drop your weapon or gopher boy here gets it," she warned Lamar.

Lamar held his pistol out and laid it on the console. "No reason why we can't be friends now, is there?"

"You didn't feel that way last year, when you busted us in that truck lot for prostitution," Tasha complained.

Then Lamar recalled the incident and remembered the three hookers by name. "Oh, come on, Tasha, you know I had to do something when I found out Peaches was only fifteen."

Suzie and Peaches entered next. Suzie carried Pitherus in her arms.

"For the record, I'm seventeen now, Sheriff. Interested in a little action?" said Peaches sarcastically.

"Sorry, Peaches, I'm on the clock. No can do."

The little girl peeked from behind the console and shrieked when she saw Pitherus. Suzie was annoyed with Claudia's scream. "Shut that little runt up."

"Mrs. Beauchamp! What are you doing here?" asked Johnny in mock surprise.

Sugar approached Claudia but Johnny scrambled to his feet. "Leave the girl alone. We'll do what you ask without any trouble," he said bravely. Sugar looked at Suzie for instructions.

"Keep her quiet and she lives. Oh, and put down the gun as well," instructed Suzie.

Johnny gestured for Claudia to come to him. He held her in his arms and calmed her. Suzie glared at Johnny suspiciously.

"So, were you really pregnant, Mrs. Beauchamp? I'm still confused about that," Johnny asked innocently.

"Don't tell me the good Sheriff didn't tell you about me," she replied arrogantly.

"He had suspicions that you were involved with the aliens but that sounded absurd." Tasha, Sugar and Peaches laughed at him.

"You're gullible, Deputy, very gullible. I might actually let you live," said Suzie. Then she ordered her girls, "Take down Jasper. I don't trust him."

Jasper sneered at her as the two grabbed his arms and forced him to the ground.

"Can you let the girl go, Mrs. B?" pleaded Johnny. "She's already been through enough."

"I don't think so. I hate loose ends and she is one of them." Suzie went to the control console and programmed several switches.

"You aren't doing anything illegal there, are you, Mrs. Beauchamp?" Lamar asked cynically.

"Just programming the ship to self-destruct. We don't want to leave any evidence of aliens, do we?"

"But I thought your boys were handling that."

Suzie was more concerned that Claudia glared at Pitherus with a crazed look in her eyes. "Your girlfriend isn't very fond of my child, Deputy."

Ignoring her remark, Johnny stroked Claudia's hair. "I still can't get over that. You never looked pregnant."

"I'm more of a woman now than I ever was. That's how I'm going to fix everything that's wrong with this world."

"What are you going to do with us?" he asked.

"I haven't decided yet," Suzie replied stoically as she finished programming the self-destruct sequence. "In a few hours, there'll be nothing left of the ship and anyone I choose to leave here."

A bright cylindrical-shaped light emanated from a round base at the rear of the control room. The light caught everyone's attention. Lamar grabbed his pistol and ducked inside one of the console cabinets. He peered out from the slightly ajar door.

Two more aliens appeared on the round base. One of them carried a device which looked like an hour glass with blinking lights. The other instinctively dove into Tasha and Sugar to free Jasper. A brawl broke out between the four of them. One of the aliens activated the small device by pressing three buttons on its top cover and placed it inside a shiny case on the table. Lamar wondered what the device could be as he spied through the door.

Suzie's tongue shot out and snared the alien around its neck. She yanked it to the ground in front of Peaches. Peaches was grateful for the opportunity and viciously assaulted the alien.

Suzie blocked the hatch to ensure no one escaped. Johnny and Claudia hid behind Pitherus' broken tank and watched. When the fighting halted, Jasper was badly injured and leaned against the control panel for support. Peaches and Sugar waited eagerly for Suzie's order to attack.

"Why are you here, Jasper?" asked Suzie.

"I spoke with Shurek earlier," he explained. "I thought you would have finished him off by then."

"It was necessary to keep him alive a short while longer to execute the next phase of my plan."

"That being the case, I offer you the support of two regiments. I see that you now have the area under control and we can move on to the next phase."

"I don't want your regiments here," Suzie informed him. "If the humans learn of their presence, they will bring their forces upon us and we will lose."

Johnny set Claudia down on the ground and placed his arm around her shoulder. She maintained a strict focus on Pitherus.

"I'm in a generous mood. Why don't you return to your ship and wait for me to contact you?" offered Suzie.

Jasper became irritated and replied, "Because it is time to initiate the next phase of our invasion."

Suzie handed Pitherus to Sugar and approached Jasper. She stood in front of him and placed her nose against his snout. "I don't think you heard me, Jasper. It's time for you to leave."

"I see," he replied reluctantly.

The little girl tugged at Johnny's arm and pointed to Pitherus. Suzie noticed and grew annoyed. "Let Pitherus have a piece of the little girl, Sugar."

Sugar grinned fiendishly and held Pitherus out toward Claudia. Pitherus' face wrinkled and frowned as he became something evil. Pitherus' legs elongated and he was no longer an infant. Sugar released him and backed away.

Jasper was horrified. "Pitherus! What have you done, Serena Luna?" he exclaimed.

"I created a family that I can trust to ensure our success."

Jasper backed away in fear. "You don't realize what you've done! The Sporatin are too dangerous to be free of their confines."

"No, Jasper, they were just misunderstood."

Pitherus' thorny tentacles shot from his torso and head. They penetrated Claudia's nose and pierced her eyes. Claudia suddenly transformed into an alien and a long tubular tongue darted from her mouth. It quickly forced its way through Pitherus' mouth and down his throat.

Johnny gasped in horror and retreated to the hatch. Lamar watched anxiously, hoping for an advantage from this outcome.

Claudia and Pitherus shrieked wildly as Sugar struggled to pull them apart. "Stop them, Sugar!" Suzie screamed frantically.

"I'm trying!"

Pitherus was in excruciating pain as Claudia's tongue yanked and twisted his organs. Two of his tentacles struck Suzie across the face and instinctively drove through her nostrils into her brain. Suzie desperately tried to pull them out. "No, Pitherus, not me!" she cried.

Sugar was knocked across the room and staggered to her feet. Pureed flesh and blood from Claudia and pureed brain matter from Suzie's head filled the opaque tentacles as Pitherus instinctively tried to drain the two of any life force. Suzie's hands fell to her side and she slumped away from the combatants.

Tasha rushed at Pitherus in a desperate attempt to save Suzie. She bit into the tentacles until they retracted from Suzie. Pitherus retracted his tentacles from Claudia and tore into Tasha's stomach. She weakened and fell to the ground as her organs were pureed by the sharp barbs and sucked out through the tentacle.

Claudia shoved her clawed hand into Pitherus' chest and ripped at his insides. He screamed in pain. Suzie crawled away from them as she looked dazed and incoherent. She suffered severe brain damage and experienced the pain inflicted on Pitherus.

Peaches lunged on top of Claudia's back and choked her from behind. Claudia retracted her tongue from Pitherus and slammed Peaches to the floor. Pitherus retracted his tentacles from Tasha and penetrated Peaches' eyes with them. She gagged and collapsed on the floor with his organs and fluid covering the floor in front of her. Claudia weakened as Pitherus struggled to maintain his tentacles inside her.

"Stop, Pitherus. Please stop," Suzie called out weakly.

Jasper saw an opportunity and attacked Sugar from behind. He tore into her neck with his razor-sharp teeth. She rammed him into the wall and valiantly fought until she weakened and fell dead.

Lamar emerged from the cabinet and raced to the shiny case. He removed the flashing device and hid it behind his back.

Pitherus stumbled and fell to the floor. The last ounce of life seeped from him and streamed across the floor toward Suzie. Suzie transformed back into her human form and reached her hand into Pitherus' blood. Tears rolled down her cheeks as she gazed in horror at her dead child-creature.

Johnny stepped out into the center of the control room and surveyed the carnage. Jasper staggered to his feet and threatened Lamar. "You're next, fat man!"

"I really don't think so," replied Lamar as he fired another shot into Jasper's shoulder. Jasper reeled backwards and clutched at the wound.

"Get back on that transporter and don't ever come back," Lamar ordered.

"Not until Serena Luna is dead. I cannot leave knowing she still lives."

The three of them studied Suzie for a moment and saw that she was barely alive.

"Why don't you take her with you? Consider it a peace offering," suggested Lamar.

"That would be appreciated," replied Jasper sarcastically. "Perhaps we'll spare you."

Lamar shouted, "Get out of here now, Johnny. I'll finish this."

"But Sheriff!"

"Johnny, that's an order."

Johnny reluctantly left the ship and hurried back to their vehicle.

Jasper dragged Suzie onto the round base and warily kept an eye on Lamar. "I won't have to worry about coming back here again because your world won't exist." He laughed sadistically as he and Suzie were engulfed in the bright cylindrical light.

"No, I think you got that wrong, Gatorface." He threw the steel box into the cylindrical light and watched as it disappeared as well. As soon as the light faded, Lamar smashed the glass power source over the base that provided the energy to transport the aliens onto the ship.

Lamar was pleased with the outcome as he glanced at the control panel. There was no way of knowing how much time before the ship would self-destruct but, at this point, he didn't much care.

Johnny started the SUV and stared in the direction of the spaceship. He couldn't just leave Lamar. He glanced at his watch and then at the sky. It was four forty-five and the sky was pitch black. He recalled the words to a song and uttered, "The darkest hour is just before dawn."

A bright explosion lit up the sky like a supernova and spread. For a brief instant, it looked like midday. "What the hell was that?" exclaimed Johnny. He leaped out of the SUV and stared at the sky.

Another explosion on the mountain sent debris raining down all around him. Johnny got back into the SUV and leaned his head on the steering wheel. A tear formed in his eye as he realized Lamar had no intention of escaping. It was, in fact, their last ride together. He wondered if it was truly over this time. Exhausted, he was nearly asleep when a tap on the window startled him. It was Lamar with that typical scowl of his.

"You gonna hang out here all night or what, Johnny? That beer's getting warm."

Johnny's eyes widened with joy as he gazed out the window at Lamar. "Sheriff, you're alive!" He jumped out of the vehicle and hugged him.

Lamar was embarrassed and pushed him away. "Now, now. I'm fine."

"What happened? I thought you were dead."

"That creature brought a little present to take care of humanity. I just made sure I did the humane thing and sent it back with them. I guess they got a real bang out of it."

"I can't believe that little Claudia was one of them."

"Perhaps the aliens didn't like the idea of Suzie taking over like she did."

"Where does that leave us?"

"Well, this time it's over."

"Are you sure about that?"

"Yes, I am. Oh, and don't call me Sheriff. My name is Lamar. We're friends." Johnny hugged him again affectionately.

Lamar reached inside the SUV and took a cigar from the center console. He lit it and inhaled deeply. "You know, I always hoped there'd be a reason to smoke one of these. Now let's get the hell out of here. It's past my bedtime."

They drove down the trail toward the highway. "So, are they really gone for good?" asked Johnny.

Lamar looked up at the sky and said, "Oh, yeah. We couldn't have asked for a better scenario - all of them in one spot."

"Suzie and the hookers?"

"Them and the alien invasion force. All in one clean sweep."

"What about the doctor at Clearview?"

"I'm sure Suzie killed him. He pretty much told me everything I needed to know about her." He took another puff of his cigar.

"I guess you still want to leave town for a little while, huh, Johnny?"

"Why do you ask?"

"Well, I was thinking that Parmissing Valley will have a whole new beginning and we have a lot of work to do."

"Why's that, Lamar?" he asked.

"I'm a new man. I took this job because I was afraid to do law enforcement where I might actually have to risk my life. After all this, I'm not afraid of anything. That means I have a lot of catching up to do."

"You have changed a lot since this all started."

"Remember at the bus station when you were on the crapper and that mutant grabbed you?"

"Lamar, shut up!" The two men laughed.

The SUV rode into town as the sun rose over the mountain. Lamar said with a big grin, "It's gonna be a beautiful day."